AMBER MAGIC

KELLY N JANE

18TH AVENUE PRESS

1

———

Ingrid swatted away the lock of blonde hair caught on her eyelashes with a huff. Overgrown branches along the game trail had tugged free a section of her braid while she forced her way down the worn path.

Ten days! Ten days of fruitless searching through the Danelaw countryside to find a woman who could point Ingrid to the goddess, Eir. The powers growing within her needed to be harnessed and disciplined, but only the Asgardian could train her to do such a thing. The few accidental uses of her magical healing gift always left her drained and usually unconscious.

Some warrior I am.

Ingrid couldn't fathom how she was the one fated by the Norns to strengthen the veil of protection around Midgard. Regardless of her understanding or lack thereof, it was the truth. Only the goddess had the answers Ingrid needed.

The worst part was only a little more than six weeks remained until Ingrid's village—her family—would pay the price if she failed. That was something she couldn't allow.

Dappled sunlight filtered through the trees of the forested area where they traveled. Chirping birds and the rustle of small creatures echoed through the leaves, but it didn't help settle Ingrid's frazzled nerves. The dark intruder encamped inside her mind swirled in a lazy circle, and it made her nauseated. It shoved against her thoughts, causing her to fight for control as she became moodier and less rational.

As she batted the wayward tress of hair from her face, yet again, she yelped as she bumped into Jorg when he stopped suddenly in front of her.

He quickly slipped his hand over her mouth. With his free hand, he held a finger to his lips and waited to let her go until she nodded in understanding. His half-elven heritage gave him enhanced skills, exceptional hearing among them.

What is it?

"Voices ahead. Stay low and follow in my tracks, one after another," Jorg whispered his answer to the question she'd asked mentally, and only he could hear.

It was the first time they'd encountered a threat worthy of concern since they'd left their village along the River Ouse and headed west, away from any other settlements. Frustration seized Ingrid over her small size. She wasn't able to see around Jorg, causing her to hesitate a step before following after him. That minor hitch in stride caused Selby to run into her back.

"Watch yourself," Ingrid hissed.

Selby's brows rose to her hairline, letting her dark eyes sparkle in the morning light. "What's the matter?" Her best friend's voice was too loud, as usual, despite Ingrid knowing she'd heard Jorg's warning.

"Stay back. I can feel your breath on my neck." The

essence pushed at Ingrid's temples and made her vision darken. She ignored it as she turned back toward Jorg and the glare he flashed over his shoulder at both of them.

Pull yourself together. Act strong, be strong.

Careful to step only where Jorg did, Ingrid moved forward once again. In single file, they would conceal their numbers and make less noise.

Minutes later, the rest of the group heard what Jorg had. Voices and laughter pierced the air. It sounded like wolves who'd cornered their prey. Ingrid could make out the tones of several males as they taunted someone. The hair on her arms raised, and the magical power resting deep within her core warmed—ready if needed.

Crouched and huddled together, they peered through the brush at the edge of a small clearing. In the center of a circle stood a woman whose hands were tied behind her back and long ropes attached to her waist. Three men fanned out from her, jerking the ropes while she fought to maintain balance.

Ingrid fingered the smooth surface of the amber bead that hung from the center of her necklace, trying to keep herself calm. Though she wanted to rush in and put an end to such revolting behavior, it was important to assess the situation first. She watched Jorg's fists clench at his sides as he seemed to battle his rising disgust as well.

With their knees pressed together in the tight space, she could hear his teeth grind, but his intoxicating scent of fresh spring grass added a flutter to her belly despite the tension. In one fluid motion, Jorg's axe gracefully became an extension of his arm, reminding Ingrid to focus.

As she studied the woman, her body buzzed with untold knowledge that the search was over. There was no sign of the woman's staff, but she somehow knew this was her. This was the woman she sought, the völva, a practitioner of Freya's magic, who could point her in the direction of the elusive Eir. The magic in the air called to her own.

We have to get her away from these men.

Jorg leaned down to her ear. "Stay here."

"We should rush them together." The words sounded more like a whine than she'd intended.

"Just stay here, out of sight, until I call for you."

He winked at her and gave her one of his grins that made his dimple flash. But this time it made her clamp her teeth together instead of swoon. He held out his hand toward Selby and Plintze, and Ingrid saw each of them nod back, accepting his command without question.

She huffed and concentrated on the scene in front of her. With his inhuman ability to slip through the brush in silence, Jorg entered the clearing unnoticed. *He's not pushing you aside; he's just better at this.*

Seven armed, human men spoke in an odd form of Saxon, but Ingrid was still able to understand enough of their words. The woman stood with her back straight and her head high, despite how they yanked the ropes and taunted her.

Long, dark hair cascaded over her shoulders and down her back until it almost touched her knees. A burgundy dress with colorful embroidery clung to her shapely form but had become filthy and torn from the attack.

Jorg cleared his throat and waited until all the men turned their focus in his direction before he spoke. "Seven men and only one woman?" Speaking in their Saxon language, he smiled at the woman, looking at her from head to toe with a devilish gleam. She answered with a grin and a flick of her eyebrows toward him.

Ingrid made a noise that could have been a growl. Jealousy snuck into her thoughts even though she knew it was only an act. Selby edged closer, reminding her to stay silent.

"This must be a special occasion. Tell me, what makes the ropes necessary?"

"Leave, Stranger. This is not your concern.'

"John . . . look at him." One man holding a rope interrupted and nodded toward Jorg. "Look at his ears." His low voice riddled with concern.

Tilting his head, he tried to see Jorg's ears. Jorg helped with a slight twist of his neck, but he did not take his eyes off the man. "Jealous?"

Ingrid cringed, and her throat went dry. She knew how sensitive it was for Jorg to show his ears. Not that long ago, he made sure they always hid under his nut-brown hair. More than ever, she wanted to rush out and stand next to him—defend him—but she waited, muscles coiled and ready.

Ingrid carefully reached for the dagger strapped to her thigh. The vine and leaf carvings on the bone handle Jorg had made molded comfortably into her palm. Selby and Plintze shifted their weight, a short sword and spear readied in their grips.

"Another loathsome sorcerer." The man named John gave a lopsided sneer as he studied Jorg. "Looks like the day is getting better."

Ingrid rubbed at her arm, the leather of her gauntlet pressed against the scar left by the dragon attack. Never again did she want to feel so helpless, and it made her squirm as she watched the captive woman. Plintze let out a low growl behind Ingrid. The dwarf's anger bubbling over gave her a boost in confidence. She wasn't the only one struggling to wait.

"Is that the woman's crimes then? Are you afraid?" Jorg shifted his weight onto the balls of his feet while he waited for an answer.

Ingrid swallowed hard as she forced her breath to stay even. *Would they think me detestable, too?*

"You don't scare me, you nithing. Your kind is a blight on our lands."

Jorg twirled his axe and grinned. "Is that so?"

He seemed to enjoy the risk in a way that Ingrid hadn't noticed in other situations, possibly because in most of those he was saving her from one disaster or another. Strength without a hint of uncertainty. She shifted her gaze to the men to keep her focus as she wiped her icy palms against her trousers.

All the other men kept glancing to John, eagerness radiated from them as they waited for the order to attack. Their leader rushed forward with a nod as his signal to the others. Those not holding ropes charged with him. The woman stood still, watching. Amusement danced over her face as the ropes slackened.

How can she look so relaxed?

In a flurry of swords and screams, Ingrid's attention snapped to Jorg as he swung his arms, spinning in a graceful set of motions with a deadly beauty. John and another man circled behind him. Jorg hooked the sword of an oncoming attacker with his axe and sent it flying just before his axe left a deep gash across the man's middle.

Ingrid's magic began to tremble, and her hands heated at

the sight of the injury. Gritting her teeth, she willed herself to push it deep into her core, and her hands chilled like she'd plunged them into snow.

Unable to wait any longer, Plintze rushed forward faster than it seemed a dwarf with a limp should be able to. The girls turned to each other, lips tight and eyes glistening, for half a heartbeat before shrieking and following Plintze into battle.

The men startled as Plintze engaged the man who'd managed to get on Jorg's blindside, giving the woman the distraction she needed. The careless captors had allowed too much slack in the ropes as they gaped at the dwarf.

The woman leaned forward and used her body to yank against one of the lines, knocking the man holding them off balance and causing him to stumble. In one swift motion, she jumped into the air, swooped her hands under her feet to the front, and untied herself once she landed.

Confused, the men stood immobile, their advantage lost in the delay. She struck out with a foot and swept the legs from under one before smashing her elbow into the throat of another.

Nearby, Selby charged one of the attackers. She easily blocked his sword and cut his thigh.

Using her shield, Ingrid buckled the knee of another. She swung again and connected against his jaw, making him crumple to the ground. Tightness gripped her chest as the urge to help the man she'd injured warred against the need to keep fighting. One thing was certain—she needed to speak to the woman. It was why she'd come so far from home.

Decision made, Ingrid whirled, ready for her next opponent. From the looks of it, they were all either engaged or on the ground. The once-captive woman held a seax—a knife for simple, daily chores—and circled a smug, seemingly unarmed man. As he turned, Ingrid saw a large dagger through his belt.

Arrogant fool to think you don't need your weapon. It will serve you right when she takes you down.

The man rushed and slammed into the woman before she could strike, knocking her onto the ground.

Ingrid shrieked, and ran forward, dagger held high. Just as she was about to swing, hoping to injure the man enough for the woman to get away, her icy fingers lost their grip, and the weapon fell to the ground.

He rounded on her and swung his arm, connecting hard with Ingrid's stomach. Air escaped from her, and she stumbled back a few steps. With a sneer, he grabbed the lost dagger before charging the woman.

Back on her feet, the woman blocked the man's arm as he slashed his personal weapon toward her throat. The power behind his swing forced her to push against it with both arms. That left the man's other arm available to ram Ingrid's dagger into her chest.

Ingrid tried to scream as the woman fell to her knees and crumpled backward. Her cries caught in her throat as she still struggled for air. A heartbeat later, Selby leaped over Ingrid, her short sword slamming into the man's belly.

His insides spilled onto the dirt as Ingrid watched. She crawled toward the woman while Selby stood guard over them, though no others were left to attack.

No! Please don't die! I need your help.

On her knees at the woman's side, Ingrid closed her eyes and called upon her healing energies. The small ball in her belly grew until it spread through her chest, down her arms, and into her hands. With tears in her eyes, she slowed her breathing, put her hands on the woman's chest, and allowed her healing glow to do its work.

Except it didn't.

A jolt of pain shot through Ingrid's arms as an image of the woman's wound, from inside her body, flashed behind her eyelids. The dragon scar on her arm pulsed, and the dark essence in her mind reeled back as if they both recognized the foreign energy.

Startled, Ingrid pushed harder to force her power into the woman's chest. Her eyes snapped open when the woman wrapped her fingers around one of Ingrid's hands, breaking her concentration.

Her hands cooled, and the warm intensity settled back into its resting place. Ingrid brushed at the woman's hand, but her grip tightened until Ingrid stared at her.

"I don't understand. What was that?" Ingrid asked as she hovered over the dying woman.

The woman pulled Ingrid closer and whispered into her ear. "Your powers from Freya are growing. Soon you'll be ready." Releasing Ingrid's hand, she reached up and tapped the amber bead that hung in the center of Ingrid's necklace. "This will guide you, but tell no one. Especially the Dark Elf or all Midgard will be lost."

"I need to find Eir, to train and understand. Do you know where she is?" The woman was dying, and if she would not allow Ingrid to help her, then she needed to provide some answers.

"You must bind the spell, no matter the cost."

"Yes, but where is Eir—how do I contact her? Tell me,

please!" A tear shimmered as it fell from Ingrid's cheek. Short, shallow breaths bounced the woman's chest then tapered off until her final exhale.

Pain gripped Ingrid as she choked back a scream. Everyone depended on her to succeed. *What am I going to do now? There isn't enough time.*

A fragile girl, who wasn't allowed to train as a shield-maiden, somehow possessed the power of Freya? Ingrid shook her head and touched the amber bead at her chest. It made little sense. She swayed as the tarry substance invading her mind oozed forward, as if pleased with her troubles.

Where is Eir? Is this her plan? I will not let everyone I love die.

Jorg startled her as he knelt beside her and laid his hand on her back. "You did what you could. No one survives a dagger to the heart."

2

———

Silence filled the clearing. The earthy scent of overturned sod mingled with the metallic tang of blood in the air. Plintze walked over to stand with the group, his sturdy frame tall for a dwarf, yet still barely over three feet. He adjusted his wide-brimmed hat that had been knocked off in the fight. Once he had it situated just the way he liked it, he rubbed his hand down his flowing russet beard, which trailed to his waist.

Ingrid glanced around at her friends, too stunned to speak. They came with her on this journey to help her follow her destiny. They'd left behind family and comfort for her sake.

Now what would happen?

A light groan sounded from a man on the ground. Jorg, Plintze, and Selby turned as one, ready for an attack. The man struggled to rise to his hands and knees from where he lay prone in the dirt, but he held no threat.

Jorg walked with Plintze at his side, flipped the man over, and put a foot on his chest. With her mind and body too numb from everything that had just taken place, Ingrid only watched from her spot next to the woman's body.

"Who are you?" Jorg's calm, even-toned voice brooked no argument.

The man coughed and glared at him, slicing a glance toward Plintze, who growled at him. A trickle of blood leaked from the side of the man's mouth, and a dark stain on his side indicated a more threatening wound. With a hard swallow, the man closed his mouth tight and set his jaw in a show of stubbornness.

"Your leader is dead, and you'll join him now if you have no other information for me," Jorg said firmly.

"Kill me. It's all your kind understands how to do, anyway."

"My kind, is it?" Jorg inhaled a deep breath before he spoke again. "What did you want from the woman?"

The man continued to glare and said nothing. Jorg stepped harder on his chest, making him wheeze for air. Wide, panicked eyes replaced the glare. "She had information we were seeking," he choked out.

"What information?"

Plintze leaned forward, capturing the man's attention. "If you won't talk, I'll turn you into a toad and fry your legs for my dinner."

Selby snorted, though she raised her brows in question. Ingrid rose from the ground and shook her head to relieve her friend's concern as they both stepped closer to the others. The dwarf couldn't truly turn a man into a toad—at least she hoped not. Resigned that the woman would no longer be able to help her, she reluctantly moved her attention to the injured man. She wanted to hear what had prompted the attack.

The man darted his eyes between each of his captors and then stared at Ingrid and Selby.

"You're human," he said, a look on his face as if he'd eaten bad fish.

"What difference does that make?" Selby snarled.

"These types have tainted our world, and need to be destroyed. Distance yourself from them if you want to keep yourselves safe."

Ingrid shook her head. "You tortured that poor woman, and for what? Because she had gifts you don't understand?"

The man curled his lip at Ingrid as he tried, unsuccessfully, to shift his weight. "You are naïve if you think their kind safe." Coughs wracked his body, and his throat gurgled as Jorg's foot pressed harder on his chest.

"Who is searching for those with powers?" Jorg asked.

Resting his head on the ground, the man closed his eyes and tightened his mouth. Plintze growled again and kicked his side where the stain darkened his tunic. The man winced and hissed in a deep breath, but refused to give in.

Plintze glared down at the man. "Tell us what you know or join your friends."

A smirk played on the man's lips, telling each of them there would be nothing more. Jorg gave Ingrid a determined, yet questioning look. Her stomach lurched at what she knew he was asking, but it had to happen.

Everyone had shielded her from the truth of battle before, which had only served to keep her weak. She wouldn't live that way anymore. Childhood was over.

The blackness in her head squeezed like a warm hug,

pleased with her thoughts. It made her hesitate with confusion over the line separating right and wrong in this situation. She clamped her jaw tight and let the heat build.

These men had killed the best chance she'd had to find Eir and destroyed an innocent woman because they didn't understand her. The more she let the thoughts swirl, the more her blood raced.

Before anyone could stop her, Ingrid lunged forward and slammed her knife into the man's neck. His eyes bulged with realization just before she removed the blade.

Blood spurted over her forearms as she sat on her knees. She braced herself with her hands against the man's chest until it stopped heaving and he stared at the sky with glassy blankness.

What is right about any of this? That some die while I search to save others?

It was different to execute someone after the battle was over, and her insides churned. The worst part was the sense of satisfaction mixed among the guilt and disgust. Shocked by her reaction, she fought against a wash of dizziness and the flashes of light circling her vision.

Strong hands reached under her arms and pulled her to her feet as she continued to stare at the dead man, dagger still in hand. Warm liquid became sticky between her fingers as she forced herself to take deep, even breaths and stand tall.

No one said anything to her as she stepped away, turning her back to the grisly scene. A slight breeze blew against Ingrid's face as she dealt with her swirling emotions. The darkness that clouded her thoughts disappeared as she accepted what she'd done.

When her heartbeat no longer hammered against her

chest, and she'd swallowed down the last bit of bile, she turned to face everyone. She was ready for judgment and reprimand, but she found neither.

"What now? Should we still find her cabin?" Selby said in a flat tone that belied her confident exterior. Her coppery brown hair was in wild tangles where it had slipped from her braid, but she made no effort to fix it.

Ingrid nodded. "I think that's best. But we should take her body with us, to bury her with what she'll need in the afterlife. We might find information in her home that could help me find Eir."

Jorg came to stand beside Ingrid. He peeled the dagger from her fingers and handed her a torn piece of cloth for her hands. While she wiped the blood away with detached carelessness, he cleaned the weapon without a word and slipped it through her belt until she could return it to her thigh later.

"We can't use a litter to pull her because of all the trees and shrubs, but if we wrap her, I'll carry her," he said.

Plintze stood next to the body of their now-fallen enemy called John and gestured the others over. "I found this in a pocket. It's Saxon, I think." A flat, golden disk stamped with a symbol the dwarf didn't recognize lay in his open palm.

Jorg took the coin and let his eyes scan over the symbol, and his brows furrowed. He looked irritated as he shoved it in the pouch attached to his belt. He turned to Ingrid. "We need to get going."

Ingrid grabbed his sleeve. "What was that?"

"I'm not sure, but it's gold and proves those men were hired. They were looking for something—not the woman, or they would have killed her fast." He darted a glance at Ingrid.

Or someone . . . No one knows about me. Do they? Her stomach rolled in on itself as she fell in step behind him.

"I'll wrap her up," she said as they approached the woman's crumpled form. It wasn't just the loss of information that upset her so much. For reasons Ingrid couldn't understand, she felt connected to the völva somehow. "We needed more time." Tears stung Ingrid's eyes, but she held them back. A weight pushed against her shoulders as the burden of the woman's final words echoed in her mind.

"I'll help," Selby said and crouched down on the opposite side of the body.

Together, they straightened the woman's limbs and used her own cloak to wrap her. The discarded ropes helped to keep everything in place well enough for Jorg to pick her up. As gently as possible, he rested her stomach over his shoulder. Once he was finished, they looked up at the sky.

Ingrid absentmindedly touched the amber bead in the center of her necklace, and it pulsed against her fingers. A tremble swept through her, and she glanced at the others to see if they'd noticed. The rhythmic sensation sped up as she turned west.

A nudge in the right direction perhaps?

"The cabin should be in that direction." She pointed and strode away, hoping she'd laced her voice with enough confidence to stave off questions.

The woman had said the bead would guide her, but she'd also said not to tell anyone. *Act strong, be strong.*

Some of the tension slipped off her shoulders when the group followed, staying in a single line due to the dense brush that surrounded the clearing. They walked in silence and let it soothe their tempers.

3

If it weren't for the dead woman splayed over Jorg's shoulder, the sunshine filtering through the leaves would have been pleasant. The red morning clouds had faded away and now it was a warm, balmy day.

The roads that crisscrossed the countryside were scarce where they traveled. From the limited information known about the völva in the village, her home was southwest. They would have to travel through rolling hills covered in forest with broad patches of open meadows. The steady thrum of Ingrid's amber agreed as she occasionally caressed it while they forged ahead.

For the most part, the undergrowth was manageable, and the trees provided cover and ample supplies for fires and food. Covered in cushiony layers of dead leaves and moss, the forest floor made their footsteps silent whispers and lined the air with the smell of damp earth, with the occasional waft of sweet flowers.

However, a sporadic stagnant pond or trapped pool of water invited the annoyance of buzzing insects. The group was relieved when they came across a large creek. The peaceful area allowed them some much-needed rest as well as refreshment from the bubbling waters.

Jorg carefully lowered the woman down in a shady spot. Her cool body now peacefully rested on soft moss within a patch of ferns, away from the others. Once he was satisfied the woman's body was safe and sound, he walked over to the creek to splash water over his face and neck. He shook his head and blew out a sigh.

"What are you, some kind of dog?" Selby yelled as she brushed water off her sleeve. With a mischievous grin, Jorg cupped his hand and sent water from the creek in her direction.

"Wrong choice, pretty boy!" Charging, Selby slammed into Jorg's midsection.

Though he'd braced for the impact, the slippery moss still caused him to stumble. Using her momentum, he righted himself while his arms wrapped around her torso and trapped her from lashing out. He flipped her upside down to dunk her headfirst into the cold waters. Angry growls turned to pleading squeals as she begged for mercy.

Laughing, Jorg returned her to her feet and ruffled her hair. "You may be stronger than average, but you should take more care in who you fight without weapons."

Plintze was off to the side and snorted a chuckle at Selby's expense. "You give her too much credit. As if she could think that fast."

Selby's hazelnut eyes popped open wide as she gaped at the dwarf. "Listen, little *man,*" she said, emphasizing the term she knew would rile him, "I can beat either of you, but he's . . . sturdier than I expected."

Ingrid giggled from her spot on the ground where she reclined against a tree. Lost in her thoughts of Jorg's muscular arms and how his laugh made her belly flutter, she squirmed against the rough bark while she twisted a green twig around her fingers.

Selby turned in her direction. Her rosy cheeks perked up as she smiled and shrugged her shoulders, then waggled her eyebrows at Ingrid. "You should have warned me."

Heat flushed Ingrid's chest, moving up her neck and into her face. She sucked in a surprised breath before looking away. A slight grin played at her lips as she tried to ignore her friend. It was harder to disregard the devilish curl to Jorg's mouth when she glanced his way, but she did her best.

Ingrid let the sweet scent of greenery and damp earth bathe her senses and calm her increasing pulse. A glance to the poor deceased woman lying among the ferns and the memory of why she'd died instantly deflated Ingrid's mood. When she faced the group again, a shimmer in the air across the creek captured her attention. Her brows drew together as she sorted the image.

Plintze noticed and followed her gaze. "Humph." Surprise laced within his favorite expression.

Selby rolled her eyes. "Looks like the dwarf is trying to speak again. Ingrid, can you translate?"

Ingrid ignored her friend's remarks as the radiance disappeared and revealed a tiny cabin hidden among the trees. "He was saying 'look over there, we found the völva's home.'"

A small grin tugged at the side of Plintze's lips, and he turned away.

"It was there the whole time," Jorg said as he stared. "That's incredible."

"What are you talking about?" Selby asked. She peered in the same direction as Ingrid, straining to see something.

"The cottage across the creek, to the left of that fallen tree over there," Ingrid said pointing so Selby could follow her line of sight.

"I don't see it." Selby threw her hands into the air and turned to face Ingrid.

Ingrid stood and brushed the small bits of leaves and moss from her trousers before walking over to Selby. "Look over my shoulder, straight ahead through that little triangle of branches. Do you see it?"

Silence filled the area as Selby's breath tickled Ingrid's neck. Intent on her search, she didn't notice how close she had leaned into her friend. Ingrid didn't want to disturb her, though she ached to move.

"No. Is this some kind of joke? Ah," Selby waved her hand and turned away, pursing her lips and rolling her eyes. "You're trying to make me look like a fool as a joke."

Ingrid rolled her ear against her shoulder with a shiver then met the confused stares of Jorg and Plintze before they each settled their eyes on Selby.

"You truly don't see it?" Jorg asked.

"Enough. I won't fall for that." Selby stomped away to stand by herself.

Plintze strode to Selby, and with a grumble, grabbed hold of her arm, spinning her back toward the cottage. He mumbled a few indecipherable words while Ingrid stared and held her breath, sure that Jorg did, too.

"Let go of me, dwa—" Selby's jaw went slack as her words faded away. Her head tipped downward as her eyes widened. "How? But, what? That was not there before." She pulled out of the dwarf's grip and spun to face him. "How did you do that? Is this some kind of dwarf trick?"

"It was there the whole time, glamoured so we couldn't see it," Jorg said. He rubbed his neck while shaking his head with an appreciative huff.

"Was the glamour connected to the woman? Wouldn't it have released as soon as she died?" Fascinated and hungry to learn more about magic, Ingrid leaned forward waiting for Plintze to respond.

"Depends on the enchantment. It's possible she designed the glamour to slip because of her close proximity to it. Or maybe there's nothing left to power the spell because of her lack of essence. Anybody's guess, but it's good this happened, or we'd have walked right by," Plintze said.

A gravelly chuckle rattled his chest. "Jorg would have carried that woman for days." The chuckle erupted into two large guffaws before it settled again into a series of muffled snorts.

"Let's get over there and set about sending her to the afterlife," Jorg said.

Sucking in a deep breath, he walked to the woman with a pinched expression. There was a grumble in his throat as he retrieved the body and moved to cross the creek.

The small structure of stone walls and a thatched roof had an arched wooden door that offered an inviting charm. It reminded Ingrid of the door to Plintze's cottage, and she peeked over at him.

There wasn't any hint of wistfulness in his expression, so she tucked the thoughts away as her own. Glass-paned windows sat on either side of the door just above boxes spilling over with blue periwinkle and yellow cowslip.

A path paved in flat stones led to the front door, flanked by blossoms of pink yarrow and white chamomile with their cheery yellow centers. Under the eaves, closest to the group, sat a bench with an empty woven basket.

"This is stunning." Selby's voice held wonder and awe. "How does a glamour work? Are there hidden houses everywhere?" A glower flashed over her face, and she flicked her eyes upward. "Or are they hidden only to me?"

"Humph."

"Aaah, there he goes again. Talk, talk, talk," Selby scolded.

Ingrid snickered under her breath, happy to hear normalcy return between Plintze and Selby despite the circumstances.

"There aren't any others," Ingrid replied as she patted Selby's shoulder.

Together, they soaked in the picturesque scenery. It hinted at a happy woman—one who had gathered herbs and mushrooms and lived in harmony with the world around her.

The darkness pestered Ingrid's thoughts once more, oozing from one side to the other as if pleased with the woman's demise. Nausea welled in her stomach, and she swallowed to keep the bile from rising.

"Selby and I can gather the items for her journey if you two will prepare a site." Ingrid's gaze landed on Jorg, and he nodded.

Without protest, Plintze followed Jorg as they wandered toward a patch of wildflowers mingled among tall grasses.

4

Ingrid pressed against the door handle, and it gave without a hitch. A waft of air filled with the scent of fresh bread and apples floated outside.

Light filtered in through the windows, allowing beams of dust to sparkle in the air as Ingrid and Selby took in the surroundings. What appeared to be a one-room cottage on the outside, belied an expansive interior.

The girls stood in an impressive entry with the ceiling stretching at least four fathoms high. To the right was a large room with a massive solid wood table and chairs. The table was made from a giant ash tree split in half and polished with enough oil to see a reflection. It rested atop an equally imposing stump as a base.

The hand-carved chairs were made from living trees. They were tall in the back with a wide seat, and the roots had been left in place, spreading out against the floor for stability.

Another grand room spun from nature opened to their left. Both friends turned in a slow arc, absorbing the sights. Beautiful golden sconces hung on the walls every few feet, although none were lit. Shared astonishment flashed between them when they faced each other.

Selby broke the silence. "How is this possible? Is it another glamour?"

Ingrid shared the awe present in Selby's voice, but something else worried her mind. It reminded her of Hnossa's home when she'd visited Asgard earlier that spring. It was grand and beautiful but filled with more peace. It was natural and relaxing where Hnossa's was shiny and intimidating.

"I don't believe so. It can't be ordinary magic, though. It gives off the same energy I felt in Asgard.'

Selby snorted. "Was the völva from Asgard, too?"

"I doubt it. I don't think she could have died from an ordinary human blade if she were. But, I would bet she knows—" Ingrid's throat caught with emotion "—*knew* others from there."

Selby rubbed her friend's arm while she scrunched her face into an attempted smile. Her gaze then broke away as they roved over the rooms. "What should we gather?"

Ingrid sighed. "Let's keep searching and see what we find." She huffed and bit her lip. "Perhaps there will be a way to find Eir." The bead rested lightly against Ingrid's chest but offered no help.

Selby slipped her hand into Ingrid's, and they took shy steps down a hallway that led from the grand entrance. They came upon a large room with slim benches along two of the walls that were waist high. In the center of the room was a large, sunken fire pit.

"Is that a meal fire? In its own room?" Selby asked.

An open window in the ceiling drew Ingrid's attention. "I believe it is."

Above the benches, dried herbs and flowers in purple, yellow, and white hung, creating beauty to the eyes and the nose. Behind them, a set of spiral stairs rose to another level.

"Where do these lead? This is unnatural," Selby said. Stretching, but getting no closer, she tried to peek up the stairs.

"There is a lot here that doesn't show from the outside," Ingrid mumbled as she moved ahead.

Selby gave a nod before following Ingrid, tightening the grip on her hand.

My brave friend has found her limit, I guess.

Ingrid tilted her head toward the stairs, and they walked side by side, pressed together between the narrow walls as they ascended to the next level.

On the next floor, they found an open area with a set of chairs and a table between them. A beautiful silver sconce hung on the wall, and a thick, multicolored woven rug squished under their feet. Two closed doors beckoned on either side of the chairs. Starting with the closest one, they walked into a large bed chamber.

An enormous bed sat against the exterior wall. On either side of the bed, crimson silk curtains covered tall windows with glass panes that looked out over the forest, filling the room with ample light.

Across from the bed was a table with a cushioned bench that sat near an imposing cabinet with intricate carvings on the doors. Scattered across the table's top sat many beauty products, and an ornate, golden-handled mirror lay face down.

Selby walked up to the table and ran a light finger over some containers before stroking the mirror in awe. "Queen

Greta, in Jorvik, had one of these. I saw it once when I walked by, but I never thought I'd see something so beautiful up close, let alone touch it."

"We should bring it and some jars," Ingrid said as she stood next to Selby, her hands tucked close to her sides.

"Let's keep looking first. Maybe this isn't her room." Selby turned and grabbed Ingrid's arm. "What if she doesn't live here alone, and someone comes back and finds us in here?" Her eyes were wide as she rubbed at her throat.

"Let's hurry, just in case." The possibility had never crossed Ingrid's mind, but Selby had a point. Being so focused on sending the woman to the afterlife and finding Eir preoccupied her thoughts and allowed room for little else.

In the hall once more, they stood in front of the second closed door. The same low hum of the amber rattled against Ingrid's chest as before. She touched the stone and sucked in a deep breath.

When she turned the handle, it didn't move. She glanced to Selby for help. Stepping up, Selby gave it a strong twist, and it wiggled, but still didn't open. Once again, Ingrid reached out and gave it another try.

Gripping it tight, she twisted with a grunted effort, and the lever sprang free. Both girls jumped, startled at the sudden motion and how the door swung wide of its own accord. A musty, herbal odor wafted out of the dark room. A puff of dust motes floated in a lazy swirl into the hall, then seemed to migrate toward Ingrid.

"I don't like this one," Selby said.

Ingrid nodded, but stepped forward as her curiosity demanded to discover what was inside. A cold chill ran up her arms despite her leather gauntlets, and she hugged herself as she stepped across the threshold.

Cluttered with bottles and jars, the room looked ravaged. Books lay scattered on long tables that were arranged against the walls as well as on another large table positioned in the center. Hanging from wooden beams were bundles of every kind of herb and flower one could imagine. Ingrid pressed her finger under her nose, as she fought to hold in a sneeze from the overload of scents.

Ingrid drifted further into the room, fascinated, as the hum against her sternum increased. Her fingers skimmed the pages of the open books, and she peered into jars of liquids and powders. Her hands tingled and warmed as she walked among the tables. A pressure formed in her middle as new connections grew inside of her with every step.

Something touched Ingrid's shoulder, and she spun to face her friend. Selby's eyes grew wide as she took a step backward. A headache pushed against Ingrid's temples, and she rubbed her fingers on either side of her head. The essence in her mind slammed against her thoughts, excited by the energy humming through the air.

"You. Your bead and your eyes. We need to leave. Now." Selby stumbled over her words as she lurched forward, grabbed Ingrid's elbow, and dragged her from the room.

Ingrid protested and tried to pull away, but Selby kept a strong grip on her and didn't let go until they were back in the hall. As soon as they were clear of the door, she slammed it closed behind them.

"What's wrong with you? I need to go back in there. It's full of magic, and I need to learn it." Ingrid's breathing was ragged, and she clenched her fists at her sides.

"It's not safe for you in there. Your bead was so bright. And you looked crazed, like a berserker. Something was happening to you." Selby did not let go of Ingrid. Instead, she reached out and took hold of her other arm as well.

She doesn't understand. There's something I need in there—I can feel it.

"You can stay, but I need to go back in. There are books and herbs I should gather," Ingrid said, forcing herself to keep a calm voice. "For the woman's burial," she added.

The pressure in her head had lightened a bit since exiting the room, but she felt like her hands were on fire and her insides were twisting into knots.

Selby cocked an eyebrow at her. "I've known you my whole life, Ingrid. You can't fool me when you're lying, and I've seen too much to believe whatever is pulling you toward that room is safe."

Ingrid closed her eyes and inhaled sharply. After several deep breaths, her heart rate slowed. The aching need that burned in her thoughts to return to the room cleared from her mind, even though the buzz of the bead still rattled low against her.

After another long breath and releasing it slowly, she opened her eyes. "Fine, for now. Let's gather the things from the bed chambers and hurry outside."

"Jorg is probably wondering where we are, and that dwarf will have grumbled so much he might want to dig two more graves if we don't hurry." Selby tried for a light, joking tone, but her voice cracked before she swallowed hard. "Besides, someone else could still show up. I'd rather not explain why we're here."

Ingrid hesitated and glanced back at the closed door, but then gave a curt nod.

They hastened back into the bedroom and gathered jars and creams from the table. When they turned to leave, something in Ingrid's gut drew her attention to the opened door.

Peeking out from the corner behind the door was the woman's staff. It was thin and almost as tall as Ingrid with an open basket at the top that was twisted into a point. When she picked it up, her heart raced and the blood in her veins thrummed through her arm. An energy pulsed throughout her body, responding to the staff on a physical level.

Dizziness washed over Ingrid, and she rested an arm against the wall before she turned to Selby. "I think we have what we need. We should get outside."

"What's wrong?" Selby stared with a pinched expression and clutched the containers in her hands tighter to her chest.

"Nothing, why?"

"Your bead is glowing again, and you look pale." Noticing the item in Ingrid's hand, she leaned back, taking a half step away. "That's a witch staff. I saw one when we were in Jorvik. Remember?"

"Of course, it is. It proves she was the völva and this is her home. There's an energy coming from it. It's odd and wonderful, like it's waking something inside of me for the first time."

"Let's get outside and get you some air. How about I hold that?"

"No! I'm fine to carry it." Ingrid tried to calm her voice and sound more relaxed after her initial outburst, but she could see by the expression on Selby's face that it didn't work. Not waiting for her to grab the staff, she hurried out the door and down the stairs.

Jorg had just finished digging when Ingrid and Selby walked up. The grave was much larger in size than the woman's body to allow the items she'd need on her journey and in the afterlife to be buried alongside her. He placed a few blankets into the pit for her to lie upon.

"What's wrong with you?" Plintze asked when he saw Ingrid.

"Nothing. What's wrong with you? Have some manners for once, Plintze." Faint whispers battled the darkness in her mind, but she mentally brushed them away and rolled her neck as she stood beside the grave.

"She's a little affected by the völva's things. I'm not sure what's happening," Selby said.

"Ingrid?" Jorg jumped out of the hole and stood in front of her. His brows furrowed as he examined her face and the white knuckles of her hand clinging to the staff.

"I'm fine. Everyone needs to quit treating me like a fragile child. I've had enough of that in my life, and I'm done with it. Now let's give this woman the honor she deserves with a proper burial."

As she spoke, her arms tightened to her body, bringing the staff in contact with the bead. A jolt of energy ricocheted through her, making her wince. With some effort, she managed to cover the effect as irritation.

Jorg flattened his lips but nodded to Ingrid before turning to retrieve the woman's body. Gently, he rested her on the blankets, then unwrapped her from her cloak. Selby handed him the various items she held, including the golden hand mirror.

"Let me see that," Plintze growled as he reached for the mirror. Jorg handed it over and watched as the dwarf examined it.

"That's beautiful filigree work in the gold," Jorg said.

"It's more than that. This is dwarven."

Ingrid stepped closer to Plintze, her eyes wide with a shining look to them. "Are you sure? How would she own something like that?"

Plintze shook his head. "I don't know how she got it, but I know for sure who made it. What was this woman's name?"

"I was never told. According to my mother, she used to travel around to different villages healing and performing rituals, but she was regarded only as a völva. I was very small the last time she was seen in our village. Word spread that she moved far away and wished to live alone."

"I want to get this finished so she can move on, and we can, too," Jorg said, holding his hand out for the mirror. Though he tried to act cool and composed, worry spilled all over his face.

Clouds moved low over the sky, bringing the smell of rain along with the overcast. The surrounding trees creaked and groaned in the chilly wind.

Plintze stared at the mirror another few seconds but reluctantly handed it over. Jorg then reached for the staff in Ingrid's hands.

Gripped by a desire to flee, she pulled the staff tighter. Her mouth went dry, and she bit her bottom lip. "I think I should keep this."

Selby edged closer to Ingrid with slow steps, her hand

held out for the staff. "Ingrid, it's *her* staff—she'll need it, and you need to give it back to her."

Ingrid's head ached, and she glanced around at everyone before staring back at the house. Retreating a step, then two, her heart pounded against her chest. She swayed and felt dizzy again.

Jorg was out of the grave and at Ingrid's side faster than Selby could reach her from three steps away. Before Ingrid could protest further, he yanked the staff from her hands, handing it off. Once Selby had it in her grasp, she retreated far enough away that Ingrid couldn't reach it again.

"Hold this, Plintze. I'll go get her some water from the barrel," Selby said, holding out the staff.

"No. I'll not touch that. It reeks of seiðr magic. I'll get the water." He marched away toward the creek before she could argue.

"Can you stand?" Jorg asked Ingrid as a little tension faded from her.

She nodded and gave him a weak smile. "I'm fine. Just dizzy, but it's better."

"Come, sit and rest. You look pale." He tilted his head, eyes focused on hers as he examined her face.

"What should I do with this?" Selby asked, holding out the staff.

"Give us a few minutes, Selby. I'll be right there to finish," Jorg replied.

"Fine." She huffed and rolled her eyes as she turned and walked away.

Ingrid settled on the bench near the door of the cabin. Jorg crouched in front of her and brushed his hand along her forehead, pushing strands of hair to the side. For a moment, her worries left, and she leaned into his hand.

"I'm sorry." Her voice was soft and sincere The ache in her chest where the staff had contacted her thrummed lightly. Disturbed by her reaction to the staff, she slumped against the stone wall of the cottage.

"You have nothing to be sorry for. The gods have asked big things of you." Jorg twisted to sit beside her and leaned back. "It's all right to trust us, Ingrid. To let us help you." He shook his head. "I will stand by your side, no matter what happens. Please trust me."

"I do." Ingrid shifted on the bench, turning ever so slightly away from Jorg. "But I need to trust myself. I'm supposed to bind the spell, protect all the realms. How can that be me?"

She rolled her lip between her teeth and absently wrung her hands together. She'd left her cloak somewhere, and her skin pebbled against her shirt with the cool air blowing around. Raindrops began to fall in a light patter, as it hit the grass.

"Because you are amazing. You have more strength inside of you than you allow yourself to believe." He laid his hand on her cheek and waited for her to meet his eyes, "I believe in you."

She smiled as he leaned in and brushed his lips against hers. For one brief heartbeat, she might have believed him.

5

Each of them stood staring at the burial mound. Ingrid glanced sidelong, first one direction and then the other, to Selby and Jorg. No one seemed comfortable speaking or even knew what to say. What did one say to send a soul into the afterlife? Was the woman worthy of Valhalla with Odin—or Folkvang with Freya? How were they to guess?

Finally, Plintze said an odd arrangement of blessings that seemed right—to Ingrid, anyway. She hoped they had done enough to send the woman on her journey with safety and success in the afterlife. With the funeral complete, they walked away.

Ingrid's mind was numb with all the thoughts filling it. *Who was she? Why do so many of her things cause my heart to race? I need more time in that workroom.*

Jorg brushed the back of his hand against hers as they walked toward the cottage. The thoughts of hiding away and being held in his arms played like a wisp of smoke from a dying fire in her mind. In the fantasy, they pretended they were an ordinary couple with a life of farming and family ahead of them.

A sneer curled her lip, and she tucked her hands across her middle. That life wouldn't be hers—*couldn't* be hers—not anymore.

Plintze huffed and stared at the darkening sky as the drops fell faster. Grumbled words muttered low into the air as he strode toward the house. Selby snorted and kept her head low as she followed him. All of them huddled together under the eaves near the door.

"Should we go inside?" Selby asked, exchanging a look with Ingrid.

Selby seemed to hesitate because the limits of her ability to cope were stretched thin, but Ingrid wanted to go back inside. A spark in her core begged for a breath of air to flame and grow.

"Yes," Plintze said with enthusiasm. "Isn't it the custom to end a funeral with a feast to honor the dead?"

Ingrid smiled as Jorg shook his head. "One day, we'll set out a feast worthy of the gods and discover who loves food more, you or Hagen. It would be a worthy contest!" A laugh bubbled from Jorg's stomach as Plintze nodded in agreement.

A tightness gripped Ingrid's chest as she thought of her brother, who was back home preparing for an attack by assassin elves if she failed. Six weeks remained before Jarrick, the dark elf leader, demanded her presence in Alfheim—or he'd send his enforcers to destroy her village. It would be over in minutes. Broken ships littering the harbor, everyone dead, and all her fault.

Why would anyone trust me to fix this?

She shouldn't have left. If she'd stayed, then Selby and Jorg would have, too. They would be safe, and maybe the elves wouldn't have cared about her. Disgust with herself twisted her gut.

She'd put on a brave face and do the best she could. Bind the spell, and then Midgard—and all their families—would be safe. Selby would have her family. Ingrid's own parents would make sure Jorg was loved, and Plintze . . .

Ingrid glanced over to Plintze as he waited with everyone. If she hadn't left, she'd never have met Plintze. Determination washed over her. She set her jaw and stood tall.

"Wait until you see inside," Ingrid said as she pushed to stand at the door first.

Selby hung back from everyone. Plintze and Jorg both glanced at her, unsure what to make of her meek and quiet posture.

"What's with you? You always jump to claim Ingrid's side," Jorg said, talking back over his shoulder as he pressed past her.

Plintze offered nothing more than his usual, "Humph."

Selby raised her eyebrows, her hands twitching as she picked at her thumbs. "I've already seen what's in there. Besides, should we really go in? What if someone else lived here with her and comes back?"

"I don't think that's going to happen. After what we found in that workroom, I'm positive this is her home, and völvas never marry. If someone else shows up, they will have less right to be here than we do. And in that case—" Ingrid set her shoulders "—we'll deal with it."

Jorg snorted but kept his features neutral. Selby nodded and focused on the ground.

With a deep inhale and a nod from Jorg, Ingrid opened the door, pushing hard so it swung wide. She stepped aside to let the males walk in ahead of her.

Plintze charged in first, as if nothing would surprise him. The smell of bread and apples no doubt fueled his hunger after the long day, but he stopped dead in his tracks after two steps.

Preoccupied with the sights in front of him, Jorg ran into the dwarf's back and nearly toppled over him. On instinct, he snatched Plintze's shoulder without looking, preventing him from falling.

"What is this?" Jorg asked. A dumbfounded stare marked his normally steady countenance.

Plintze gaped one direction and then the next, his feet firmly planted where he stood. The rest of the group shifted around him further into the room. Selby and Ingrid stepped toward the massive dining table and allowed the boys a better view of the overwhelming interior.

"Now do you see what I meant?" Selby asked.

"How is this possible? It looks so small from the outside. One room—no more." Jorg turned in a circle, taking in the space.

"This is not natural. That was no ordinary witch," Plintze said.

"Völvas train to use Freya's magic, don't they?" Ingrid asked.

Her heart pounded, unnerved from the dying woman's words that rattled in her memory. *"Your powers from Freya."*

What did that mean? Ingrid caught herself and glanced quickly to Jorg.

Thankfully the sights preoccupied him enough that he didn't notice her mental conversation. The woman had said to tell no one, and if that included Jorg, she should be more careful. Especially since she wasn't sure if the part about Freya or the bead possibly guiding her was the secret. Better to keep it all to herself than risk it.

"Yes, but your average völva doesn't have the power to create this. It's almost . . ." Plintze's words trailed off, and his brows knitted together.

"What? What is it?" Selby asked in a shaky voice.

The dwarf fidgeted and shifted his weight from foot to foot. His unsettled behavior made all of them jumpy.

"We're sure this is the woman's home? Maybe we made a mistake in thinking it was," Jorg said.

"Nah, this is her home. Her scent is all around the place. But there's something else, too. I've not been around too many of the gods, but Asgardians are distinct. That woman, or someone else from there, made all of this." Plintze crinkled his nose as if the idea was unpleasant.

"My mother told me Eir is a norn and a valkyrie. One who weaves the fates of men and helps choose who lives on the battlefield. Maybe she was here?" Ingrid turned to Plintze with wide, anxious eyes. "But a dagger wouldn't kill someone from Asgard. Would it?"

Plintze shrugged. "I don't know. I've never tried."

The other three stared at the dwarf, silence filling the rooms. Before long, Selby couldn't help herself and rasped a small chuckle. "And why not? I'm sure your charming personality could entice a god to challenge you to a fight."

Ingrid and Jorg looked down to the ground, trying to hide their grins while Plintze gave his customary grunt.

"The woman died, so she must not have been a goddess. She had powerful magic though, or access to it," Jorg said as he looked around. "It's getting late, and I say we find places to sleep and come up with a plan in the morning. The rain is heavy now, and I'm happy to have somewhere dry to sleep for the night."

"Sleep? Here?" Selby's voice held a higher pitch than usual, and she rubbed her arms as she rocked on her feet.

"I will not rest until I eat." The dwarf folded his arms over his chest and stamped his leather-clad foot, his mustache and beard folding together as he set his lips tight.

"Come on, there's more to see, and you'll like it," Ingrid said, ignoring the swirling wave of nausea pushing against her stomach. *Act strong, be strong. I can do this.* "It will be good to stay inside for a change, Selby. We won't wake up with morning dew all over us." No matter the cheeriness she conjured into her voice, Selby's expression stayed grim.

It will be all right, really.

Jorg's smile, complete with a dimple, flashed at her as he stepped close to her side and entwined their fingers. The small gesture and his solid presence settled Ingrid's nerves as they walked.

Before they made it to the cooking room, Ingrid glanced over her shoulder and noticed that Selby had not followed them. She remained in the front entry, picking at her nails. Even at a distance, Ingrid could see her friend's chest was rising and falling too fast as she stared at the ground in front of her.

Plintze sighed when they walked into the large room that still smelled like warm bread. "This will do." He strode straight to a door Ingrid hadn't noticed before. Arms loaded with vegetables and a large hank of smoked ham upon his return, he nodded over his shoulder to Jorg. "There's more back there for you."

Jorg smiled and gave Ingrid a wink before he followed the dwarf's lead, disappearing into the dark room.

With a meal underway, Ingrid turned back to talk with Selby. "What's the matter? Plintze found a bunch of food, but you'd better hurry if you want to get any of it."

"'What's the matter?' How can you ask that?" Selby clenched her fists at her side, her breath ragged. "We are in the home of some sorceress or a goddess from Asgard. Or maybe some other realm. Why not!" She threw her hands into the air and paced toward the door and back while Ingrid stood silent and waited. "We are to eat and sleep here like it's nothing? No. We should keep moving and find somewhere *else* to stay."

"None of this make sense, and I can't explain it, but I'm *supposed* to be here. Whatever magic that woman used, it's calling to me. It's part of who I am."

The revelation smacked against Ingrid like a shield. She expected to train with Eir, to learn skills, but a persistent tap against her insides yearned for something more. Something more than mere training, but she couldn't understand, not yet.

"That's not helping. Something happened to you—up there." Selby flicked her eyes toward the ceiling. "But, are you sure what you feel is safe, Ingrid? What if it's dark magic calling to you because of that connection you have in your brain to Jarrick? He could sense it and want to push you toward it for his own benefit."

Ingrid rolled her bottom lip between her teeth as she thought about what Selby said. It was true that the essence Jarrick shoved into her was a mystery. And while the powerful magic in the house was overwhelming, the sticky substance had retreated.

This is right. I'm sure of it. There are answers here that I need.

"I agree that whatever he did binds me to him somehow, but what is here in this house is not his kind of magic. The darkness doesn't press on me, it shrinks back." Her fingers rubbed at her forehead while they both stood in silence for a few seconds.

Ingrid lowered her hand and stood tall. "Trust me in this, we are safe here. Come, get something to eat . . . that always helps. Then we can make more plans." Ingrid offered her hand. Selby hesitated before grabbing hold of it and following along, her expression still sour.

The girls halted abruptly upon entering the cooking room. Food was spilled all over the large table, and the pot hanging over the fire bubbled with what smelled like stew. "How did this happen so fast?" Selby asked. Her voice held a hint of disappointment that she'd missed the action.

"A motivated dwarf is a sight to behold when he is hungry," Jorg said with a hint of laughter in his voice. "It is delicious. Come and join us."

Selby shuffled forward and shrugged her shoulder toward Ingrid. With a roll of her eyes, Ingrid filled a trencher. Jorg was right. Everything tasted rich and flavorful.

Ingrid slouched against the table and savored a bite of

carrot glazed in honey. "I could eat these every day. Thank you, Plintze."

"Humph." His hands were busy pouring thick gravy over a mound of sliced chicken and a slab of bread covered in butter.

Ingrid smiled at him. *I love that cranky old dwarf.*

Jorg snorted but kept on eating.

6

After eating, everyone made their way upstairs. Ingrid had described the workroom, and Plintze was as hesitant as Selby to see it. But being from another realm, he was the best one to possibly understand the mysteries it held, and she needed answers to the room's secrets.

Ingrid's skin tingled as they ascended the stairs. Part of the sensation was good, while sometimes the tingling felt more like she'd fallen into a patch of nettles. At the top, Selby plopped into a chair.

"Once was enough for me. I'm not going back into that place, but Jorg—" she stared at him with pain and worry swirling in her eyes "—keep a hold of her."

"I can take care of myself." *No one seems to remember I killed a man!* Anger rose in Ingrid's chest at the implication she was helpless. The dark pressure surged against her temples and then receded to the back corner of her mind.

"That room is full of magic. It pulses through me from here. Are you sure you need this?" Plintze looked at Ingrid with a hard stare. "If you do, I will help, but it would be better to stay away."

His hesitation and the danger he implied made Ingrid's insides cramp into a tight ball. She forced herself to focus on his face. She'd believed her whole life that she was meant for something. Something great, not the fate of all humankind perhaps, but if that's what the Norns had chosen for her, then she was ready for it.

"I need the knowledge that's in there. If I don't learn to harness my power and secure the veil of protection, it won't only be our families that are in danger. Jarrick wants to create a new leadership among the gods. To do that he'll have to start a war, and everyone will suffer."

Ingrid clenched the edge of her tunic into her fists to keep her voice steady. "If I can learn what I'm supposed to do before the deadline, then maybe it will stop him for good, and I won't have to go with him at all."

Plintze gave a small, curt nod and walked over to the door. The handle turned without a hitch, and he strode through.

A buzzing in her stomach grew stronger as she stepped closer, and it drowned out everything around her. She heard the others, but only as if their voices carried through water. She didn't care what they said.

Jorg rubbed her shoulder, and she thought he'd said something, but she couldn't quite make it out. When she didn't return the warmth, she noticed his brows knit together. Ingrid sighed. His touch felt familiar and warm, but she needed to prove herself capable, to everyone—maybe even more so to herself.

With a deep inhale, Ingrid stood tall, but her hand wandered out and found Jorg's, anyway. The tiny action was more for his comfort than hers. She felt fine. He squeezed, and they moved forward as one, entering the room.

Again, the scents assaulted Ingrid—mint, lavender, sweet honey, and spices that burned the small hairs in her nose. But there were others, less familiar, coming from the various mortars and pestles set around on the table. Releasing Jorg, she made her way down the middle table, allowing her hand to caress its smooth edge.

A book lay open next to several glass bottles with stoppers resting inside their slim necks. Ingrid stopped, and as her fingers skimmed over the delicate vellum pages, soft and velvety calfskin under her touch, the words made sense to her.

She'd never learned to read the runes, let alone seen any other written language, but the knowledge was there. It sang to her like a bard, a rhythmic thrum unlocking secrets stored in her mind.

The room was no longer shrouded in darkness but illuminated in clear detail. There was a reason and order among the chaos, and it all made sense. The cadence matched her heartbeat as she glided further into the room, swaying to a feverish beat as the need to absorb everything overwhelmed and burned inside her chest.

Then came the pain.

Searing hot agony filled her as darkness pierced her vision and tore at her. Screams rang through her ears as she fought against the torrent of sounds and images. Dizziness washed over her, and she reached out to steady herself against the table.

Ingrid's hand slipped, and she fell against a wooden box. Blood trickled down her forehead as she righted herself.

Shouts assaulted her from behind, and she spun away from a hand that reached for her. Jorg's face, full of alarm, stood in front of her. Over his shoulder, Selby stood in the doorway with a panicked expression.

When Jorg stepped closer, Ingrid threw her arms in front of herself to stop him. His body immediately flew backward as if flung from a violent current.

Selby disappeared from the doorway, and a crash sounded in the hall. Ingrid's chest tightened and breath wouldn't come. Tremors rattled her body. Icy fingers seized her middle. Then the smell of pines, of spring and freshly turned earth filled the air. She lunged forward and clutched her fingers into Jorg's tunic. Dark splotches tunneled her vision until there was nothing.

Ingrid could hear her name in the distance. It was faint and frantic. *Why*? Her head ached, and she couldn't clear her thoughts. As the sounds grew louder, Jorg's voice penetrated into her consciousness, and everything flooded back to her. The sensations in the workroom had been too much for her to process. Her body had betrayed her and shut down against it.

The cool air hit Ingrid as she awakened and shivered. Jorg pulled her close to his chest, a relieved sigh pushed against her cheek.

"Thank the gods," he whispered as he buried his fingers into her hair.

As her strength returned, she pushed against him to sit up on her own. "What happened?"

"That's what you need to explain to us," Jorg said.

Over his shoulder Ingrid spied Plintze shifting from foot to foot, and the little bit of his face not covered in hair looked pale. Twisting, she looked for Selby. They were sitting on the floor of the hallway, the chairs and table where she'd last seen her friend lay scattered. "Where is Selby?"

"I'm here." A voice smaller and weaker than could possibly belong to her boisterous best friend croaked out from the corner.

The pain in Ingrid's head throbbed as she stood, but she ignored it. Her feet felt as heavy as iron as she stumbled closer to Selby and fell to her knees. The memory of Selby's silhouette disappearing from the doorway flashed through her mind.

What had she done?

"Where does it hurt?" Ingrid could barely force herself to look into Selby's eyes. Whatever injury she had was Ingrid's fault.

"It's not so bad. I think I hit my shoulder against the chair is all."

Ingrid didn't hesitate in pulling off her gauntlets, letting the familiar warm tingle of her healing energies flow down into her fingers. Selby flinched and glanced between Ingrid's hands and her face. Tears threatened to form as she realized Selby was afraid of her.

"I'm sorry. I don't understand what happened, but please let me try to help."

Selby's weak smile did not agree with her eyes, but she nodded. Before she could change her mind, Ingrid placed her hand on Selby's shoulder and felt her tense. With slow, deep breaths, she concentrated on the area.

There wasn't an outer wound like she'd worked with before. This was an unseen injury, and when she closed her eyes, it appeared in her mind's eye. The muscles and tendons from the top of Selby's shoulder down her back to the blade were inflamed and bruised.

The joint had been pulled too far. It was close to dislocating. Ingrid calmed the angry tissues and eased the separation until everything resumed healthy function.

"You'll still be sore for a while I think, but it should be better." Ingrid slumped back on her heels. The expense of using her power when she was already so drained from the experience in the workroom caused her to almost fall over as she reached to pick up her gauntlets.

"Let's go downstairs where we can rest farther away from this place," Jorg said. He gently took hold of Selby's good arm and helped her to stand before he scooped Ingrid up into his arms.

"I can walk by myself," Ingrid mumbled without conviction.

"Fine, but I still want to hold you." Jorg kissed her temple and tightened his grip on her.

"All right. Let me get in front of you two. My shoulder hurts, I don't need to have a queasy stomach, too," Selby said.

"Yes, anywhere is better than here." Plintze hustled passed Jorg, then stopped in front of Selby. "Lean your hand on my shoulder so you stay steady," he said with a glance back at her. "I don't want you tumbling down onto me."

Both Ingrid and Jorg grinned at his less than concealed concern.

Downstairs everyone settled onto the surprisingly comfortable benches made of moss-covered stone in the room across from the large dining table. Inside, the silence rained down as hard as the water from the skies poured outside.

Selby fidgeted and finally spoke what they all wanted to ask. "What happened in there?"

"I'm not sure exactly. I'm not even positive I remember it all." Ingrid rolled her bottom lip between her teeth and paced. "The magic sang to me with power and wisdom." Her chest heaved as her breaths quickened. The essence in her head pushed forward as if it, too, were listening.

"The light from your bead was so bright it was hard to look at you. Like it wrapped around you and pulled you away," Jorg said in a low voice while he stared at the floor. His arms rested on his knees as he wrung his hands. "You spoke in a language I didn't understand."

"I think it was the language of the gods," Plintze said. "No one outside Asgard understands it, but I heard some of the words once, long ago."

More shaken silence filled the room while they thought on what he'd said.

"How did you hear it, Plintze? Were you in Asgard?" Selby asked as she shook her head, stunned by the revelation.

"No, it was in my realm, but that's not important right now. I could be wrong."

"There was a piece of information, something important, but I can't remember. I need to go back in there," Ingrid said, ignoring their comments and trying to focus on the memory of what she'd read. "That's the only way I can do what's expected of me. With that magic. It will tell me how to bind the spell."

She scooted off the bench and paced, her eyes roaming

around the room in haste, never landing on anything or anyone as she spoke. "Of course, I can't do it on my own. I need to carry the power in there with me."

Selby stood and grabbed her friend by both arms. "Ingrid, look at me." She shook her slightly until Ingrid focused on her face. "Whatever you felt when you were in there, whatever you heard or saw, it's dangerous. You can't go back in there. Do you not remember what you did? To me or Jorg?"

"Yes, I can. Don't you see? This is what I've been searching for. Eir said to find her, but maybe I don't have to. I can learn what I need here." Selby's question didn't penetrate through Ingrid's thoughts. "The power to do what the Norns destined and stop Jarrick. That's the only way I can save everyone."

Selby let her hands fall back to her sides. A single, silent tear slid down her cheek. "Maybe, but isn't that why we're searching for Eir? Isn't she supposed to help you figure out how to use that magic, or whatever it is, so you don't get hurt by it? Or hurt anyone else?"

Ingrid stared at her. A scowl crossed her face as she shook her head. "You don't trust me. You don't think I'm strong enough to handle it." She moved backward with small, hesitant steps.

"I trust you. If I didn't, I wouldn't be here," Selby said.

"Ingrid, we *all* trust you, we're just worried for you," Jorg said from behind her.

She heard Plintze sigh as she stared at the floor, bile rising to the back of her throat as the pressure built inside her head. Her dark companion pulsed at the friction between them, and the sensation at the base of her skull clouded her vision.

"No, you don't trust me. How can you? I don't blame you. I'm not capable of doing anything. We've seen that over and over. Fragile Ingrid—Meyla, the little bird. But not when I was in there. That magic is supposed to be *mine*. It's the only way I'll grow strong enough."

"Stop and remember what happened in there. Ingrid, please—"

"No, *you* can't understand. Not like the rest of us," Ingrid yelled, cutting off Selby's words.

They held each other's gaze in uncomfortable silence before Selby spoke, her voice low and thick as she nodded. "Yes, that's right. How can I understand anything about you? I'm just a regular human, plodding along after the rest of you like a dumb hound." Selby pulled her mouth tight, and silver lined her eyes as she spun and strode toward the meal room.

7

No one spoke, and the surrounding air grew thick and heavy, pressing on Ingrid like a shield wall. *Selby didn't deserve that.* Her head throbbed, and she rubbed her temples. *She's wrong, though. I need that magic, or I'll never finish this.*

"Ingrid." Jorg broke into her thoughts. "What happened in that room—what it did to you—it's a magic that none of us understand how to wield. Not me, and even Plintze wasn't affected like you." He'd taken small, slow steps toward her while he spoke. He was now within touching distance, but he didn't reach out for her. "Without doubt, the Norns have fated you with extraordinary gifts. That means those of us who care for you need to guard you."

Ingrid rolled her eyes and moved to turn away from him, but Jorg grabbed her wrist. "Selby loves you. She has a house full of sisters, yet she sticks by your side." Relaxing into his touch, Ingrid shifted closer to him. "You did something, in that room . . . and it scared all of us. Selby most of all, maybe.

Go talk to her. Plintze and I will go look for some reasonably dry wood and get a fire going to warm this place."

"What? I'll not go out in that deluge." Plintze crossed his arms over his chest where he sat on a stool in the corner and made a growling noise.

Jorg raised a brow at the dwarf and gave a sharp nod toward the door. Plintze grumbled and hopped to the floor, muttering the whole time as he stomped out into the rain.

Once the room was empty, Ingrid absorbed the silence. It frustrated her that she couldn't remember the words from the books or handle the magic she'd experienced. But that was no excuse to attack her friends. With a sigh, she turned and went to search for Selby.

"I'm sorry." The words flew out as soon as Ingrid saw the way her normally stalwart friend sat with her shoulders slumped on one of the stools. Selby rested in front of the large table, still a mess from their meal.

"You were right." Selby's head hung forward and she picked at the broken skin on her thumbs without looking up.

Ingrid sat down on a stool next to her. "No, I wasn't. No one has ever supported me more than you. I wouldn't be able to even hold a weapon if it wasn't for your training." Ingrid lifted one of her hands and looked at the leather gauntlet that covered it. "You looked past all of this and treated me like I was normal."

"I never understood why it was an issue. You had cold hands, so what? Why did everybody worry about it?" She chuckled under her breath. "But, it is a big thing. It's because you're missing part of yourself. You're special, Ingrid. At least that part I've always known."

Ingrid shrugged. "I'm just me."

Selby snorted. "And Plintze is just a dwarf, Jorg is just half-elf, and I'm just a regular human."

"I'm human, too. I didn't choose this." Ingrid reached over and took Selby's hand. "Something inside of me has awoken and now I need it. It scares me sometimes."

"I'm sure it does, but I also believe that you can handle it. You've always been aware that you were meant for something great . . . I recognized it, too." She flashed a shy smile toward Ingrid and sighed. "So now what?"

"Plintze and Jorg are going to build a fire, and I think we'll stay down here for the night and decide what to do in the morning."

"You're sure no one will come here looking for that woman?"

Ingrid huffed and shook her head slowly. "I don't think anyone else lived here with her, but am I sure? I'm not sure about anything anymore."

Plintze and Jorg's voices carried to the girls as they began building a fire in the other room. Selby leaned over and pulled Ingrid into a tight hug.

The fading embers of the fire glowed against the walls as a chill crept back over the quiet room. Ingrid lay staring at the dark ceiling, her mind whirling through too many thoughts: Jorg's arm that rested over her stomach, the scent of apples and fresh bread that constantly wafted through the air, and the restless rumble in her gut that wanted to pull her back up the stairs.

Why shouldn't she go back and look around again? The

others were over exaggerating the effects it had on her. Surely, she could handle it if she concentrated and gave it more time. It was probably why the goddess hadn't shown herself yet. Ingrid needed to figure some things out on her own first.

Jorg shifted and rolled over, his arm slipping away. Selby's snores created a comforting blanket against the rumble of the storm outside. The flood of indecision was coursing through Ingrid.

She looked sidelong at Jorg and held her breath. If she was going to go, it needed to be right then. Decision made, she double checked that she could slip away unnoticed, then rolled to the floor and crawled on hands and knees toward the hall.

A vague curiosity rose to mind that she hadn't heard Plintze's snores, but she brushed it away and hurried onward. After she'd made it far enough away, she rose to her feet and padded quickly up the stairs.

The door loomed before her, and she hesitated once more. Was she doing the right thing? Should she really go in? *Yes*. This was her life, and she was the only one who could find the answers she needed.

The handle felt warm in her moist hand as she turned it. Once again, the musty smells hit her in the face. There was no turning back.

The box Ingrid had fallen against earlier was perched over the edge of the table. She pushed it back to a safer position, and her fingers jolted with electricity. It was as if she couldn't lift her hand away, but she didn't want to anyway.

Biting her lip, she pushed open the lid of the box. Runes carved onto small stones that fit into Ingrid's palm filled the interior. Each had a separate symbol.

Ingrid had never been allowed near any of the travelers who occasionally visited the village and would claim to do rune castings to tell the future. Her parents always offered them a night's hospitality, as was required of the village leaders, but then they would insist the visitors continue on their way early the following day.

Her hand hovered over the stones until finally, she scooped up two. They warmed in her hand, or her hand warmed around them, she wasn't sure. The symbols were hidden so she used a finger on her opposite hand to turn over the first stone. Dagaz. The symbol for home.

How do I know this?

With a tremble, she flipped over the second stone. Thurisaz. Protection. Ingrid sucked in and held her breath. It was the reason for her journey—to protect her home and loved ones—and the runes confirmed it.

As she contemplated choosing a third stone, the air thickened and pressed in around her. Afraid to lose the stones, she clutched them tight in her fist, while she gripped the table's edge with her other hand. White knuckles kept her upright as her vision faded.

A heartbeat later, she blinked against the waning brightness of twilight, yet she still felt the smooth edge of the table under her fingers. All around her, men yelled and swords clanged. Dust clouds swirled among the throng of feet busy at battle.

What is this? How can this be?

A warrior charged straight toward Ingrid, and she dodged sideways to avoid the blow of a raised sword. The man still swung with a grunt and met the edge of an answering blade from a man just behind Ingrid's shoulder.

It was as if they didn't acknowledge she was there. Was she there? *No*. It was a vision. Past, present, or future?

Quickly she looked around, and a weight lifted from her shoulders when she identified that it wasn't her home village. It was a large open area surrounded by a palisade.

A tingle skittered down Ingrid's spine, and the little hairs on her neck stood on end. The disturbance came from somewhere behind her. Moving slowly, she slid her eyes as far over as she could and let her neck follow until she saw what it was.

In the middle of the melee stood a tall figure dressed in a dark leather sleeveless tunic with black trousers. Long blond hair hung straight down his back with tall pointed ears jutting through. As if caught in a net, Ingrid stared, unable to move.

The male lowered his arms and ignored the battle raging around him. *Jarrick*. She'd never seen him before, but she knew it was him. The dark elf smiled at her. Not toward her, but *at* her.

Ingrid's chest heaved. Suddenly, she couldn't get enough air into her lungs. How could he see her when she wasn't really there? Her knees wobbled, and her hands gripped the table harder to keep herself standing. She was stuck between the real world of the workroom and the vision before her.

A tremendous boom cracked through the skies. She wasn't sure if it was in the real world or within the vision. A scream rang through her ears.

Everything went dark again. A heavy weight against her chest burned. The scream persisted as the murky darkness of the workroom reappeared in her view. She realized it was her own voice a heartbeat before strong arms grabbed her shoulders. Spun around, she came face to face with the wide, wild eyes of Jorg.

8

Ingrid sagged against the weight of Jorg's hands around her arms as her knees buckled. Silence surrounded them as he pulled her close and hurried them both out of the dark workroom.

With the door shut behind them, he kept one hand firmly on Ingrid while he righted one of the chairs in the hallway. His arms encircled her in a vice-like grip, but his body trembled against hers as they sat together, neither saying a word.

"What were you doing in there?" Jorg asked after they'd each let their emotions settle.

"I couldn't sleep, and I needed more time." Her palm still encircled the rune stones, and she squeezed them harder.

"You were screaming and wouldn't let go of the table. Your eyes had a glow to them. Bright, like shining turquoise stars. They did it earlier when you healed Selby's shoulder also." Jorg closed his arms tighter around her. His breath hitched before he continued. "Something in you is changing, and I'm afraid for you," he whispered.

I'm still me . . . I think.

The words were too heavy to rise to her throat. A single tear slipped down her cheek as she pressed closer against Jorg's chest.

Bent over her pack, Selby adjusted the contents and didn't look up as Ingrid and Jorg made their way back downstairs sometime later. The rain had stopped, and she looked like she was in a hurry to leave.

"Where's Plintze?" Ingrid asked.

Selby straightened up and put a hand on her hip, a questioning expression on her face. "That's all? Stroll back downstairs and act as if nothing happened? We all heard you, Ingrid."

"Oh." She didn't know what else to say.

How could she explain what she'd seen in that vision? Was it something yet to come? Was it just a way for Jarrick to contact her and scare her?

The sound she'd heard, that boom in the air, still rang in her ears and she wasn't ready to face it. Though in the back of her mind, she knew exactly what had made the sound. "I needed . . . to see. To understand more . . ." Her voice trailed off, and she stared at the ground.

A heavy sigh filled the air, and Selby touched Ingrid's arm. "Are you okay?"

Ingrid nodded and did her best to hold back the tears. Everything was as frightening to her as it was to her friends, but she needed to keep herself under control.

Act strong. Be strong.

Jorg snorted before he spoke. "The sun will be up soon. Since we're all up anyway, we should get a start toward Jorvik. It'll be a long walk from here."

Jorvik? "Why would we head to the capital?" Ingrid snapped her head up and stared at Jorg. "If Eir wanted to meet me there, I'm sure she would have told me. My bead—" she swallowed what she was about to say and wrapped her fingers around her bead. It was cold to the touch and lifeless. "That's not the way to go. I'm sure of it."

"That's where she came to you the first time. Why not go there again?" Selby asked.

"Because things are different now. Where is Plintze anyway?" Pressure built within Ingrid's temples, and she pressed her fingers against them.

Before either of the others could answer, the door creaked open and Plintze tip-toed inside. A shocked look crossed his face when he saw everyone turn toward him. His mustache twitched a few times as he closed the door, but he said nothing.

"Getting away from this place then? Good, I'll get my things." He strode over and picked up his spear and small pack without another glance to anyone.

"How long have you been out?" Ingrid asked. *And why do you seem guilty?*

"Not long, just went for a walk. Are we going or what?"

Selby huffed and bent down for her own pack. "I, for one, don't care where we go, but I'll be happy to be away from here."

With a deep breath, Ingrid stepped over and packed up her things, while Jorg did the same with his.

Once they were all outside, Jorg turned to Ingrid. "So,

which way should we head then? You decide, and we'll follow."

Clutching her bead again, Ingrid closed her eyes. Every muscle in her body tensed as she inhaled. She turned to hide her face from the others, but as she faced the west, her bead pulsed to life. Small tingles ran through her fingers and forced her eyes open.

"This way." Relieved, she squared her shoulders and marched forward, not waiting for the others to respond. The sounds of their footsteps behind her were enough to create a slight grin and a spring in her step.

After a short time of trudging through undergrowth, they'd found a game trail to follow. Ingrid led the way with Selby behind her. The early morning dew on the leaves of the shrubbery gave off a pleasant mixture of sweet berries and earthy musk.

Within a few heartbeats, several things happened at once. Jorg called out to Ingrid in a loud whisper, his hushed tone laced with urgency from his position behind Selby. A strange huffing and snorting sound came from the trail ahead.

The tangy scent of copper and crack of breaking bones assaulted her senses. Ingrid, not heeding Jorg's warning to stop, rounded a bend to stand within thirty paces of a large brown bear hovered over the carcass of a freshly killed deer.

Everyone came to a halt and froze. The humid air squeezed Ingrid's throat. For seconds that seemed to stretch like hours, no one moved a muscle. As if the world stopped with them, Ingrid could hear no sounds or see anything other than the hulking figure swaying its head side to side in front of her.

From deep within the bear's chest came a growl that sounded like thunder. The rumble passed through Ingrid as she held still, frozen in place. The beast bounced on its forelegs and lunged forward in a mock charge. Behind her, Ingrid heard the crack of branches as at least one of her friends intelligently ran away.

But she couldn't.

Her body stilled as her mind went numb. This was unlike any other danger she'd ever faced. A man with a sword or a shield could fall, but a bear was different. More than one man she'd known had fallen victim to a bear while out hunting, and they were experienced with far more strength.

Jorg called to her. She heard more rustling in the brush, but she still couldn't bring herself to move.

With a burst of surprising speed and fury, the bear made a real charge. Ingrid raised her hands, a warm tingle flaring to life in them. It felt much like healing but slightly more energetic.

Branches crushed behind her just as hands grabbed hold of Ingrid's shoulders. She was spun to the side as the bear swiped its large paw across her back.

A flash of light blinded her at the same time razor-sharp claws ripped into her shoulder blade. By the time her mind wrapped around what was happening, she was in the air. She landed with a hard thud to the ground as the air whooshed out of her lungs. Twigs poked her in the ribs and thigh, and the wounds on her back felt hot as the pain mounted every second.

The roars and snarls of the bear were mere background

noise to the throbbing pain radiating throughout her left side. Shiny spots danced around the edges of her vision, and her breath returned with heaving effort.

A failed attempt to sit up left her panting with her head resting on the musty leaves that covered the ground. She squeezed the watery film out of her eyes and used her feet and good arm to crawl her way into the cover of a hazel bush. The nutty smell acted like a balm to her senses.

She curled herself into as small of a ball as she could and tried to focus on the tingle of magic that still sputtered in her core. It prickled against her like the air sizzled just before lightning struck.

Deep and quivering, she couldn't reach it. Her head pounded too hard to concentrate. She was going to die under that bush, unable to heal herself. Blood dripped down her back and over her ribs. Tremors began to shake her arms and legs as she sank deeper into the ground cover.

When something nudged her leg, she kicked out and tried to fight, but the pain was too much. It mercilessly slammed into her, bringing the contents of her stomach up into her throat. All her efforts to stay calm were then forgotten with the fight to stay conscious.

"Ingrid, it's me," Jorg's voice called out in a low raspy tone.

The tears she'd held back sprung forth, and she wriggled out from the bush. Her hair caught, and the branches scraped against her face, but she forced herself to ignore it.

"It's going to hurt, but I'm going to pick you up now, okay?"

Ingrid let her eyes close as she nodded and took slow breaths through her nose to brace herself. Though his arms were gentle, she still bit her lip hard enough to taste blood. As soon as he had her settled as best as he could in his arms, they were quickly moving through the trees and didn't stop until they were in a small clearing under a large oak tree.

Jorg lowered himself to the ground and kept Ingrid cradled in his arms. She couldn't say anything or move for several minutes while she willed herself to push away the pain. Her powers still reluctant to heal her.

"We need to make a poultice or something to stop the bleeding." Selby's worried voice penetrated through Ingrid's addled mind. "We should look for some yarrow"

"I'll be okay. Let me rest a minute, and I'll fix it." Suggesting she needed the helpful herb only made her more intent on healing herself. The pain was so intense that Ingrid huffed a laugh, unsure if she had spoken out loud or if she was starting to dream.

Maybe I'm having a vision, and this isn't really happening.

"It's real, Hjarta. Stay still and rest. Let us help you until you regain your strength," Jorg whispered against her temple.

He was right, she knew, but she wasn't going to lay there like a helpless child. No matter how many times he called her 'my love,' or how hard it made her heart flutter.

Ingrid concentrated on all the warmth she could muster from her center and pushed it toward her left side. Unlike when she'd healed others, she had to direct the energy instead of following it. Beads of sweat rolled down the back of her neck as she pushed. Her shoulder and back blazed with heat, and she clamped her mouth tight as she struggled to keep from whimpering.

When the pain subsided enough to let her relax and Jorg's

arms no longer hurt where he held her, Ingrid opened her eyes and looked around. A pair of green eyes with swirls of gold stared back at her. Jorg's forehead was creased deep in worry, and she smiled.

I'm better. You don't need to worry.

His chest rumbled, and he shook his head. "Have you healed yourself instead of resting?"

"I did enough for now." She didn't want to admit how much trouble she had drawing on her powers. Ingrid twisted to look over her shoulder at Selby who crouched next to them. "Are you all right? Did you get hurt?" She faced Jorg again. "Did any of you?"

Selby huffed a laugh. "No, we are all fine. Not a scratch on the rest of us. You concentrate on yourself. Your tunic is a bloody mess."

With her good arm pinned next to Jorg, Ingrid couldn't twist enough to find where the gigantic paw landed against her. "If we come across a creek, I should wash it out, so it doesn't stick to me."

I need to sit up on my own, please.

He pressed his lips thin but helped Ingrid to move off his lap and lean against the giant oak tree. Ingrid spotted Plintze sitting farther away and silently wringing his hands in his lap.

"Plintze, did you get injured?"

"No. I'm fine," he growled. "I lost my pack. I'm going to go search for it." He stood and stomped away before anyone could stop him.

"Are we far enough away from the bear? Should you go after him?" Ingrid asked Jorg.

"We're at a safe distance, and his pack is next to that tree over there. I think he's embarrassed because he ran."

Her brows furrowed. "He shouldn't be. That beast was huge."

"He'll be fine. He just needs a minute to soothe his temper. I'm going to get a fire started. You're shivering," Jorg said before standing to gather sticks.

9

Ingrid couldn't remove the chill that had settled deep inside her. It was as if her whole body had grown as cold as her hands. The power coiled in her middle was at rest.

Maybe I'm just drained from my injuries?

Her back, from shoulder blade to waist, still ached. The wounds had closed completely, but she hadn't been in any condition to take care of everything. While she sat, huddled toward the flames, she reached inside of herself and called upon her abilities. The ball began to uncoil, but then fell back into place. The warmth surged forward and then disappeared.

"What's wrong?" Jorg asked and scooted closer to her.

"Nothing." Ingrid bristled at his concern as pressure built inside her head. She was trying to figure it out for herself and not having an answer struck a nerve.

It was still early, barely past midday. Plintze returned after Jorg had the fire going and offered Ingrid a pouch of water. He'd found a rushing little creek not far away, and the crisp cold water had soothed her throat but added to her sense of cold. He also had a handful of yarrow.

"There's more by the creek," Plintze said and handed it to Selby's outstretched palm.

Selby crawled forward and sat on her knees in front of Ingrid, fidgeting with the plants in her hands. "Maybe we should find that creek and wash your wounds. That tunic is probably stuck to you by now, and it's going to hurt if it's pulled away without soaking it in water first."

The idea of leaving the warmth, made Ingrid shudder, but she nodded.

"We can all go. You're not in a position to help Selby if something comes at you," Jorg said quickly with an arched brow.

Ingrid pressed her lips tight. He was right; she would be a hindrance to Selby in a fight in her condition and possibly get her friend killed. Ingrid silently growled at her own weakness. The tension woke the dark ooze in her mind which flowed from one temple to the other as if swaying to a slow drum beat.

"Whatever you need to do. Selby, let's find that creek." Ingrid stood and refused to wobble, although her legs threatened it.

The oak tree was a solid hand hold as Ingrid reached out for it. A sense of peace soaked into Ingrid's fingers as the rough bark under her palm pulsed with ancient wisdom. It gave Ingrid a sense that they were not alone in this forest.

Plintze led the way as they headed to the creek. "You two stay back here. We'll be done when we're done," Selby said and waved her hand for Jorg and Plintze to keep guard while she and Ingrid trudged down the embankment to the small rush of water.

While the pain was tolerable and the skin was sealed closed, Ingrid still felt the ache of her muscles. Bruises pulsed below her skin. Several ribs had broken, which she'd only set together but not completely healed. Nausea rattled her stomach when she moved, making her wish she'd stayed by the fire.

"Which do you prefer? The shock of cold water or the sting of your tunic pulled from your skin?" Selby asked as they reached the creek's edge.

Ingrid stared at her for a moment and then looked around. "Which one would make me seem the bravest?" She chuckled more to herself than anything, but she hissed from the pain it added to her ribs. "I'm so tired, Selby. Can you make the decision for me?"

Ingrid huddled by the fire after dressing in a spare, dry tunic from her pack and wrapping herself in both her own cloak as well as Jorg's. After the humiliating tears she'd spilled while Selby cleaned her back, she wanted nothing more than to warm quickly and head out on the trail again.

Selby's touch had been gentle. In fact, the experience had reminded Ingrid of her mother—focused and determined, yet kind—as her friend had cleaned and then pressed mashed yarrow and hazel against her wounds. But the process had drained her further, and she needed to rest.

Jorg sat next to her, but she could see the worry on his face and how his hands would rise and then fall back to his lap when he wanted to pull her close. It seemed he was afraid to touch her and cause more pain.

Even though the herbs felt good against her skin, it bothered her. *Why can't I heal myself?*

"Maybe it has something to do with what you did to the bear? It could have drained you more than you realized," Jorg offered in answer to her internal struggle.

"What do you mean? What happened to the bear?" Ingrid twisted to give him her full attention.

"As soon as it swiped you, it fell backward, roaring and snarling like it was in pain. It kept shaking its head and wobbled like it was drunk as it tried to run away."

"It even left the carcass," Selby added.

"There was . . . something . . . like a flash behind my eyes." Ingrid shook her head. It didn't make sense, and there was no way she was going to figure it out on her own. Her huff was enough to tell the others she was done with the discussion.

"I've been thinking. We are helping you search for Eir— or waiting for her to find us, possibly—but I don't even know what she looks like," Selby said, breaking the silence and changing the topic.

"She's tall and slender with long brown hair and pale blue eyes. Beautiful, but very serious." Ingrid spoke while she stared into the flames, remembering the goddess she'd met before when traveling in Jorvik. "When she stood in front of me, power radiated from her."

"As tall as me or taller, like Jorg? Because, well . . . *everyone* is tall to you." Selby chuckled as she poked the fire and added a few sticks.

Ingrid twisted her mouth to the side to attempt a look of annoyance. In truth, she couldn't help but enjoy Selby's teasing. It kept her from being lost in her own thoughts and stopped the dark influence from sending her into a bad mood.

"She never told you where to meet her?" Selby's expression was more curious than frustrated.

"No. She said I'd find her when the time was right." Ingrid shifted and tried to stretch, wincing as she moved.

"Eir is a goddess. When she wants you to find her, you'll find her." Plintze's calm voice interjected. Other than the "humph" at Selby's short joke, he hadn't said a word since they'd settled by the fire.

"Mama told me she was a norn and a valkyrie, too. I wonder if she lives in Asgard? Will she take me there to train? Have you met her before?" Ingrid's voice pitched higher as she assailed the dwarf with questions, only a few of the many clogging her mind.

Plintze stared at her and raised his bushy eyebrows when she stopped talking. "I don't know," he said slowly and deliberately.

"But you know who she is. Why haven't you said anything before? Have you met her?" Ingrid was getting agitated, and her headache returned in force.

"Eir is the goddess of healing, a handmaiden of Frigg—"

"What does that mean? The gods are immortal. Why would they need a healer?" Selby interrupted.

"Immortal beings can die with the right weapon." Plintze huffed at Selby's question before turning his attention again to Ingrid. "Most of Frigg's handmaidens wait for a summons when needed. Eir is independent, from what I've heard. I've not met her, but basic education for dwarven younglings teaches about the other realms."

"I've called for her. Why hasn't she come?"

"How would I know the will of a temperamental Asgardian?"

Ingrid nodded and let his words sink in. "I can't wait for whenever she chooses to find me."

Act strong, be strong.

The runes felt heavy in the pouch on her belt. Dagaz and Thurisaz; home and protection. There had to be a way to force the uncooperative goddess to show herself.

Several days later, after trekking through the underbrush along more wildlife paths, the group came upon a wide road at the edge of the trees. Old, abandoned Roman roads criss-crossed the countryside, and it was a relief to leave the prickly brambles and constant shade behind.

A variety of non-vital topics passed as conversation while the group strolled along. Selby carried most of the discussion, as usual.

When the sun dipped low on the horizon, a clearing opened into a great view of the fells. Rounded hills full of green were sprinkled with yellow gorse and periwinkle, lilac, and pink wildflowers. The sun's rays cast a scenic glow over everything.

"Those don't look difficult to pass. Not much different from where we graze the sheep." Selby's face softened into a dreamy, faraway gaze.

Plintze grunted. "We should find a place to camp and eat before it gets too dark."

"Yes, let's not allow the dwarf to get cranky. Except, we're too late," Selby teased.

Ingrid giggled and squeezed Jorg's hand and tugged him forward. "Let's get to the base of the hills before dark."

When they topped a small hollow, flickering campfires dotted the view, and laughter could be heard in the distance. Everyone halted and stood as still as startled deer, straining their ears to listen.

Distracted by Selby's chatter, Jorg had neglected to heed the sounds around them, and Ingrid could see how much it bothered him.

We're far enough away and safe. Everything will be fine.

He glanced at her and released a long breath through his nose, although his muscles stayed tight.

"Should we go around?" Selby asked.

"Humph." Plintze growled, the rumble in his chest abnormally aggressive. "Something's not right."

"We should get a look and find out who they are," Ingrid said.

Bile rose in her throat as the memory of the dagger in the woman's chest popped into her mind from the last time they'd encountered strangers on the path. The eager pressure of the tarry substance inhabiting her brain, rolled in delight.

Before they could step off the path to circle the group ahead, two men broke from the brush to stand a stone's throw in front of them.

One man called out words that made no sense to any of them.

Immediately, Jorg, Plintze, and Selby fell into a fighting stance, while Ingrid held her hands forward. An unfamiliar, yet comfortable, tingling sensation buzzed through her palms, and they warmed like when she healed

The men raised their weapons slightly at the response, but the same one spoke again.

"Dia dhuit."

Different from the first time, the language was still strange, and no one understood their words.

"Hello there," the man called again, this time the words were recognizable, but the accent was thick.

"Hello to you," Jorg called back, glancing over his shoulder at Ingrid. "Saxon," he whispered, and she nodded without taking her eyes off them.

The man leveled his gaze at Jorg but kept sneaking quick glances toward Plintze. His companion openly stared at the dwarf. A growl came from deep inside of Plintze, and Ingrid lowered one hand to his shoulder, which made him shift his stance and calm slightly. She doubted the men could see Jorg's ears with their distance and the fading light, but she kept at the ready just in case.

"We are traveling and have stopped here to rest for the night. From where do you hail?" The offered information held a friendly tone, but the man's expression stayed austere.

Woolen cloaks draped the men, but leather greaves covered their shins, and shields peeked out over their shoulders. The armament of warriors. Their hands remained concealed, poised to draw their swords.

"From west of Jorvik," Jorg answered without giving further information.

"Norsemen? What brings you this direction?" The men stiffened, and the one who spoke lost the casualness in his voice.

"This is still Danelaw territory. What brings *you* through these lands?" Jorg asked.

The man staring at Plintze shifted on his feet nervously, occasionally darting looks to the rest of the group and his companion.

They'd stayed ready for attack while Jorg spoke with the strangers, and the warm energy that spread through Ingrid continued to tingle in her fingers.

"We had business in Mercia and now travel back toward home in Ireland."

The men took a few steps forward, and Jorg raised his hand. "It's best we keep our distance. Consider it a safeguard. A recent altercation has us quick to draw weapons. Since your companion can't take his eyes off my friend here, I believe it might be in all our best interest to leave each other be."

Ingrid peeked at Jorg as he spoke. He stood so tall and proud, speaking with authority and keeping them all safe. Part of her loved what he was doing, but another bristled at herself for not taking the lead. The internal battle stirred up the darkness oozing in her mind.

Act strong, be strong. With a deep inhale, she forced her mind to clear and ignored the pressure as she straightened her shoulders.

"That's understandable, however, you are welcome to join us for a meal and warm yourselves by our fires. I'm sure you must be weary."

"Why would you make such an offer to a group of strangers?" Jorg asked cautiously.

A hint of something resembling amusement in crossed the man's expression. "You don't have an army hiding in the bushes, do you?"

Jorg pinched his brows together. The muscles in his arms flexed as he clenched his fists by his side.

Ingrid leaned toward him, enough to brush her hand next to his. *He knows we don't.*

Jorg shot Ingrid a sidelong glance and exhaled. "No, just the four you see here."

"Then our prince—"

His companion snapped his head toward the man fast enough to interrupt his speech.

"And our king," the man added hastily, "would expect us to offer hospitality. We insist that you join us."

"I smell roasting meat," Plintze answered.

Selby groaned. "If we make decisions based on the dwarf's stomach, we are inviting a *lot* of trouble."

"It won't hurt to have a hot meal and some conversation, don't you think?" Ingrid whispered toward the ground, so the men couldn't hear her. "They don't seem like the others."

Jorg continued to watch the waiting men. "No, I suppose not, but no one—" he turned and stared hard at Ingrid "—*no one,* lets their guard down. Agreed?"

"Agreed," Ingrid answered with a smirk. *What's with that look? I'll track any danger just like you.*

"Agreed," Selby and Plintze said together.

"If someone has a splinter, you'll run off alone to help without a second thought, and that can't happen," Jorg said, his voice low while still staring at Ingrid.

"All slivers will fester then. Will that do?"

Jorg smiled wickedly at her. "Yes." Turning his focus again on the men, and sliding a neutral expression back onto his face, he called out, "We accept your *invitation.*"

10

The men walked forward, the speaker with a fast stride and the other hesitantly falling in behind. Jorg also closed the gap, and the rest kept step with him until they were within arm's length. The speaking man extended his hand to Jorg, and they greeted each other.

"I'm Bremen, and this is Greer," he said.

About as tall as Jorg's six-foot frame, Bremen appeared near the same age, yet broader through the shoulders and equally muscled. His hair was a lighter shade, a sandy blonde, and was drawn up in a knot at the back of his head.

Several days' worth of stubble covered his angular jaw in the same shade, framing a full set of lips. Under long, dark lashes, hazel eyes sparkled with confidence and independence.

Jorg introduced himself and went around the group offering all their names. He scrunched his brows at Selby, who had a doe-eyed expression while looking at Bremen. She blushed when she saw the twitch in Jorg's mouth as he fought a knowing grin.

"It is fascinating to meet a dwarf. I've only heard tales of your kind," Bremen said.

"Are you going to share that meat with us?" Plintze asked, ignoring Bremen's comment.

Ingrid and Selby both winced. "You'll soon discover that dwarves are better companions when they are well-fed," Jorg offered by way of an apology.

Bremen only laughed. "Then let us move on to the fires where, yes, there is roasting meat, and you may have as much as you'd like."

"He didn't mean that, Plintze. Behave yourself," Ingrid said in a rush.

Bremen laughed again, harder than before, and Ingrid snapped her head to Selby as she giggled along with him. Greer kept a grim expression, but the entire group moved toward the campsites in a tense yet sociable mood.

Ingrid bumped into Selby's side as they walked toward the camps. "You giggled," she whispered.

Selby blushed and stared into the ground, not offering explanation or apology.

"I don't think I've ever seen you like this before, not even over Hagen." Ingrid grinned and shook her head. Leaning in closer, she whispered, "He *is* rather handsome, though."

Jorg tipped his head and looked over his shoulder before turning back to the front with an eye roll. *Not as much as you, of course.* She snickered under her breath when she saw his dimple flash.

Bremen stopped the group and spoke to Greer. "Hurry forward and make everyone aware that our new companions will be joining us, so there is no concern when we arrive."

"Yes, s—"

"And," Bremen interrupted, "be sure to remind everyone that the prince's whereabouts are still to remain hidden. Is that understood?"

Greer scowled for a split second before giving a quick nod. "Yes, I understand, and I will prepare the way for everyone's arrival."

Ingrid shivered. Something about Greer bothered her. Whether it was his small raven-like eyes or his constant scowl that even his full beard and mustache couldn't hide, she wasn't sure. But, he made her uncomfortable.

Bremen turned back to the group as Greer jogged toward the camp. "Better to give warning than cause a commotion."

"Why, if I may ask, is your prince in hiding?" Jorg asked. Stiff with coiled muscles, he stood taller than he had a few minutes before.

"Unfortunately, that was a necessary precaution as we traveled through unfamiliar territory. We thought it the best way to keep him safe."

Jorg studied Bremen with a slight grin. "It's a shame that we won't be able to meet him," he said.

Bremen nodded. "Yes, it is." He held himself with a strong posture yet seemed relaxed as he held Jorg's stare with the competitiveness worthy of a Norseman.

"Are we going to stay here all night?" Plintze grumbled.

"Pardon me, let's continue," Bremen said, marching forward and leading the group while Jorg moved to follow behind Ingrid and Selby.

When they neared the camp, Plintze, who had been striding with purpose, slowed and drifted back to Jorg's side.

"There are more fires than it looked like before."

"I noticed the same thing," Jorg whispered. Neither of

them broke their gaze from the large number of men ahead of them. "You travel with a lot of men," Jorg called to Bremen.

"Yes, well, it is an unsettled time in Ireland. It requires the king's attention, but even so, he insisted on a large showing in Mercia."

"How fortunate he had so many men to spare at such a time."

Bremen gave Jorg a questioning look but nodded. They reached the outskirts of the camp, and many men rose to their feet when the small party walked by, creating an uneasy tension. Even Bremen appeared uncomfortable with the actions and occasionally made motions for them to stay seated. Ingrid and Selby walked a little closer to each other when they saw the unexpectedly large number of men.

Hidden somewhat between the others, Plintze walked unseen through the men sitting around fires, until a few nudged their companions and pointed. Plintze ignored them, but as they made their way toward the middle of the encampment, a low rumble of mutterings rose around them. By the time they reached the center near the largest tent, a crowd was following them to get a look at the dwarf.

"I apologize, Plintze, but I don't believe the men have seen a dwarf before." Bremen lifted his chin and bellowed toward the back of the gathered crowds, "These are our guests! Go back to your fires!"

The men dispersed while still trying to sneak wary peaks in Plintze's direction and mumbling among themselves.

"Humph." Plintze kicked his toe in the dirt, looking uncomfortable with someone coming to his defense. But, he raised his head proudly and stared at Bremen, gave a slight nod, then asked where the roasted meat was.

"Clear the area and guard your fingers," Selby said in her robust voice, and Bremen let out a hearty laugh, surprising Jorg and Ingrid. They chuckled and looked between their friend and their new acquaintance with interest.

I've never seen her act like this with anyone, and no one laughs at her jokes but me.

Jorg stared and shook his head, seemingly confused at the turn of events.

Bremen slipped the strap of his shield over his head and flipped one side of his cloak over a shoulder. A young boy hurried to help untie the two pieces of the heavy leather corslet covering his chest and back, then bent to do the same with his greaves.

It was similar armor to what Ingrid had seen the men in her village wear for battle. When the boy ran off with the shield and all the leathers, Bremen returned the cloak to the front, and Ingrid spotted the sword still hanging from his belt.

Then again, each of them still had their weapons strapped to their bodies as well. Ingrid noticed that Greer continued to stand and did not remove his battle gear. His dark eyes glinted as they darted around the group, a slight curl to his lip as if the air held a foul odor.

"Sit. Let's enjoy each other's company," Bremen said as he sat on one of the many cut logs arranged around the campfire.

Still somewhat uneasy, the four sat as several young girls rushed forward with trenchers filled with roasted grouse, vegetables, and hearty slabs of bread. Though Ingrid's stomach rumbled when she smelled the aroma of rich spices, it also reminded her of home, and she hesitated to eat as she thought of her family.

As a distraction, she watched the serving girls who spoke quietly to the men and hurried away as soon as the meal was served. Their language was one that Ingrid had never heard before, even in the bustling capital.

"Is that your native tongue the girls speak? I don't recognize it," Ingrid said.

"The servants all speak Gaelic. Most of the men speak Saxon as well, but not all. None understand the Norse language." Bremen paused and glanced at each of them, settling on Jorg. "I have met a few Norsemen, but those didn't speak Saxon. It's convenient that you do." A question laced his words as he stared at Jorg.

"Our village chieftain believes it is best to learn several languages It makes doing business easier," Jorg said.

Bremen paused but then gave a tense nod. "We've had many Norsemen land on our shores to do business." The cool tone permeated the air, and everyone stopped eating, even Plintze.

Jorg held Bremen's stare over the rim of his cup. "There are many forms of business, but we are on a personal journey if that eases your mind." After hesitating for a moment, Jorg continued. "You've traveled across the sea and south as far as Mercia. What did the king there offer that warranted such a display of strength?" Then added, "If you don't mind my asking."

The air grew thick around Ingrid's shoulders as she mentally noted which direction held the best escape route.

"Not at all." Bremen bit off a large bite of bread and chewed slowly, speaking again only once he'd swallowed.

"We negotiated a treaty with the king. We have similar interests in keeping our shores and lands protected."

Jorg bobbed his head and accepted the answer, letting any further comments go unspoken. It seemed to appease Bremen, and some of the tension faded into the air. Ingrid let her hand travel back to her bread from where it had rested on her thigh, above her dagger. After the meal, everyone relaxed as they became less concerned about each other. Much to Ingrid's delight, stories began from Bremen's travels. Even Greer seemed to loosen up as he joined in with the storytelling and laughter. Mugs of ale clinked together while the fire burned bright and the night wore on.

11

More than once, Ingrid found Bremen waiting for Selby's reaction or gazing at her longer than necessary as she asked questions. He seemed enthralled by the entertainment. Selby, for her part, was equally coy with the engaging young man as he strutted around and gestured to make the stories come to life.

Ingrid knew the pain Selby caused herself as she pined away for her brother through the years. It was good to see her affections turned in a new direction, yet she wondered if becoming smitten with a stranger from another land was any better.

As the evening wore on, fewer and fewer men continued to sit by the fire, most finding their way to tents for the night. Several men, upon Bremen's insistence, erected a small tent for Plintze when he grumbled about a place to sleep for the night, which he promptly crawled into and snored.

"So, my new friends, we have captured the whole evening with story after story about our own adventures. I would love to hear some of yours," Bremen said and lifted his mug toward Jorg.

"It's been a pleasure to listen to you since I've not met anyone from Ireland before. I'm sure our stories would pale in comparison," Jorg answered.

"Perhaps, if it is not too forward, you might share with us how two young women, a dwarf, and another male," Bremen hesitated, "find themselves this far away from home?"

Silence filled the air as the remaining men around the fire stared at the three and waited for an answer. Some even stopped their mugs midway to their mouth, apparently having lost interest in their drink.

We shouldn't tell them everything.

"It's a simple story, I'm afraid, but we are looking for a lost relative of Ingrid's, and our search has brought us this way," Jorg said.

The tension in the air grew thicker as smoke from the burning logs trailed up and coiled around Ingrid's throat. She didn't drink ale much—she didn't like it—but she still put the mug to her lips occasionally to appear indulgent. But at that moment, she swallowed a long draw of the bitter liquid.

"Seems a long way to search for a relative. Must be someone important."

"She is dear to my mother and me, but our settlement is small, and we couldn't spare more people." Ingrid sat taller and smiled, the ale inspiring a bit more courage than she may have previously.

Bremen quirked his lips and nodded, then rubbed at his jaw as if he were thinking about what Ingrid said. "And the other one, Plintze, he's from your village as well?"

"No, we met on a separate trip, and he became a friend," she replied.

Selby groaned and rolled her eyes. "He is a pain in the . . . backside, but I trust him to protect Ingrid—and all of us," she added hastily.

Ingrid rolled her lip between her teeth and looked into the fire. *I knew she loved him, too.*

Jorg slipped his hand into Ingrid's.

"And how about you, Jorg? Did you join these two adventurous women, like Plintze did?"

Jorg met Bremen's gaze across the flames, neither backed down from another stare challenge. "I'm from the same settlement. Why do you ask?"

Bremen gave a gentle point in Jorg's direction. "Well, one can't help but notice the ears, now can they? I'd love to hear the story about those."

"I was born with them. That is how you got yours, isn't it? Or does it happen differently in Ireland?" Jorg grinned and raised his glass.

Ingrid sucked in a deep breath through her nose and squeezed his hand while keeping a neutral expression on her face. The secret of Jorg's elven heritage was still fresh and raw. He embraced it well, keeping his ears uncovered now instead of hiding them under the dark waves of his hair.

I'm glad you let them show.

Bremen's expression cooled, and his smile slipped away. Jorg stiffened, and tension radiated off of him as he gripped Ingrid's hand a little stronger.

Finally, Bremen gave a loud laugh. "Well, enough then. It's been a pleasant evening, and we wouldn't want to ruin that, would we?"

Jorg tipped his head in agreement. From the corner of her eye, Ingrid saw Selby's shoulders lower as she sighed under her breath.

"There was talk in Mercia of a druht, a private war band, hunting enchanted beings," Bremen said. "I didn't give it much thought at the time. But, now that we've met, I would hate for you to run into any of those misguided souls and put the lives of your lovely companions at risk."

"We've already met a few of that druht, as you call it. Not a friendly sort, it seems they are hired by someone, but we persuaded them to leave us be just fine," Jorg said.

"Oh? Please do tell how you convinced them to give up their wages. I've not met men willing to do that before."

"Elves can make people do things by speaking to them in their dreams or singing to them, like the faeries," Greer blurted out.

Bremen inhaled a deep breath and sliced a glare to his friend. "Our homeland has strong superstitions about the fae realm. I fear that may influence many opinions of you within the camp."

"Is it true? Can you make men do your bidding?" Greer asked.

"Greer, that is enough," Bremen snapped. Authority oozed from his voice as if he expected immediate obedience.

"I have never tried to force anyone to do my bidding, nor would I, if that settles some of your fears. And, I don't even know if I can sing—I've never tried." Jorg let out a whiff of amusement. "The persuasion I spoke of was the kind that uses weapons. You've asked quite a few questions, Bremen, do you mind if I ask one for myself?"

"Of course."

Ingrid's pulse pounded against her skin, and a trickle of sweat rolled down the center of her back. The tar pressed hard as her heart raced faster. The uneasy truce between them balanced on a dagger's edge as the conversation continued.

Jorg glanced around beyond their fire to the many tents. "You're obviously a leader among your men, Now we sit next to the largest tent within view, yet you look no older than me, younger perhaps. How does someone of your age end up in such a position over a group this large?"

Greer fidgeted and looked agitated, but Bremen remained calm and composed. "That's fair enough. I grew up among the king's men and showed a special affinity for sword play at an early age, granting me the ability to begin my training younger than most."

There was a small silence while everyone stared into the flames, small pops from the wood released sparks into the dark night. The conversation had grown less jovial, and Ingrid tried to remove her hand from Jorg's, but he squeezed lightly for her to stay. She picked at a non-existent loose thread on her trousers with her free hand. It was Selby who finally broke the silence.

"Why would the druht hunt down those with magic? What could be their reason?"

"From what I heard, their leader is a man from Wessex who has a deep hatred of all magic because of personal experiences. He believes someone with magical powers, will help those from the otherworld bring death and destruction to all humans. A reward is offered for any information about who it might be, so they can be stopped."

There are stories about me? Why didn't anyone say so before we left?

Never learning who she was had made her more vulnerable. Ingrid fidgeted and rubbed her hands together in her lap, wanting to pace or at least slip into the dark and hide. Her parents thought they were protecting her by hiding her connection to Freya's spell as she grew. But now there were too many unknowns that left her exposed and defenseless.

Selby sat close enough to Ingrid that she reached out a hand and brushed the side of Ingrid's thigh. "We saw their questioning methods," Selby said. Even in the glow of the fire, her face paled and her mouth clamped tight.

Bremen peered at Jorg with a mixture of agitation and concern. "What happened?" he asked through his teeth.

"They had a woman bound and tied like an animal. We helped release her, but one man put a dagger in her chest before we got to him."

Bremen leveled his sight on Selby. "I am sorry." He continued to stare at her, as he tipped his face toward Jorg. "Did any of them get away?"

"No."

Bremen inhaled and nodded. "Good."

The conversation floated into Ingrid's ears, but she couldn't hear the words. The realization that those men searched for *her* and the woman had died because of it—because of her— had her head in a spin. She sat tall as she battled for control against the dark pressure making things worse.

"I need to rest now," Ingrid muttered. "Can you show us where we should set ourselves up for the night? Anywhere out of the way is fine."

"A tent is ready for you, as our guests." Bremen stood and called out to an older woman, who stepped out of the shadows where she'd been waiting. "An féidir leat na mná a thaispeáint go dtí a bpobal." He spoke in her native tongue before turning back to the others. "Moirin will show you to where you can retire."

Selby, Ingrid, and Jorg stood as one and turned to follow the woman. "Jorg, would you mind staying to talk with me for just a few more minutes?" Bremen asked.

Ingrid stared at Jorg, and he brushed her cheek with the back of his knuckles. "I won't be long."

Jorg sat back down, with what Ingrid believed was a smile of assurance. She followed Selby and peeked back at him, spying his wink before she slipped into the shadows. They walked past three tents until they came to one that looked as if it should lodge at least ten. But when they ducked through the door, there were only two pallets covered in straw and furs, and even had a woven mat on the floor.

"This is just for us?" Ingrid asked Moirin, but Ingrid could not decipher the mutterings she made.

The woman, in turn, couldn't understand Ingrid either. She gave up and began trying to help Ingrid out of her clothes, gasping when she pulled off the gauntlets. Moirin ran her hand along the length of Ingrid's dragon scar, muttering more words in her own language before pulling her hand away and resting it in a fist at her chest.

Touching her head, chest, and each shoulder before

kissing her fingers, she shuddered and then handed Ingrid a nightdress that appeared from a trunk.

Selby hurried to undress and redress herself before Moirin could help her. The older woman was unfazed, apparently back to business after her reaction to Ingrid and then shooed them both onto their respective beds. Brushing against Ingrid's hands, she produced another blanket and tucked it in tight.

Without another word, Moirin left the tent, and the girls thought they'd seen the last of her only to discover her a few minutes later hurrying back to put a warm stone wrapped in a cloth under the blankets near their feet. Once Moirin had them settled with the warmth of the stones creating more heat than was tolerable, and no way of saying so, she blew out the candles and left for good.

Selby giggled and reached down to remove the heat source near her feet. "I don't know about you, but I could get used to someone taking care of me like this, even though it's like sleeping in the middle of a hearth. Do you think this is some kind of pre-roasting ritual as we sleep, and they'll serve us for breakfast?"

"What? How do you come up with such things? I think she was trying to be nice. At least you can move. I think she might have sewn me in somehow. Can you help me?" Ingrid whined.

Selby slipped out of the covers and helped Ingrid to loosen all of her coverings. "She obviously felt your hands."

"Yes, she did that earlier, too, when she handed me the meal. She didn't take our packs, did she?"

"No, they are still here. Do you want your gauntlets?"

"Yes, I would rather wear those instead of all these coverings." Ingrid slid the sleeves over her arms, securing a loop around her middle finger to keep them in place. "What do you think is happening to Jorg? Do you think that Bremen really wanted to talk with him? What if they do something to him because they fear he'll use his elven magic to control their minds, like Greer worried about? Maybe we should go check?"

"*Now* who conjures up stories? Bremen wouldn't do that, he's not that kind of man. I'm sure of it. Although, he seems to think we can't take care of ourselves, so he probably wanted to talk to Jorg without us there."

"You're sure of him. Would that be the reason you were all smiles whenever he looked at you? You giggled at a joke. Someone is a little affected, I'm betting."

"Well, how could I not be? No other man I've met can rival Hagen in looks and leadership. Do you see the way the men listen to him?"

"I noticed that no one else was giving any orders. Why do you think that is? That seems odd. What if *he* is the prince and just doesn't want us to know it?"

Selby was quiet for long enough to hear the crickets outside the tent before she answered. "It doesn't matter. We'll leave in the morning anyway, but he was handsome to look at." Selby sighed and settled herself down into the covers. "It's nice, though, to have a warm place to sleep. I'm glad we came this way. It was enjoyable to be around plain humans, too, even for an evening."

Ingrid thought about that, and a ball formed in her stomach. "Why do you say that?"

"I love you, you know that, but I feel like I don't belong sometimes." They both stared up at the ceiling and let the words hang in the air. "It's nothing. I liked their company; that's all." Selby rolled toward the outside wall of the tent and scooted deeper under the furs.

There wasn't anything Ingrid could say. She also felt like she belonged nowhere and understood Selby more than her friend would believe. After the fight they'd had in the cabin, she hoped the evening gave Selby some peace.

I hope I've chosen the right path for all of us.

As the sun rose the next morning, Moirin hurried both girls out of their beds . She motioned for them to get dressed while she gathered the stones and muttered to herself. She grabbed hold of Ingrid and lifted one hand then the other, examining her fingers. Ingrid watched her in utter confusion as she continued to mumble.

Ingrid shrugged her shoulders, not understanding a word the woman said. Selby matched the motion, and they both tried to hide their giggles while they dressed. Ingrid gathered her knives and started to leave, but she didn't make it far.

Moirin tugged her back into the tent and sat her on the bed, twisting Ingrid's shoulders so she could work on her hair. Once Ingrid realized what she was doing, she sat still and cringed more than once when the woman insisted on removing all the tangles.

Selby tried to sneak away, but Moirin rushed in front and forced her to sit on her bed to wait for her turn as well.

"I guess we need to make a better impression today," Selby chuckled. "Maybe we'll get to meet the prince."

"Or, maybe we already have? *Ouch*. Which would be odd, though, so probably not. *Ouch*!" Ingrid called out as Selby snickered at her pain. "Just wait! You're next, and she is, forceful." Ingrid slammed her eyes shut and bit on her lip to brace herself for the discomfort.

"Yeah, it would be odd." Selby looked off into the distance, contemplating what Ingrid had said. Soon, Morin broke her concentration by twisting her shoulders to begin her hair treatment. "*Ow*! You weren't joking."

Ingrid giggled. "What do you think? Was it worth the pain?" She stood before Selby and turned a circle.

Selby twisted her mouth. "Unfortunately, yes. You look great." Scrunching her eyes closed, she endured the removal of her tangles as well.

When the girls finally stepped out of the tent, they each wore single woven braids that cascaded down the center of their backs with a smaller braid circling each side of their head like a crown. Moirin had even adorned the back of the crown with golden pins. Dressed back into their trousers and, they looked a mixture of fine noble and tough warrior.

At the same campfire they'd sat near the night before, Selby enjoyed the grin that eased across Bremen's face as they approached.

"I think I might keep this look," Selby whispered to Ingrid. As usual, it was loud enough to have traveled to the ears of everyone nearby. Ingrid closed her eyes and shook her head, but a prickle on the back of her neck made her uneasy. Neither Jorg nor Plintze was anywhere in sight.

"Good morning," Selby said.

Bremen stood as the girls approached, his focus solely on

Selby. She sat on a log to Ingrid's left and scooted to the center when Greer walked up eyeing her with a smirk.

"Where are Jorg and Plintze?" Ingrid asked, scanning the area.

Bremen spoke something in Gaelic to Moirin who grumbled before she hustled away. He chuckled to himself then turned his attention to Greer. "Where were you off to so early?"

Jorg, where are you? Ingrid didn't know if Bremen had been too distracted by Selby to hear her question or was deliberately ignoring it. He seemed relaxed, but the hostility she'd perceived from Greer the night before saturated the air again like a heavy dew.

"I was checking in with the men to be sure preparations have been made to move out this morning."

"Have you seen Jorg or the dwarf, by chance?" Bremen asked as Greer settled onto a log, finally addressing Ingrid's concern.

"His name is Plintze." Ingrid heard the growl in her voice, but she didn't care. *He has a name after all.*

Bremen clearly wasn't asking out of the same concern she had. He probably only wanted to keep an eye on them as a threat. *As you should. I'm sure Jorg could beat you in a battle.*

"Yes. Plintze. Have you seen them?" Bremen asked Greer again, a tight smile on his face that didn't match the challenge in his eyes at Ingrid's tone.

"No, I don't believe I have seen the—*Plintze*—today. I saw Jorg heading out that direction early this morning." Greer swept his hand in a lazy arc away from camp. "I didn't care to stop him and ask why."

There was no way Jorg would have left without telling Ingrid. She knew that to her core. After his outburst the night before about elven abilities, Greer's gesture seemed too casual.

"I'm sure they'll show up. We'll head out soon since the journey is long." Bremen dug into his meal as if there was nothing to worry over.

"As Jorg mentioned yesterday, we must go our own way. While we enjoyed the warm beds a great deal, we need to find my relative." Ingrid fidgeted with her bowl. A worried shakiness in her stomach troubled her appetite.

Where are you? I'm not getting a good feeling about these men. Darkness seeped throughout her thoughts, and she struggled to sit still.

Bremen looked at her casually. "After we spoke last night, Jorg agreed to stay with us, at least for a time, since your path is through the fells, same as ours."

Ingrid swallowed down a lump in her throat and stared at the bowl in her lap. A sidelong glance to Selby rattled her nerves as her friend also appeared uneasy. *Act strong, be strong.*

Determined not to reveal weakness, she lifted her chin and straightened her shoulders, ignoring the trepidation. Perhaps Jorg was scouting the area or hunting, as he did sometimes in the early morning. She would wait a while longer, though frustration bubbled within.

As they ate, Ingrid kept noticing Greer hiding a yawn, as did several others sitting near them. Tents were being struck all around them, and as men walked by, more than one stared at their group, many of them stifling yawns as well.

"Several men appear exhausted this morning. Did we

miss a celebration after we left last night?" Ingrid asked, trying to make polite conversation to ease her nerves.

All the men around their fire grew silent and stopped eating, their faces marred with angry scowls. Ingrid swallowed the bite she was chewing and sat still, realizing she had said something wrong.

"As I mentioned last night, superstitions run deep. Many of the men stayed awake," Bremen answered, "so they wouldn't dream."

"Ah." Ingrid then remembered how they thought Jorg could control their minds and actions while they slept. A chill ran down her spine, and she wished again for Jorg to join them.

Then as if by force Ingrid's eyes jerked up to stare at a man dismantling a nearby tent. Rather than lay the crossbeam to the ground, he let it fall.

Time slowed as Ingrid watched it land against a branch, the force of the beam lifting the branch into the air. The man lost his footing and tumbled down, the branch ripping through his thigh.

Before the entire incident had finished, Ingrid was on her feet letting her trencher clatter to the ground. The thrum of energy pounded against her chest as the bead on her necklace bloomed and glowed. A bright amber tinted her vision yet made every detail vivid and distinct.

The promise she'd made to Jorg echoed in her thoughts as she kept her feet planted. Blood pooled under the man's leg enough for her to see from where she stood. She stayed anchored in place though her hands blazed like fire, and she wrapped them around the bead.

A flurry of commotion sent men scrambling to help.

Tearing shirts and pressing against the gaping wound. Bremen called out orders and hurried over, bending down to speak in the Gaelic tongue.

From the corner of her eye, Ingrid saw Selby take slow steps closer toward the panicked group. Creases lined her forehead as she stared over her shoulder at Ingrid.

Drum beats sounded in her ears as Ingrid's heart raced, and the air squeezed from her lungs. A shake of her head pleaded with Selby before her friend turned away from her. These men couldn't discover her identity. If they found out who she was they'd give her to the druht. No one would pass up an easy reward.

"Ingrid can help!" Selby shouted over the din.

Her voice slammed into Ingrid like an axe.

Bremen stood and spun in her direction, moving with haste to stand in front of her. "What does that mean?" Staring at Ingrid, his eyes grew wide. "Are you a healer?"

Selby nodded. "She is, let her touch him."

"Selby, don't." Ingrid hated the way her voice sounded weak and pleading as her chest rose and fell quicker.

Before Ingrid could run, Bremen snatched her arm and dragged her toward the crowd, yelling for a path to clear. Selby followed behind.

Ingrid's knees squelched into the mud made by the man's blood as she fell next to him. Overwhelmed, her instincts took over. She ripped off her gauntlets and placed her hands against the pulsing injury. The torn flesh showed inside her mind behind her closed lids.

First, she concentrated on knitting together the torn veins where the blood flowed profusely, then she watched as tiny splinters released and washed away before each side of the gash folded together and closed, leaving unmarred skin.

No sound penetrated her mind, only the warm, sticky blood on her hands and the coppery aroma of it filling her nose. The tingle of energy flowed from deep inside of her to the damaged skin.

As the wound completed its healing, sounds drifted back to her consciousness. The distant hammering of boards, the camaraderie of the men as they worked, the ragged breaths of the man under her palms, and the cool shade of bodies huddled over her blocking the daylight.

As she lifted her hands away from the man and opened her eyes, his panic-riddled expression stared back at her. A hard lump formed in her throat that she swallowed down and sat back on her heels.

"You will be fine now."

The man shook his head at her, unable to form words. More white than color shown in his eyes as he gaped.

Ingrid felt herself sway, exhaustion washing over her as she sat. The energy sank back into her middle, drained and cooled.

A voice sounded in her ears, distant though she could feel breath on her cheek. Strong arms pulled her to her feet, and she turned her head enough to see Selby out of her peripheral. Together, they walked back over to the fire, and Ingrid settled onto a log.

Shouts and the ruckus of an angry crowd formed at Ingrid's back. *They are going to turn me over to the druht. If they don't kill me first.*

She'd never see her home again. Everyone in the village would die. She hadn't proved herself worthy enough for Eir, and now all of Midgard would be left vulnerable to the evils of the other realms.

Ingrid stared at her friend. Tears stung the backs of her eyes as she fought to understand. "Why?" she asked through the thickness in her throat.

"He is alive because of you," Selby answered, ignoring the bigger issue.

A cool cloth was shoved into her view, and Ingrid glanced up to see Moirin nodding for her to take it. She reached for it and wiped at her fingers. The cloth turned red, but her hands remained stained.

Bremen crouched in front of Ingrid. The muscles in his jaw popped as he clenched his teeth before he spoke. "You are not an ordinary healer. Who are you?" His tone clipped, but not angry.

Behind Ingrid, the dissent among the men began to grow louder. It wouldn't be long before they hauled her away, tied in ropes like the völva. Ingrid held Bremen's stare but said nothing.

"Can you protect her?" Selby asked. A wobble to her words said she was close to tears.

Ingrid tensed further. Selby shouldn't have made her do that. Let her cry for what would come next. How could she even beg for protection when she had caused the need?

"I'll sort out the camp and calm the men, but then I'll be back, and you need to explain what happened." Authority returned to his voice, it was not a suggestion but a command.

Bremen's voice boomed over the shouts, and quiet rippled through the camp. Ingrid shifted to watch, to see the moment her fate changed.

Selby sat on a log next to her and tried to take the cloth, but Ingrid gripped it tighter. At least it was something to hold. A cold, bloody piece of cloth to use as comfort.

"I'm sorry." Selby's words floated into the air, but Ingrid ignored them.

She had to stay focused on the scene in front of her. Whatever happened next would decide if she'd be able to continue the path that led to her destiny or if she'd doomed herself, and everyone else with her, when she chose this route to find Eir.

A small group had formed among the men, headed by Greer. A space open between them as Bremen stood in front of the larger crowd. Ingrid was too exhausted to deal with Selby's guilt and the battle forming in front of her.

Once again, she pleaded in her mind for Jorg to show himself. The thought of not seeing him again before they hauled her away stole her breath.

"She has unnatural powers, like the others. We shouldn't have let them among us," Greer shouted at Bremen. The ten or so men behind him grumbled their agreement and shuffled their feet as they cast uncomfortable glances in Ingrid's direction.

"Martin would be dead now if she hadn't been here. We owe her our thanks," Bremen said, raising his voice only enough to be heard, but he kept it controlled and even.

"Still wonder where the prince is?" Ingrid asked Selby in a low voice, the words bitter in her mouth.

"There are more men on his side. They'll listen to him

and understand that you're not a threat." Selby focused on the arguing men. "If they don't, we'll leave. I won't let them hurt you."

Though she felt her strength returning, Ingrid fought back the sting of tears at Selby's words. If she had to fight her way out of this, she would lose. The darkness in her head oozed forward in lazy agreement.

"Greer, we have been like brothers, but you need to step aside. We invited Ingrid into our camp as a guest, and she has done us a great service. I will not hear any more of this." Bremen stepped closer to Greer, and the men behind him pressed in as well, surrounding the smaller group.

"You are making a mistake and bringing danger to us all," Greer said, but he no longer shouted. Ingrid had to strain to hear him.

"It is my mistake to make then. We need to finish breaking camp and be on our way. There will be no more of this dissent, or you can leave my service."

The men who had stood with Greer seemed to fade into the larger crowd, leaving he and Bremen in an open area in the center. Greer glanced around and must have accepted he was defeated because he nodded to Bremen but said no more.

Ingrid stood, her trousers sticking to her legs as the blood on them dried. "Bremen," she called out, and all heads turned in her direction. Selby rose at her side, staring at her as well. "Where are Jorg and Plintze?"

Those men knew where they were, she was sure of it, and she needed answers before they went back to their work. Something wasn't right. Jorg wouldn't have left her alone this long.

"Do you know anything about where they have gone?" Bremen asked, his gaze leveled at Greer.

Most of the men turned their focus toward Greer, but a few stared at the ground and shuffled their feet. The same men who'd stood with him moments earlier.

Rested and restored to strength after the healing, Ingrid strode forward with Selby on her heels. She shoved through the circle to stand near Bremen, although Ingrid could sense the unease at her presence. None of the men stopped her.

"Many of us disagreed with allowing an elf and dwarf among us. After hearing all the talk in Mercia, we questioned the appearance of two creatures none of us had ever seen in person. I chose to question them after you retired. As one of your personal guards, it is my duty to keep you safe." Greer spoke with his head held high as he stared at Bremen.

Towered over by all the men around her, Ingrid stiffened and stood as tall as her petite frame allowed. She took a step closer to Greer and spoke between clenched teeth, "Where are they?"

13

———

Greer ignored Ingrid and continued to stare over her head at Bremen. *If I had my hammer right now, you'd pay attention to me.* When he didn't answer her after several seconds of silence, Ingrid launched herself at him.

Startled, Greer raised his arms to defend himself and caught her midair. He pushed her away, knocking her off balance as she punched and kicked at him. Ingrid landed with less of a thump on the ground than she might have thanks to both Selby and Bremen stumbling to reach her and break her fall.

Ingrid recovered quickly and hopped back to her feet. Faster than anyone could grab her, she once again rushed at Greer. This time, he was ready for her and swung his arm, so the back of his hand landed against her cheek, sending her into the dirt.

While on her hands and knees, blood began to fill her mouth. She ran her tongue over her teeth to check if any were missing. Specks of light, like tiny shooting stars, danced around the edges of her vision from the pain radiating through her jaw.

With determined effort, she rose to her feet, widened her stance, and stood firm. The flood of her emotions seemed to excite the dark essence, and Ingrid's body shook as she struggled to control it.

"Ingrid, please stop." Selby's eyes were wide as she took hold of Ingrid's arms. "Don't get yourself hurt. He'll tell us where they are."

"Get out of my way!" Ingrid struggled against the hold, trying to free herself.

Before she could get around Selby, Bremen's fist landed on Greer's jaw and sent him backward into the men standing with him. "Tell us where you've taken the others."

Whether he was defending Ingrid or angry over Greer's actions, Ingrid didn't know or care. She relaxed slightly as the throbbing in her jaw caused her to second-guess her attack strategy.

Those loyal to Greer helped him to stand and then continued to hold him so he didn't strike back at Bremen. He spat and smiled through bloody teeth. "Find them yourself. You're so willing to discard those who have been loyal to you. I have nothing more to say to you."

"Should I put him in chains or run him through?" a man standing next to Bremen asked.

"Neither," Bremen said as he scrubbed his hand over his face and blew out a long exhale. "Greer, you sadden me. It didn't need to come to this. Just leave. You're no longer in my service, and those of you who joined him in this, you need to go also."

"They should *not* go free," the man said again to Bremen.

"I understand, Gavin, but let them crawl away like the dogs they are."

"Where is Jorg? You can't just let them go before they tell us!" Ingrid screamed at Bremen. Selby continued to hold Ingrid to prevent her from throwing herself at Greer again, but it only made her angrier. "Let me go!"

"I saw some of these men walking back to camp early this morning from the south. I can go look in that direction," Gavin said. He turned toward some of the other men and nodded for them to follow.

"We'll all go," Bremen said to Ingrid, then turned back to Greer. "Be gone before I return, or you won't have the opportunity to walk away again."

Seething that Greer was going free, Ingrid jerked her arms away from Selby and turned her back on all of them. Bremen continued giving orders as if her whole world wasn't crashing around her.

"Gavin, lead the way. The three of you fan out, and we'll follow. The rest of you—" Bremen turned and focused on a few individuals but addressed the rest of the men who remained as Greer and his followers slunk away "—continue striking the camp so we can get on our way."

"You can't just let them go! What if we don't find Jorg and Plintze this way? They just get away with whatever they did to them?" Ingrid hurried to stand in front of Bremen.

The idea that Jorg and Plintze might need her—need healed—and she didn't know where they were, hit Ingrid like a blow to the gut. Unsettled, she sliced a glance at Selby, the one person she'd counted on for unwavering support.

A life without Jorg was incomprehensible. The scraggly

dwarf, with all his gruff exterior, was a fierce protector with a heart of gold. Now she stood alone, without any of them.

They had to find them. Why hadn't Bremen insisted that Greer show them the way? Maybe he knew where Jorg was already. Maybe he'd been part of whatever they'd done to him. Ingrid tasted the blood in her mouth from the blow she'd taken from Greer.

If you don't take me to them, I will gut you. Closing her eyes, she inhaled, surprised by the intensity of her reactions but not afraid of them.

After Jorg and Plintze returned, there would be time to figure out Bremen's motives—or not. It wouldn't matter anyway. Once she was back with those she trusted, they could leave together and put all of this behind them.

Bremen marched after Gavin with Selby on his heels, but Ingrid stayed a step behind. He'd ignored her questions, and she preferred to keep them in front of her. If this whole situation turned out to be a ruse, she wanted options for fighting her way to freedom.

She almost chuckled to herself. Jorg would be proud of her warrior mindset, though he'd probably grumble about the need for it. With a jut of her chin, she shook off the thoughts and concentrated on the search. She couldn't let herself become distracted.

Beyond the farthest tent, among the trees where there was no underbrush, they came upon two men standing guard. As they approached, Ingrid caught sight of something that made her heart pound, and she struggled to inhale. Someone was lashed to a tree ahead, back against the trunk and arms tied behind. She could only see the hands, but she knew they were Jorg's. Without hesitation, she ran forward.

The guards stood between where Jorg leaned, slumped against the rough bark, and Gavin. They argued until Bremen came into view. The men paled, and all voices went silent. No one stopped Ingrid as she slid past them.

Cuts on Jorg's cheeks marred the smooth skin of his face, which was smeared with blood. One eye was swollen shut, and his mouth was split in several places. His tunic had tears in it, and blood soaked the thin shreds of fabric that remained. It looked as if it had been slashed by a whip.

Ingrid stopped several feet from him, while her chest heaved and legs wobbled at the extent of his injuries. *What have you suffered because of me?*

Jorg's dark, angry expression turned to surprise, then concern when he saw Ingrid. She stepped within touching distance, but he grunted and tried to lean harder into the tree, away from her.

"Don't." He flicked the gaze of his good eye over her head at the men before meeting her stare.

"They already know," she whispered. A single tear slipped down her cheeks while she roved over the cuts and purple bruises blooming on his face. Pain tore at her heart for what he'd endured. *This is all my fault.* "I'm sorry."

"You're not responsible for the ignorance of others. Besides, they hit like a bunch of old women. I've taken worse from Hagen when we train." A crooked grin tried to form, but he winced and licked his lip. Red-stained teeth peeked out from his mouth, causing her to swallow hard at the sight.

"Yeah, but Hagen never broke your nose," she said, staring at the crook in the center of his face. "And, if I recall, he always yielded." She closed the gap between them but kept her hands at her side. The heat radiating off them was nearly unbearable.

Jorg coughed and turned away to spit bloody mucus before he continued. "He's not like the cowards who kept my hands tied."

A small, sad curve touched Ingrid's mouth but did not spread to the rest of her face as she raised her fingers to Jorg's jaw. A hiss escaped from between his teeth as he sucked in a deep breath when the heat brushed against his broken flesh.

Before she could do more than reduce the swelling, someone startled Ingrid by touching her arm. She instinctively spun and struck out with her hand, making contact with the chest of her attacker.

Although she hadn't intended it, her power had rushed through her fingers to slam into Gavin. The jolt flung him backward onto the ground. The noises around her were muffled, and dizzying sparks danced around the edge of her vision while the essence in her head swirled. Lightheaded and unsteady, she took several deep breaths.

The others rushed to Gavin and helped him to his feet. He rubbed at his chest where Ingrid had punched him. With some help, his tunic was unlaced at the neck and exposed an indented patch of skin, puckered and angry, from what looked like a burn. Bremen reached to touch it but quickly recoiled as Gavin flinched.

Bremen turned to Ingrid. "You've injured him."

"I will help him . . . *after* Jorg," Ingrid said, clamping her lips tight together to stay strong. Though she longed to apologize, she couldn't appear weak for Jorg's sake.

Her mind reeled from what had happened. *I had no idea I could do such a thing to someone.*

"I was going to release him for you," Gavin said through gritted teeth.

With a heavy sigh, Bremen rubbed his face with both hands. "If you'll step aside, I'll do it myself," he said to Ingrid.

A weight pressed against her chest, and she couldn't speak as she stared at Bremen. She only nodded as she took a single step to the side. Part of her knew she hadn't meant to do any harm, but another part that whispered in the back of her mind suggested something different.

No.

She wouldn't listen—wouldn't let the darkness slither deeper into her mind. Jarrick's essence, or whatever it was, was a bother and a headache. Nothing more.

Bremen moved forward and kept his eyes trained on Ingrid as he stepped around her. When the knots released, Jorg groaned as his arms struggled to function after being held behind him for so long.

Snapped from her internal battle, Ingrid hurried to Jorg. She let her fingers trail over his jaw and up to his brow, watching as the red, puffy skin returned to its normal shape. Both hazel eyes, bright as they swirled with green and gold, held her gaze.

Next, she skimmed over his nose. She smiled as best she could with her own swollen jaw when the bridge of his nose straightened. As her fingers slid over his lips, Jorg closed his eyes and kissed them. When she hesitated, a moan only she could hear rumbled from his chest.

The sound drew her attention to his torso, where she placed both hands over his shredded abdomen. The cracked skin and red, sticky ooze seeped between her fingers until the smooth, sculpted curve of his muscles reappeared.

Her brows pinched together as she searched beneath the skin to find more damage, but it was hazy. Unlike earlier, when she could see Martin's bones and tissue as she'd healed him, Jorg's wounds were murky and left her unable to find the damage.

"Ingrid," Jorg's voice called to her softly. He whispered her name once more, and she raised her chin to meet his eyes. "I'm fine now. Let the rest go before it drains you."

"I don't understand why I can't see it."

"It doesn't matter, and you've done enough. Your eyes look like gemstones." His dimple flashed as he shook his head slightly. "Gods, you are beautiful." After a few seconds, or hours, she didn't know or care, Ingrid let her hands fall to her sides.

A sharp realization stabbed at her, and her eyes went wide as she spun around. "Where is Plintze?" Panic laced her voice. *You fool, how could you forget about him until now!*

"What did you do with the dwarf?" Bremen asked one of the men who had stood guard over Jorg.

"We kept them apart to question them, but the dwarf escaped before we could ask him anything," the man answered.

Ingrid noticed that neither he nor his companion held weapons any longer. The news of Plintze's possible safety allowed her shoulders to drop in mixture of relief and fatigue. Exhausted from the multitude of emotions and the healing, she swayed and stumbled backward until she leaned against Jorg.

Jorg grunted with the effort, but he wrapped his arms around her and kept her tight against him. His sweet grassy-pine scent enveloped her, and she sighed. "What happened to your jaw?" he whispered in her ear.

There was still a little power flitting through her core, and her hands were still somewhat warm. She placed one against her cheek. She managed to reduce the swelling and ease the pain, but as before, she couldn't finish the job.

"How is it that you knew nothing of this?" Selby, who'd been silent since they'd left the camp, stood off to the side.

Ingrid glanced at her friend, which drew her away from musings about why her own injuries were giving her abilities trouble. A narrow, angry expression was fastened to Bremen as they both waited for his answer.

"If you are implying that I would torture someone who I'd offered hospitality to—" Bremen clamped his mouth shut and moved three slow steps closer to Selby before he continued "—it can only be excused because you do not know me. If I needed information, I wouldn't hide among the trees." He stepped even closer, his eyes pinned on hers. Selby didn't flinch or waver but stood her ground.

"I'm to believe that, because you've been so open and honest with us, is that it?"

That stopped Bremen no more than a couple paces away from Selby. He stood completely still as he stared at her, locked in what appeared to be a battle of wills.

Ingrid felt a nudge of forgiveness toward her friend for forcing her to show her abilities in front of everyone. Selby had always been a warrior, strong and protective. Especially of Ingrid. One slip that saved a man's life wasn't worth damaging their friendship.

If the druht found out who she was because of it, so be it.

Jorg would be fine, and they would deal with whatever came their way.

Selby's hands twitched at her sides. Ingrid knew her friend well enough to recognize she had a limit for how long she could stand still. It was only slightly longer than she could stay quiet.

"It was convenient that you knew just which direction to look. You can't blame any of us for being suspicious," Ingrid said, stepping out of Jorg's grasp to stand on her own.

Selby must have been thinking similarly to the way Ingrid had earlier, and she didn't need to stand up to the prince by herself.

Gavin made his way to Bremen's side. The other guards also stood ready to defend him, inching closer to his back.

"I'm the one who saw the men come from this direction at daybreak." Gavin turned away from watching Selby to answer Ingrid directly. "I didn't think anything of it at the time."

The extra voices broke through the standoff, and Bremen shook his head. "I was unaware of this. I had no reason to think my men would do such a thing." He stared again at Selby while he spoke. He then lowered his chin and studied the ground in front of him before turning to face Ingrid and Jorg.

"I did not order this to happen, nor did I have knowledge of it, but my men's actions are my responsibility. I offer my apology, if you'll accept it." Bremen looked only at Jorg as he spoke, his posture tense. The expression on his face was that of a man unaccustomed to the act of asking for forgiveness.

"I believe you didn't know what your men were doing," Jorg said. It wasn't an acceptance, and there was an edge to his words. Ingrid understood why. He wasn't defeated, and he wouldn't give Bremen the satisfaction of thinking of him as weak—in need of amends. "We will leave, so as not to call attention to your lack of leadership. That will be apology enough."

Ingrid stiffened. She agreed with Jorg's right to be angry, even enjoyed his Norse lack of deference, but he might have pushed too far. Bremen's face turned hard, and he blazed with indignation.

"The agreement we made last night still stands. Nothing has changed since our discussion before this debacle took place." Bremen scratched at his chin, a questioning pause lingering in the air as he stared at Jorg. "I took you for a man of his word." He took his turn to push too far.

Jorg went rigid as stone. Ingrid held her breath, certain she'd heard Selby do the same. Nothing mattered more to the men in their village back home than their word. It was a concept ingrained into their laws—and Jorg.

Selby moved closer, positioning herself nearer to Ingrid, but also between Jorg and Bremen. Ingrid accepted the silent declaration of her loyalty but hoped the situation would not come to blows. Still, her hands found the handles of her daggers, just in case.

He's not from our lands. He doesn't understand what he said.

Jorg's eyes shuttered, and he turned his head toward Ingrid slowly. "He did. He is a prince who came to discuss treaties with a king. He understands the customs of many cultures—including ours."

This standoff needed to end—preferably without violence. Jorg needed time to gain his strength back and so did Ingrid. Gavin and the other Irishmen waited silently, but they, too, had their hands on the hilts of their weapons. No one bothered to correct Jorg's statement of Bremen's identity.

"What agreement did you two make? Why would we stay with you—after all this?" Ingrid asked Bremen, making an arc with her arm that gestured to the entire area, including the tree where Jorg had been bound.

It was Jorg who answered, but Ingrid didn't take her eyes off Bremen. "I agreed that we would travel through the Fells with Bremen and his men since we are all headed that way anyway. I thought the larger number of men might offer more protection."

"We can defend ourselves just fine," Selby said. She sounded offended, and Ingrid let out a small huff of air in agreement. Selby turned to Bremen. "We can move faster on our own. Why would you invite our kind of troubles? They don't concern you."

That broke his stalemate with Jorg. He blinked several times, the hard glint of his stare softening as he focused on Selby.

"That may be, and I didn't know all the details before. But with others searching for Ingrid, you would be safer to stay with me. With us . . . our larger company." The prince stuttered, and deep lines creased his brow as he answered.

It was true. They could move faster alone. Two weeks had passed, bringing the deadline nearer to the moment when Jarrick would demand Ingrid go with him to Alfheim. He had plans to use her powers to start a war among the gods of Asgard in order to restore the old gods of Vanaheim. If she refused to help, he'd destroy her village, and with it, all those she loved. She needed to find Eir and prevent that from happening.

Greer and his men have left the camp. I think we should stay and use their numbers like you wanted to. Especially until we find Plintze. You can say I still need time to recover from both healings today.

Ingrid tried to give Jorg a way to save face and heard the rumble from his chest as he contemplated the message only he'd heard.

"For the time being, we will stay. I will honor the agreement, but only until I am certain that Ingrid is at full strength."

Bremen nodded his acceptance, and Ingrid caught a glimpse of the relieved expression on Selby's face.

Jorg took her hand and turned toward the camp without another word.

14

———————

Jorg squeezed Ingrid's hand and pulled her closer to his side. "Two healings? Did someone get a sliver?" He gave her a sidelong glance as he referenced her promise before they'd joined Bremen on the road.

Ingrid bumped him with her shoulder and huffed. "It was bigger than that." The idea that she'd waited to help and may not have until Selby had called her out pecked at her. *I should have helped sooner than I did.*

"What happened?" Jorg's voice was softer, no longer the teasing tone that hinted at irritation.

"A man fell and punctured his leg. I forced myself to stay back, like I'd promised—" she glanced up at him quickly "—and then Selby shouted to Bremen that I could help him. I'm sorry I couldn't keep my word to you." Ingrid's feet shuffled through the damp leaves in the shadows of the forest floor, a waft of earthy musk rising into the air.

"I'm glad you helped him. You shouldn't hide who you are —and I shouldn't have asked you to."

"Greer knows about me. They all do. Someone will tell the druht about me for the reward, it's only a matter of time."

"We'll face that if it comes about. I won't let anyone hurt you again." Jorg let the tips of his fingers trail lightly along Ingrid's jaw. Neither of them wanted to say anything more.

They walked on in silence again. Behind them, the low voices of Bremen's men could be heard as tensions subsided. Everyone was eager to move on. Selby was back there, too, though Ingrid hadn't heard her voice. She assumed that if she were to turn around, she would find her friend standing near Bremen.

"Is that where you left your gauntlets?" Jorg asked. "Your hands are like ice."

The question brought Ingrid's attention to their entwined fingers. "Yes."

They'd reached the outskirts of the camp, and as they continued forward, those they passed halted their conversations. An unease brewing in their wake.

Jorg tilted his head as if he heard something, then a small grin flashed across his face as they walked through the men.

What was that? How can you smile at a time like this?

The dimple in his cheek dug in deep, and he winked at her but said nothing. Ingrid rolled her eyes at his ability to accept his circumstances as if it didn't bother him. Meanwhile, she struggled to maintain clear thoughts with all the pressure and frustration rolling through her.

Bremen called out to Ingrid and Jorg, so they waited for him to catch up with Selby at his side. He faced Jorg with a cool expression. "I would like to move forward in peace. It would help the others—" Bremen made a slight motion toward the watching men around them "—if we make a show of calling a truce." His voice was low enough for only the four of them to hear.

An understanding passed between them louder than words when Jorg nodded his acceptance.

Bremen stepped back, opening the space between them, which gave everyone standing around a clear view. He straightened his shoulders and asked, louder than necessary, "Will you give me your word that you will travel with us in peace?"

With his arms relaxed at his side, Jorg let his voice carry for all to hear, "I have no objections with remaining together for as long as we are heading in the same direction."

"Rumors may not hold any truth to them, or maybe they do. I'd like your word that you will not use any other abilities you may have against me or any of my men."

Jorg held his stare. "I give you my word." The tone tinged with the remainder of his frustration from earlier.

The muscles in Bremen's jaw tensed, and he hesitated but stuck his hand out to seal the bargain instead. "Let's be on our way in friendship."

Jorg raised his face to the sky and ran his fingers over his jaw, as if contemplating the truce. Somewhere, probably during his capture, he'd lost the tie in his hair, and it flowed in free waves to the top of his shoulders. Ingrid forced herself to keep focused. "It sounds as if it's a truce then."

Several men had moved in closer and watched as Jorg accepted the handshake. An uneasy peace floated through the air and settled ruffled nerves for the time being.

The deal struck, Bremen turned to Selby. "Would you— all of you—walk at the front?" Bremen asked, correcting himself quickly and shifting his feet.

Selby shot a quick glance to Ingrid, before she focused on Bremen, and a soft expression settled over her face. "I'm happy to stay near you."

Jorg made a very Plintze-sounding huff and shook his head. Ingrid nudged him. *Leave her be.*

With no further words, they stepped out. The long line of warriors, wagons, and servants began the trek through the fells. Not long after, Gavin joined them at the front.

The grim memory of what Ingrid had done to him still troubled her. "I'm sorry for what happened earlier, Gavin. How is your injury?"

"I'll be all right," Gavin said. "It doesn't hurt too much." He flashed a quick glance at Ingrid. "If the need ever arises again to come up behind you, I'll be sure to have your full attention first."

Ingrid grinned politely. Maybe it wasn't the best time to help him anyway. Ingrid didn't need to have anything else go wrong for a little while. She had no idea what might happen if she tried to heal an injury her own power had caused. It would be better to wait until she wasn't under the watchful eyes of so many others.

A hand touched Ingrid's side, and she turned, ready to defend herself, startling Gavin into raising his weapon. But then they each relaxed somewhat as a small servant girl stared at them with sparkling gray eyes. She gently held out a pair of knitted, fingerless gloves toward Ingrid without a word. Ingrid's shoulders lowered a fraction more, yet the churning unease of being startled stayed and caused her hand to shake as she took the offering.

Without time for Ingrid to thank the girl or find out why she'd given the gift, she ran away to walk next to Moirin. The older woman nodded, and Ingrid squeezed the soft garments to her chest before she slipped them over her hands.

Not long after, Jorg and Gavin were in a deep conversation about the perfect shape of a dagger handle when Selby came to walk next to Ingrid. "We need to find Plintze. I can't believe I'm saying this, but I miss his grouchy face."

"I'm worried that we're getting too far away. One of those men—" Ingrid sucked in a deep breath to stop the rise of anger while thinking of what had happened "—said that he escaped before they could question him. What if he went in a different direction?" Ingrid halted suddenly. "Maybe we should turn around and go look for him."

Her heart pounded in her chest. How she could be so callous to head off without thinking that through?

Both Gavin and Jorg turned to stare at Ingrid. "Are you talking about Plintze?" Jorg asked.

"Yes. How could we have left before we found him?"

"He's fine, I'm sure," Jorg gave Ingrid a look that seemed to say more, but she didn't understand. "Let's just keep going, and if he doesn't find us in a couple days, we can make plans to search for him."

"What if he doesn't find us? Or doesn't want to?" Selby asked.

"He will," Jorg reassured.

"I'll pass the word along to the column to make sure everyone's aware that he is welcome, if that helps," Gavin offered.

"It might, but he won't know that." Ingrid fiddled with her necklace and looked into the forest at the side of the road. The bead was cool between her fingers.

Jorg took her hand and forced her to look up at him. "Trust me. He's well."

Ingrid narrowed her eyes at the message he was trying to get her to understand. *You know where he is?* A playful quirk of his brow was her answer.

"Fine. But we search if he isn't here in two days," Ingrid said firmly.

"Agreed," Selby said.

Bremen walked up to the group. "Is there any trouble?"

"The ladies were expressing concern over their missing friend," Gavin said. "I offered to send a message down the line that he is welcome if he meets up with us again."

"That's a good idea. I am sorry he is missing," Bremen said. "We can send out scouts to search."

"A kind offer, but not necessary. Plintze is resourceful, and he'll decide when he wants to return," Jorg said.

"If you think that's best, I'll leave it to your judgement. Perhaps you can tell me more about where you're from as we continue." He swept his arm toward the road, and the group began walking again. The manner of his gesture was both friendly and commanding at the same time.

"We told you last night that we're from a village north of here, on the River Ouse," Jorg said with a sharpness to his tone. Ingrid suspected it was a remnant of the other part of the night and the questions he'd had to endure.

"Yes, I guess I'm interested in finding out more of how Ingrid was able to take care of such grievous injuries as I've seen her do twice today. That doesn't seem to be something learned in a small farming settlement."

"It isn't," Ingrid said.

"You don't have to say anything," Jorg growled. "The less information others have, the better it might be.'

"I shouldn't have forced you into the open this morning," Selby said, facing the ground in front of her.

Rolling her neck and straightening her shoulders, Ingrid ignored both of them. "I'm glad I was able to help Martin and Jorg. There is a power within me to heal injuries and more, yet I don't understand it. I only have a few more weeks left to find a woman who can help me develop my abilities.

"There is a dark elf who has given me a deadline to join him instead of completing the task expected of me. He will send his followers to destroy my village if I fail to meet him as planned. As to the men searching for me, I don't know who they are or what they want. Several days ago, they killed a woman who could help me find Eir, and that's when we learned of them."

The truth spilled out of Ingrid like a flash flood. Some tension left her shoulders, but pressure still squeezed her chest and made her edgy.

Bremen stared at her, but his expression changed from hardened suspicion to curiosity. "That was a lot of information. There is a dark elf, and he has a task for you?"

"There is a veil of protection around the human realm, provided by the gods. It is weakening. When the spell was cast, the fate of a human was woven into it. One who would add the strength of Midgard and bind the spell for all time." Ingrid stared into the air, looking at nothing. Her chest constricted, and her pulse screamed in her ears. "I am that human."

From her side, Ingrid heard Selby release a nervous whoosh of air. The tension rippling off Jorg hit her in waves.

Bremen scratched at his beard and looked sidelong at Ingrid. "I've heard tales of an unrest in the otherworld that will settle at the hand of a maiden."

Ingrid nodded at the way his Irish beliefs were similar. "I thought I was to be a shieldmaiden, fighting on the battlefield, earning honor and glory, but now I know different. A constant drum beat within me as I grew, telling me that I was meant for something great. The Norns chose me. I'm searching for Eir, a goddess of Asgard, to complete my training. If I don't learn to control my abilities in the next few weeks, not only will we lose our village, but evil will unleash on all men."

As the afternoon stretched on, Ingrid explained to Bremen all that had happened: the first time she'd healed a boy on the docks, how she had persuaded Selby to stowaway on her father's longship, the adventures they'd had in Jorvik, and then the shipwreck.

When she explained meeting the trolls, Bremen's eyes widened, and he held up his hand for her to stop. "Wait, trolls captured you? How is that possible?"

"That's one reason I have to find the woman I'm looking for. As the veil weakens, it's easier for wicked creatures to slip through again. The dragons have returned as well."

"This is a lot to take in," Bremen said and rubbed his jaw.

"Why is it that when we first met, you were careful to tell us that the prince was not among your men?" Selby asked. Her voice startled Bremen so much that he stared at her without answering. "The answer is your safety is important. You have a role to fulfill for your father, for your kingdom."

Selby looked down at her hands. "Ingrid has a role to fulfill as well. Not everyone wants to see her succeed, as I'm sure you can understand, but what she says is all true. Believe me when I say that you never forget the smell of troll." She shuddered.

Ingrid turned over her arm and pushed the knit glove down to reveal the shiny pink scar in full view. "I promise you, dragons have returned." The recollection of the attack that almost ended Ingrid's life flashed through her mind and stabbed at her heart with the need to find Plintze.

"No one has seen a dragon in many generations, and there are no stories of survival when they attack," Bremen offered.

"It wasn't an ordinary dragon. The dark elf used magic to control the dragon's mind and speak into mine. When I refused to join his cause, he attacked. Plintze found me and saved me."

There was so much more she could have said, but the memories choked her voice. And it looked as though Bremen had heard enough.

"Now you can see why we need to keep moving. We need to find the goddess, so Ingrid can fulfill her part in everything," Jorg said to Bremen.

It was all Ingrid could do to stand firm and keep her eyes focused on Bremen's, holding his stare as an equal as they paused in their walk. The heat of Jorg's body radiated off him. He didn't stay by her side because she needed protection, but in solidarity. Because he believed in her.

She felt ten feet tall. If her hands weren't shaking or the pressure wasn't building inside of her that she'd not find Eir in time, she would have let a grin slide over her lips. Instead, she said nothing and waited, letting Bremen decide what would happen next.

The Prince nodded at her and exhaled a deep breath. It was enough.

Later, after the evening meal while everyone was bedding down for the night, Ingrid stood by herself near the edge of the forest. She'd felt restless and needed some time to herself. Her body was exhausted from the journey and her head ached, but she couldn't stop pacing.

The darkness pressed hard. The presence that splashed between her temples swelled unbearably. The stars covering the night sky like a blanket disappeared from her vision, and she pinched her brow with tight fingers. A strangled cry caught in her throat as her knees cracked against the ground.

Then . . . It all released. Her limbs felt boneless as she tried to brace herself on her hands and knees, but she instead slid to her belly. The pressure was gone, yet her breath came in ragged bursts from the earlier pain.

"That appeared uncomfortable. My apologies."

A voice, sticky and terrifying, spoke from near her side. A voice she'd heard before—when it spoke through a dragon.

Jarrick.

Ingrid willed her strength to return. She slowly rose to her feet and turned to face the dark elf.

She stood in what felt like a dark pit. Her feet were firmly on the ground, and she had plenty of space to move, but the darkness pressed in on her from all sides. There was nothing to see. No sounds penetrated the air, nor did she smell the earth, even though she'd just had her face on it. It was as if she were in total blackness, the absence of everything except terror.

The figure of a man was barely visible in front of her. At first, she thought he wore a dark cloak, but she then realized he was absorbed into the shadows. They encircled him as if one was part of the other. He took a step closer, and the shadows slipped to the background.

The male towering before her had the same perfect, smooth skin as Jorg, but it had a shimmer about it that made it visible regardless of the darkness. Hair so light blond it was almost white fell in a straight cascade down his back and was tucked behind elongated ears that rose several inches to a sharp point.

"Jarrick." Ingrid's chest squeezed, and she couldn't breathe.

"Hello, Ingrid. It's nice to finally meet you face to face."

"How is this possible? Where are we?" Ingrid couldn't run; she couldn't move. She didn't seem to be trapped, just paralyzed from her own fear. Except, something was familiar.

The darkness slithered through the space from Jarrick to Ingrid and back. A vibration rattled through her body, like a silent purr as it swirled.

"This is from my mind." Stunned, but sure of herself, Ingrid said the words out loud. The pouch on Ingrid's belt seemed to get heavier, as if the runes were pressing against her body, uncomfortable and distracting.

"I knew you were a clever girl. We can accomplish great things together, Ingrid." The swirls of smoky shadows danced higher in lazy circles around Jarrick as he spoke. "You have a gift. It makes you special and powerful. Others want to hold you back, to keep you from your potential, all under the pretense that it's *better* for you. But, I know you. I've been with you—when you recognize you are capable and yet held back."

A non-existent wind ruffled Ingrid's hair. It was a tendril of the darkness. Instead of feeling like a foreign invader, it caressed her skin and even brushed her hair away from her face. It was familiar. The ache inside her head, the one she'd battled since the tarry essence entered her mind, eased.

"You have more power than any of your petty companions can comprehend. They make decisions for you, tell you what you can or cannot do, and why? Their own fear. It has nothing to do with who you are because they don't understand. I do."

A sound in the distance drew Ingrid's attention. Did she recognize it? Her skin prickled with coldness, and breathing grew difficult. Her name? Was that what she'd heard?

Ingrid slipped her hand to her waist to touch the runes in her pouch, but the space between her and the dark elf squeezed closer, even though neither had moved. Her hand fell to her side, the runes forgotten.

Jarrick smiled at her but did not reach out for her. Weightless, she was once again relaxed and warm. As if she could close her eyes and float on the wind. As light as the touch of a butterfly, the darkness . . . or Jarrick . . . whispered into her ear. *You can. Let go.*

Lifting her chin, she let herself fall backward, and the smoky swirls caught her. She smiled, enjoying the sensation of pure weightlessness. With a sigh, she righted herself and stood once more in front of the powerful elf.

"You search for Eir, but she will limit you. Control you like all the others. I want to free you. Your powers are strong, perhaps even stronger than Freya. Nothing about you is weak, Ingrid. The lies you've been told are to hold you back. To keep you from deciding your own fate. You don't need to be trained; you need encouraged to practice, to explore, to discover.

"Think on what I've said. With me you'll have no limits. You'll be a queen. Unlike the rest of them, I want *you* to be in control. Come to me, Ingrid."

Jarrick reached out his hand but did not touch her. He wasn't trying to grab her or steal her away but let her decide for herself. That's what she'd wanted from the beginning. To learn how to use the gifts she had without being treated as if she weren't strong enough. Like she was too weak.

Then it was there again, the sound. This time it bit into her with a sharp pain, frantic. It was trying to pull her away from where she stood. To take her away from the ability to choose her own fate.

"Ingrid. Take my hand!" Jarrick's voice was hard, demanding. "Choose now!"

The shadows swirled around her faster, pressing in on her again. She couldn't breathe. She was suffocating, choking as if she'd been pulled underwater. A scream leapt from her throat as pain crashed through her body. Then she was no more.

15

───────

Ingrid groaned as the sensation of spikes being driven into her temples continued to grow. The scratchiness in her throat made it hard to speak, and her skin pebbled from the cold. On top of all of that, she was alone.

What had pulled her from the darkness? *It wasn't me . . . there was a voice.* Bitter tears stung her eyes. Someone had taken her choice from her.

Unwilling to face the pain of opening her eyes more than a sliver, she tried to focus on where she was. Though it was dark, it was familiar. Just out of reach, a campfire had dulled to little more than embers. Snores from sleeping bodies rattled through the air like a pond full of bullfrogs.

With a sigh, Ingrid forced herself to sit, wincing and clenching her fists as she did, trying to mitigate the lingering headache.

"Are you hurt?" Jorg's voice traveled to her from off to the side, well away from any hope of warmth from the fire.

"My head is pounding, and my throat hurts. Can you

come closer, so I don't have to raise my voice or twist to see you?"

There was no movement or hint that Jorg had heard Ingrid's request. She was about to repeat herself when he finally came into view. Before he sat down, he stoked the fire and set a couple smaller branches on the coals, the dry wood caught quickly and cast an ominous orange glow around his silhouette.

When he finally sat down, out of reach, he wrapped his cloak around him and said nothing. The awkwardness was new. Even before they'd discovered their fondness for each other, there had always been an ease between them. No matter how much her brother and his other friends teased or ignored Ingrid as children, Jorg would make a point to be considerate.

"Are you the one who ripped me out of my vision?" Ingrid asked.

"I found you on the ground and thought you'd been hurt. Tremors were shaking your body, and your eyelids fluttered but never opened." His voice was low and raw. Ingrid watched the flames and waited for him to continue.

"There was one point when I thought you were waking, but then you went completely still. Your body was cold, so I tried to shake you and bring you back to me." Jorg rubbed his hand over his face. "I thought you were dying." His voice was barely more than a whisper shrouded in pain.

"I wasn't." She wanted so much to tell him that she could hear his concern, but, she was so angry.

Eir seemed to have abandoned her, and Jarrick had offered Ingrid a way to save their people. Deep in her gut, she knew Jorg didn't understand that he was stopping her from deciding her own fate. She knew he was worried because he loved her.

"That's when you started screaming and thrashing. I tried to calm you. Selby tried to calm you, but nothing worked. You finally fell unconscious for . . . It must have only been seconds, but it felt as if it were hours. It tore me apart. Then you opened your eyes and stared right at me. Told me never to touch you again and that everyone would die now because I didn't let you choose." Jorg sat slumped and didn't move a muscle.

Across the small remaining flames, Ingrid saw Selby. At some point, she'd either sat up or scooted closer, but remained on the other side of the fire. Tears lined her cheeks and shimmered in the dull light.

The weight of everything seemed to land on Ingrid's shoulders. No one understood what it felt like to have the pressure of saving everyone she loved, and not know how to do it.

Jarrick had offered her control and freedom. The ability to grow stronger without restrictions. How could that not help everyone? She didn't remember screaming or saying those words to Jorg, but did she really feel that way?

In part, yes.

The part of her that had a job to do—one that was far too large for her—certainly felt that way. But, the other part? The other part wanted him to pull her into his arms and tell her that it would all work out. The silence settled around them like a haze, thick and suffocating.

Ingrid sighed and shook her head. Was Jarrick really offering her all those things? What did he want from her in return? His voice echoed in her mind. The way he'd sounded at the end, before the vision was ripped away, when he'd insisted she take his hand. Cold so deep it felt like daggers crept through her body. She reached for the runes in her pouch. They were as cold as ice, and she snatched back her fingers.

"It was Jarrick," Ingrid whispered and then swallowed down the burn in her throat. "He said he would show me how to use my magic. That he'd let me choose."

From the corner of her eye, she saw Jorg raise his head and his chest beginning to rise and fall faster.

"Time is running out. He was giving me a way to avoid the death of everyone back home—unlike Eir who won't even show herself to me. Everyone thinks they need to protect me, to make decisions for me. He was allowing *me* to be in control."

"Did he take you somewhere, like when you went to Asgard to speak with Hnossa?" Jorg's voice was tight, the words pressed thin.

"No, it was dark—frightening at first. There were all these shadows that seemed to be alive."

He sighed, but not from frustration. It was more out of worry. "It was dark magic, Ingrid. He was confusing you, luring you away so you can't do what you need to."

Ingrid snapped her eyes to Jorg. A bitterness stung her tongue. *I'm too weak, that's what you mean. I'm not able to make a decision on my own.* "He treated me like I'm capable. Why hasn't Eir shown up yet? What do I have left to prove to her? Everyone wants to protect me and *help* me, but *I'm* the one who has to bind the spell."

A coughing fit wracked her body as her voice gave out. When it was over, silence filled the air. Frustration rolled through her like thunder clouds when she caught the pity in her friend's eyes.

"Ingrid, no one wants to hold you back. We all believe in you." Selby's voice had never sounded so quiet and compassionate—or small. At some point during Ingrid's rant, she'd moved closer. She reached out and touched Ingrid on the shoulder. "Please understand that."

Ingrid wanted to throw her arms around her best friend and sob, but she stayed firm. Selby was right. She'd nearly made a terrible mistake. Jarrick had made sense and confused her. Where was the goddess?

Ingrid rolled her shoulder to dislodge Selby's hand. It was too much, and she was too tired. Any more conversation could wait. "It's late. We should rest." She pulled her cloak tight around her shoulders and laid down with her back to the fire, and to her friends.

Two hours on the road, and still, no one spoke to Ingrid. Whispers and wide-eyed stares she pretended not to notice had followed her all morning. When anyone noticed her looking at them, they'd suddenly become very busy and needed to scurry off. Even Jorg decided to join the crew who helped the wagons when their wheels careered into a deep rut. Something which happened continuously, making the travel pathetically slow.

By early evening when the caravan stopped for the night, it had been the longest day of Ingrid's life. Never had she been so lonely despite being surrounded by people. Selby had sat near her at their midday rest, but spent the time chatting with Bremen. Jorg had stationed himself alone under the shade of a tree.

Now, they'd stopped for the night, and she still didn't know what she was going to do. Her heart ached to put the whole mess behind her, but how could she? Spending the whole day alone with her thoughts had only made her more confused.

Jarrick wanted to destroy Asgard in order to build up the Vanir once more—the original gods, who all but disappeared after Odin took charge. Did they want to rule again? Evil was already slipping into the human realm. Midgard wouldn't survive in the middle of another civil war between the gods. Would it? Could her abilities provide a helpful advantage?

The other option was to train to bind the spell, keep the Asgardian gods in leadership, and let the human world continue in peace none-the-wiser. That would require Eir, and she wasn't helping.

Focused on her internal argument, she stared into the brush alongside the road, and movement caught her attention. Remembering Jorg's assurance that Plintze was safe, she tucked her chin to hide her grin. She could use the dwarf's grumpy wisdom.

Selby and Bremen stood near each other, talking as if they were the only two around. Selby kept tucking a piece of her hair behind her ear even though it never moved, and Bremen held his hands in his pockets as if he was trying to keep from touching her. Since no one was paying attention to Ingrid, she sauntered closer to the edge of the road and slipped into the woods.

The rich smell of the forest soothed Ingrid's senses as she walked farther into the brush that grew sparsely between the tall trees. At least, she felt calmer until the sting of another scent assaulted her nose. It was familiar, yet didn't belong to the surrounding nature. The musky scent of body odor slapped her back to reality just as a man slid out from behind a tree.

"Hello, my dear." The man was taller than Ingrid, but not by much. He had short cropped hair with an oily sheen that was noticeable even in the dim light. Scrawny in appearance, yet he had a look about him that said he'd manage well enough in a fight. Ingrid took a step backward, her pulse beating against her throat. "Now, don't run off. We won't hurt you. You're worth a hefty purse."

"You must be mistaken, no one would pay ransom for me," Ingrid said.

"It isn't ransom; it's *reward*. And you are exactly who we're looking for," a low, gruff voice said from behind Ingrid. One she recognized. Ingrid turned slowly to face Greer.

She'd expected to find Plintze and had let herself become surrounded. A flash of fear coursed through her but quickly turned to anger. Her lip curled into a snarl. She shrieked and lunged forward.

The smaller man was closer, and she surprised him when she smashed her outstretched hands against his unguarded chest. The tang of magic coated her tongue as he flew several feet away and sprawled on the ground motionless. Ingrid spun before Greer could reach her and bolted back through the undergrowth to the road.

Jorg stumbled into Ingrid, as soon as she emerged, his eyes wide and wild. "You screamed—are you hurt?"

"Greer . . . Druht . . . in the trees," she huffed the words as her chest heaved with every ragged breath and the buzz of power still coursing through her veins.

Overhearing her words from where he'd come to stand behind Jorg, Bremen spun and shouted orders as he ran toward his men. Ingrid and Jorg followed him, relieved when a trunk full of weapons opened in front of them.

Jorg grabbed Ingrid's face, squishing her cheeks in his strong fingers. "Fight hard and stay alive."

The gold in his eyes swirled within the green, and the muscles in his jaw popped as his grip tightened. She nodded, and he whirled around to join the fray. He didn't command her to stay behind him or to wait on the side, but to join the battle. Finally, he showed a little trust in her.

Ingrid absorbed the mayhem around her. Strangers swarmed among Bremen's men in the fading light as they scrambled to pull their weapons and return the attack. Thick shadows cloaked the path, and bodies slammed into each other in the narrow space. Ingrid was stunned at the over-whelming numbers of men jumping from the tree line.

Power rose from within her, fighting to be let out again. *Act strong, be strong.* Ingrid pulled her daggers and rushed into the fray.

A man charged in from Ingrid's right, and she turned in time to block his hand when he reached out to grab her. She sank a dagger into his arm. Blood spurted over her face as she jerked the weapon free. As he stumbled forward, she drove her other blade into his chest. The sputter of her powers in reaction to the injury made her falter until she shoved it down and kept fighting.

Ingrid slashed against the dagger of another attacker. The metal clanged together and hissed as they slid apart. A wicked sneer crossed the man's face as he licked his lips and circled around Ingrid.

Careful to turn with him and never letting her eyes leave her target, Ingrid smiled at him only a moment before the tip of Selby's sword pierced his chest from where she'd thrust it through his back. Shocked, the man stared at the blade before crumbling to the ground.

The girls nodded to each other, before turning to continue the fight. In the distance, Ingrid could make out Jorg slicing through a crowd surrounding him. Near him, a squat figure used a spear to cut through the intruders, and she knew Plintze had returned.

"Is that Plintze?" Selby asked as they charged toward their next victim.

"Yes, but there's something else, too. What is it?" Concern spiked Ingrid's words as she watched a colorful light streak through the air near Plintze. Whatever it was, the question deserted her mind when one of her daggers slipped from her chilly hand to the ground.

Short of breath, she scanned around her feet quickly and spied it in time to duck the swing of a man close to her. She picked up the wayward weapon and struck under his ribcage as she rose. He grabbed at Ingrid, his hand wrapping around her braid as he pulled her to the ground with him as he fell.

Air whooshed from Ingrid as the hard earth slammed against her back, and her neck snapped backward with a crack. With strength she didn't realize she had, she pushed the lifeless body off her and jumped to her feet only to face off with a giant of a man. Ingrid stepped backward while raising her daggers, ready but wary.

Close as they were, the smell of sweat and coppery blood

wrapped around them. Ingrid thrust her dagger toward her new opponent, but he lunged out of the way. Her foot slid in mud churned up by all the trampling feet.

Unable to get up when the next blow came at her, she dropped and rolled toward her attacker. A loud scream rang out as she sliced through his thigh. The man fell to his knees, clutching his wound. Ingrid jumped up and drove the dagger down into the side of his neck.

Selby screamed from Ingrid's left, and she turned in time to see her friend swing an axe into the side of a man twice her size. Blood trickled down her face where she'd suffered a hit, but she snarled with victory and moved closer to the group at the front.

A band of druht fighters outnumbered and surrounded Jorg, Plintze, and several other men, including Bremen. Most of the skirmishes had been settled. The outnumbered druht were either dead, injured, or retreated, and theirs was the final group in a face off.

Ingrid raised her dagger to charge forward, but she froze as a small figure burst from the brush and dove at the crowd.

Screams followed the creature as men grabbed their faces or throats where slashes tore open their flesh. Selby reached Ingrid, and together, they spurred each other ahead when they saw that the only men injured by the small flying beast were the druht.

They struck from the edge, and the beast rushed between. The invaders broke off the assault and fled into the darkness of the brush. Whatever it was that chased them left a spray of sparkling light in its wake.

Ingrid let her arms fall to her sides and released a heavy sigh. A mix of mud and other vile substances coated her face and slipped into her mouth, making her gag as she tried to wipe it clean.

Selby rolled her neck from one shoulder to the other in both directions before wiping her short sword clean against the chest of the nearest fallen druht and returning it to its rightful place on her hip.

16

Exhausted, but oddly refreshed. The frenzy of battle had allowed Ingrid to release her anxiety and fears. Fighting with Selby at her side reminded her of what was at stake and what she never wanted to lose. A quick overview of the men near her found what she sought—Jorg. He met her gaze with equal measure of concern and relief.

Before she could walk toward him, what appeared to be a small child stepped out of the woods to stand in the middle of the road. Gasps and muttered curses sounded behind them when everyone else saw the girl.

Plintze shoved through the crowd and stood defensively at the creature's side. The pale moonlight rising over the trees shone enough to see that whatever she was, the girl was not human.

She was a beautiful female, a little shorter than the dwarf, who looked like a young child with large, round eyes in a crystalline lilac color. Thick hair flowed around her shoulders, beginning as a pale sky blue shade at the root and turning a deep violet at the ends.

After that, the human-like characteristics ended with light spring green skin that shimmered when the light hit it and two sets of iridescent wings that protruded from between her shoulders. A dress the shade of daffodils wrapped around her body, under her arms, then fell softly past her knee to mid-shin. It fluttered in the breeze like the air itself.

"Plintze, you should introduce us to your friend," Jorg said.

He'd walked up to stand behind Ingrid. She wanted to lean into him as his grassy scent covered the stench of battle, but she squared her shoulders and maintained composure.

"Are you the one who helped us during the battle?" Bremen asked, standing near Selby in the same protective manner as Jorg. Gavin and the others pressed forward but did not move past them.

"This is Lazuli. She's an old friend of mine," Plintze said. Lazuli smiled and clasped her hands in front of her while she twisted back and forth playfully. "She is the sprite I told you of back at my home, Ingrid. The one who helped me after the dragon attack."

Murmurs buzzed through the crowd at the mention of dragons. Ingrid stepped closer, and Jorg followed. "I remember you said you got help, but you didn't say it was from a sprite." Turning her focus to the childlike figure, Ingrid smiled. "It's nice to meet you. Thank you for your help when the dragon attacked me and also for today."

With her head tucked at a coy angle and her shoulders swinging merrily from side to side, she could have looked like a sweet, innocent little girl—except, blood splatters covered her from head to toe. When her smile broadened at Ingrid, jagged teeth showed red to match the smears across her face.

"Plintze spoke often about you. I'm glad that you recovered." Her voice tinkled into the air like the chimes in a breeze.

"Often?" Ingrid turned to Plintze, which took considerable effort to look away from Lazuli's effervescence. "How long have you been in contact with each other?"

"I find time when you are busy with those two." Plintze gestured between Selby and Jorg. "But when these fools turned on us, I needed a place to hide for a while and stayed with Lazuli."

Selby, Jorg, and Ingrid stared at the dwarf with blank expressions, until Selby finally spoke. "Dwarf, I think I just gained a little respect for you."

"Humph."

"Lazuli, I'm sorry we're so shocked, but Plintze has not talked to us about you at all," Ingrid said.

"Why would that cause you distress?" Lazuli turned to Plintze. "Humans are funny. Let's go play now. There are places I still need to show you in the hills that no human has ever seen. We can play without being interrupted by their petty arguments." Lazuli pulled on Plintze's sleeve with an excited tone in her voice.

"We can't, not now," the dwarf grumbled.

"Why?" The sprite's bottom lip pushed out, and she looked as if she were about to cry.

His eyes met hers. "We need to stay. The humans still need our help."

"It will only be for a little while. Let's play, and then we can come back." A serious, well-practiced, whine rang in her voice

"I like this girl," Selby said with a chuckle.

"I'm not a girl. I'm a sprite," Lazuli said and flew closer to Selby, a mischievous glint in her eye. Bremen stepped to Selby's side, his hand on the hilt of his sheathed sword. "Do you want to go play with me?"

"No!" Bremen and Jorg both yelled at the same time.

Lazuli glared at each man. "You are not nice. I do not want to play with you," she said with both hands on her hips.

"We need to stay and help the humans to safety. After that, we can go play," Plintze said in a kind voice that caused all the others to gape once more.

"Promise?"

"Yes." Plintze turned his focus to Bremen. "Am I going to have any more troubles with your men, or can we clean up from this mess and get going?"

Bremen stared at Lazuli with a thoughtful expression. "Lazuli, will you promise not to hurt any of my men while we offer you hospitality?"

Lazuli peered around Bremen to the men standing behind him, her gaze narrow. "Do they think like the others? Do they want to tie me up or run me through with a sword?" A small grin crossed her face. The invitation to let them try made Ingrid shudder.

Bremen shifted slightly to block Lazuli's view of the men and bring her focus back to him. "No. You're safe with us if you will promise safety for them as well. Do we have an agreement?"

Ingrid peeked at Bremen, his voice strong and brave, but she noticed a trickle of sweat slid down next to his ear. Regardless, she couldn't help but feel a little appreciation for the man who was so willing to accept those he couldn't possibly understand.

Lazuli stood as tall as her little body allowed, and her lips broke wider across her face. The jagged teeth, outlined in crimson, made Ingrid's stomach clench, and she heard Jorg make a noise behind her as well.

I wonder if she knows how to smile without showing her teeth?

"Maybe you can tell her it's a game to play with the men," Jorg whispered into her ear. Ingrid sucked her lips together to keep quiet.

"I accept your terms," the little sprite said.

She fluttered her wings to lift herself off the ground and move closer to Bremen, arm jutted out for a handshake. His shoulders stiffened, but he engulfed her small hand with his large one and gently accepted the truce.

Not far away, in the taller grasses next to the churned path, Ingrid's attention snapped to the sound of a moan. "The wounded need attention."

Somehow Ingrid didn't think a truce with a sprite was a trustworthy bargain. But maybe if they could keep her busy, she'd stay out of trouble. Ingrid dragged her gaze over the crowd and spied Selby.

"Lazuli, would it be all right with you if Selby helped you to clean up? You got a lot of blood on your dress." Ingrid gestured to her friend as she spoke.

At first, Selby's eyes sprang open, but then she softened and stepped forward. "I'll wash, too. It'll be fun." Her friend picking up on the need to give the worrisome newcomer a new focus.

The sprite buzzed over to hover in front of Ingrid. "You are nice, too." Lazuli ran her hand over Ingrid's arm, making it tingle as if her skin danced at the light touch. "We will be friends." Then, as she hummed a little tune, she zipped back through the air to Selby.

Together, they sauntered down the path. The nervous men parted in silence to allow them passage as they searched for a water barrel.

Shocked from the turn of events, everyone stood rooted to the ground. Bremen turned to the group, breaking the daze. "While Ingrid tends to the injured, let's prepare to move out. Leave their dead by the side of the road, and we'll push on to stop in a more defensible area for the night."

Murmurs floated through the crowd, but everyone hustled to obey. Ingrid roused herself from her thoughts and hurried to those with the worst injuries first. As she moved from person to person, she healed the most severe injuries, but left the milder ones to ensure sufficient energy for everyone.

Jorg followed her, helping with supplies and moving bodies until no one else remained. Two of Bremen's men died, and six others had serious enough wounds that it would require them to ride in a wagon and rest after Ingrid's touch. Others resumed their posts along the line, many with a new reverence for the petite healer.

Three of the druht with injuries too intense they couldn't escape were propped up against each other after Ingrid helped them against their will. Bound by their hands and feet, they could not stop her. Ingrid hoped they would regret their actions when they understood how she could help them, but hatred burned in their eyes even more for it.

"We should have run them through," Jorg growled, agitated that Ingrid had drained herself for their kind.

"Yes, it's what they deserve. But maybe they'll think differently of us now," she said. Although she knew they wouldn't, the healer and warrior within her couldn't reconcile just then.

Jorg huffed and shook his head. Raising an eyebrow, he leaned down and stared into her shining eyes. "We are Norse, and they *should* be afraid."

With a roll of her eyes and a small wince of homesickness, she surveyed the rest of those around her to be sure she'd found all the wounded.

Jorg smiled. "It is amazing to watch you heal."

"It's getting easier. I'm only a little tired this time. Are my eyes bright again?" she asked, turning her face to his.

Softness filled Jorg's expression as he nodded. His eyes were wide but filled with awe, not fear. "Your bead only glows while you are in the middle of the healing, then it fades. But not your eyes—they are like turquoise gems glowing in the sun."

"Hmm." Ingrid could tell it was meant as a compliment, but she had no explanation for why it happened. She didn't understand how any of it worked.

No closer to saving her village and binding the veil, another wave of frustration hit that she still hadn't found Eir. Or, more likely, the goddess hadn't found her. What more did she need Ingrid to prove?

"Greer led those men against us," Jorg said. "He wasn't among their injured or dead, so he'll be back."

Ingrid was exhausted but had finally settled down to eat and rest after they'd found a safer, more defensible area for the night. She glanced over to Plintze, a sense of relief spilling over her that he was back and safe.

"I'm sure he will." The words were quiet and left to fade into the air. Deciding how to deal with Greer when he came after her again was a conversation for tomorrow.

A peaceful quietness wrapped around the three of them. There was too much silence. Ingrid twisted around searching the other fires with suspicion.

"Where is Selby?"

"I'm sure she'll show up." A playful grin tugged on Jorg's mouth that he tried to hide.

"Humph."

Before Ingrid could question the two, who seemed to be enjoying a secret, Lazuli zipped through the air and stood in front of Jorg, startling all of them.

"Are you an elf? You kind of look like one," Lazuli said. Her eyes narrowed, and in a blink of an eye, she was in the air hovering near his ear.

"Whoa!" He leaned back and scowled as he waved her away. "You don't just fly into someone's face like that."

Lazuli closed her eyes and sniffed long, loud, and dramatically before she buzzed back to stand by Plintze. "You smell like an elf. Are you a halfling?"

"Lazuli, that's terrible manners," Ingrid said in a polite voice as if speaking to a small child.

"Why?"

"Well . . ."

"Humans worry about ridiculous things like that," Plintze said.

"Why are you worried? You are a halfling!" Lazuli's eyes lit up, and she clapped her hands together. "I've never met one of those. You would be my first." Again, she flew over into Jorg's space and flitted all around him as if she were inspecting a new horse.

"Stop that, or I will tie your wings down," he said, swatting at her.

"You wouldn't dare!" She clenched her fists and sneered to let her spiked fangs glisten in the low light before flying away without another word.

When Lazuli returned, her arms were loaded with several blossoms of a white, night-blooming flower. She dumped them in Ingrid's lap before proceeding to place them into her hair.

"I've never seen these flowers before, Lazuli. They are beautiful. Where did you get them?" Ingrid decided it was better to accept the sprites ministrations than decline and make her upset.

Lazuli just hummed and fluttered around Ingrid's head as she worked without an answer. When Ingrid tried to turn her head to speak again, a strong pull of her hair changed her mind. The little sprite continued to work, buzzing around to the front and back of Ingrid, sometimes scrunching her face as if she were creating a piece of art before resuming her efforts.

What is she doing?

A small jolt of nerves pinched Ingrid as she realized it was the first time she'd used the one-way bond she had with Jorg since her vision. A swift response of pressure from the dark essence still residing in her mind at the thought of Jarrick gave her an instant dull headache.

Jorg smiled in response to hearing the words but leaned forward, placed another small branch on the fire, and said nothing. Ingrid let out a heavy breath and resigned herself to Lazuli's creative fussing. The sweet scent of the flowers helped to soothe away her unease.

Not long after, Bremen appeared from the dark and came to sit at the fire, choosing to sit near them rather than one with his men. Ingrid started to say something but stopped as Selby wandered out of the shadows from a spot near where Bremen had emerged. She walked up to sit near the flames but stared at Ingrid instead.

"Selby," Jorg said. A smirk played at the corner of his mouth as he quirked a brow at her in greeting.

She ignored him as she watched Lazuli work. "What's happening here?"

"You were busy—" the sprite glared at her "—and I wanted to play. Doesn't she look nice?" Lazuli answered.

"Oh yes, lovely." Selby bit back a giggle and settled onto a log next to Ingrid's after scooting it over so their happy little friend could continue her work.

"What happened to *your* hair?" Lazuli buzzed near Selby, tugging several small twigs and leaves from the back of her tangles and held them in front of her face. "These are not pretty. I will get you some flowers instead."

With that she flew away, and Ingrid couldn't help but release a snicker at the berry-red color of Selby's face. But it was when Plintze snorted that a chain reaction began, and within a few heartbeats, everyone was laughing.

Lazuli returned laden with more blossoms and began to work on her next subject. "There!" the little sprite exclaimed, turning all eyes toward Selby once again. Fluttering in front of the girls, she looked from one to the other with a big grin. "You look much better." She clasped her hands together at her chest and sighed with a smile. "I'm going now." When she darted over to Plintze, kissed his temple, and disappeared into the trees, the movement was so fast it took everyone by surprise.

Silence filled the circle as everyone gaped at the dwarf. "Ach, I'm going to sleep," Plintze growled and stormed off.

"It is late, but I wonder if you wouldn't mind hearing a thought that I have," Bremen said as the four of them remained seated near the fire.

"Of course," Ingrid answered, curious and wary of what he might say.

"The attack today will not be the last. Greer knows who Ingrid is, and he'll have spread the word to the leader of the druht of her whereabouts." Bremen glanced at Selby and then to the others. "I think we should let the majority of the men continue to protect the supplies and servants. But we should go on ahead at a faster pace and get to my home where it is more secure."

"I agree and look forward to a quicker pace." Jorg leaned forward and casually stoked the fire.

"Yes, well then, we'll leave just before daybreak." Bremen peeked at Selby, hesitated, then reached his hand out to her with a steady gaze. Selby stood and entwined her fingers into his, and the two left together.

Ingrid wrapped the cloak around her shoulders a little tighter. "It will be a short night," she said a little more sharply than she intended. Rather than amend her tone, she blamed her residual irritation on the exhaustion of the day.

She laid down with her back to the fire and tried not to think about the hurt that flashed over Jorg's face before he'd nodded to her.

17

Bremen had gathered a group of six other men to accompany them to the monastery he'd purchased when he'd arrived in Northumbria the year before. He'd explained how he'd left a contingent behind to restore it.

"So, it's a castle for the prince now?" Jorg teased.

Bremen tightened his lips into a line, but otherwise ignored the comment. He also hurried along the servant boy who was helping to tie the leather greaves onto his shins.

Ingrid turned her focus to the camp to hide her amusement and instantly sobered as one of Bremen's soldiers stood a few feet away looking very nervous. He shifted his weight from one foot to the other and darted his eyes up to Ingrid and then back to the dirt.

"Excuse me, my lady, but," the man hesitated and looked around again as if trying to decide if he should keep talking. "I was wondering if you could come and have a look at a friend. He's struggling with a pain and doesn't want to complain for fear he'll be dismissed from service. If that happens, he'll lose his land back home. He didn't ask me to come to you, but I was wondering if you'd look at him just the same."

Ingrid stared at the man for a few seconds, letting his words sink in. Her heart fluttered that someone was asking for her help, and a smile spread on her face. "I'd love to." She followed the man with Jorg joining by her side.

The man paled, and his eyes grew round as he looked at Jorg. "I don't mean to offend, I'm a friend to the fae. I swear," he stuttered. Jorg fought to keep a twitch in his lip from curving up.

Selby groaned at the comment as she and Bremen walked up to the small gathering.

"You're Colam, is that right? Who is it that needs care?" Bremen asked.

"It's Finian. He's got a terrible pain. Had it since before the attack, but it's been worse since then. He didn't want me to ask, but now, he can't walk or eat," the man gushed, keeping his eyes focused on the ground and visibly trembling. Colam darted a glance to Ingrid and then Bremen before swallowing several times.

"It's good that you came to his aid before we left. Let's all go see Finian, shall we?" Bremen turned to the side and motioned for Colam to lead the way as he fell into stride with Jorg behind the girls.

Finian was toward the back of the long line of men, near a wagon ready to begin the daily trek. They found him on the ground leaning against a wheel with his eyes closed.

"I've brought the healer to see you, Finian," Colam said kneeling next to his friend whose eyes snapped open.

"You shouldn'a done it," Finian said. He tried to push himself up and grabbed his side, yelping in pain.

Ingrid immediately fell to her knees in front of the man. "I'm glad he came to get me. May I touch you? I think I can help."

"No, please stand and don'a waste your time wi' me."

Ignoring his response, Ingrid laid her hand on his shin and closed her eyes. Whether everyone stopped talking or she was blocking them from her hearing, she didn't care. She only allowed the warm golden glow inside of her to enter her mind. It soaked through her and then filtered outward into the man to search for what caused his pain.

Within seconds, she found the source: one of his organs was leaking and poisoning his body. Drawing in a deep breath, Ingrid exhaled until a glowing ball formed near the injury inside the lower right side of his abdomen. She then directed all the poison into it.

She concentrated on the worm-shaped tube but couldn't find what had damaged it or a way to restore it. Without hesitation she drained the rest of the fluid and forced it into the golden ball, causing the organ to shrivel in on itself. Directing the orb to travel up into Finian's stomach, she then let natural reflexes take over to expel the poison from his body.

Opening her eyes, Ingrid told Finian to roll to his side. She stood quickly, ordering everyone to back away just in time as the poor man wretched and vomited profusely. When he had finished, he sat up again and leaned back against the wheel. Ingrid turned to Colam. "Can you find him some water or ale, please?"

Wide-eyed, he nodded and hurried away.

"How do you feel? Is the pain gone?" she asked Finian.

"I think 'tis, but I'll be sure after the ale comes," he said, wiping his face with the back of his sleeve.

"I don't think you'll have any more trouble, but I'd like you to rest, perhaps ride in the wagon for a while when you leave."

"You didn'a do anything that will change me, or nothin'?" Finian's pale forehead pinched, but in his weakened state, it was hard to tell what concerned him.

"Change you?" Ingrid's brows furrowed, confused.

"The magic, it doesn'a change a man to," he paused, and his eyes flicked up to Jorg and back to Ingrid, then he lowered his voice to a whisper, "to somethin' else, does it?"

Ingrid bit the inside of her cheek to keep her face neutral when Jorg snorted behind her. "No, I only made your injury better, I hope."

"Thank ye, I'm much improved already."

"Don't just say that. I need to know the truth," she said.

"No, m'lady, I wouldn'a lie. I am better."

At that moment, Colam arrived with a flask of ale and handed it to his friend. Finian sucked down several large swallows before he wiped his beard with the back of his hand. The lines in his brow relaxed, and his eyes were bright.

"Please rest. Promise me, Finian." Ingrid gave him a hard stare, and the man nodded vigorously. "You should feel restored soon, but that's all I can do." She brushed her hands against her trousers as she stood.

"Finian, you heard the woman. You'll ride in a wagon until you are well, and it will not go well if I hear reports that you didn't follow that order." Bremen spun to face Colam. "Be sure he does." Both men nodded their heads eagerly.

"Thank you, m'lady," Finian said before taking another long swallow of the ale.

Bremen tipped a thank you to Ingrid and strode toward the front. Jorg put his hand on the small of Ingrid's back and prodded her to follow him.

"I'll just follow back here, by myself, as usual," Selby complained. Ingrid and Jorg snickered at her familiar commentary, but Bremen halted and turned around making all of them stop and stare at him.

He skirted around Ingrid and Jorg to stand in front of Selby who stared in silence with her eyes wide. Bremen turned to stand by her side and offered an arm.

Selby looked at his elbow sticking out toward her and then back up to his face with a shocked expression. Slowly she slipped her hand over his forearm while keeping her eyes focused on his. A smile brightened his face, and one slid across hers in return. The couple walked past Jorg and Ingrid without giving them a glance.

"Well—" Jorg looked at Ingrid with a glint in his eye and put out his elbow "—m'lady?"

Ingrid grinned. "I might get used to that." She slid her hand through his offered elbow and looked up expectantly when he didn't walk.

"I'm sorry about before. It tears me up inside to see you in pain. I believe in you—and I trust you to make the right decisions. Wherever you go, I'll go." He closed his eyes and drew in a deep breath, letting it out slowly before he continued. "Ingrid, you can think me a weak fool, because I love you, but I don't want to control you."

Ingrid felt herself wilt. "What if I don't find Eir in time?"

I'm afraid. What if I find her and it's not enough? What if I'm not enough?

Drawing her closer, he held her chin. "You are more than enough." He kissed her, forcefully enough that Ingrid's knees wobbled, and she braced herself against his chest.

"What was wrong with that man?" Jorg asked after they'd each had a few moments to settle their nerves and continued walking toward the front.

"I'm not sure how to explain it. One of his organs leaked poison into his body so I gathered it up and made him expel it. I couldn't fix it though, I just made it stop working."

"Stop working? How is that possible?" he asked with obvious confusion in his expression.

"I don't know." She threw her arm into the air. "I don't understand how any of this works. It was the only way I could get it to stop hurting him."

Jorg pulled her tighter to his side and rubbed the hand resting on his forearm. "I don't like you healing the men when it's not from a fight. What if something goes wrong, and they blame you for it? You should wait until you've had more training."

Ingrid turned her head and raised her eyebrows at him. "You aren't telling me what to do, are you?" She pulled at her hand, but he held her tighter. A thin line formed where his lips usually were.

"I'm not *telling*. I'm *suggesting*—" he arched a brow "—that you wait."

Ingrid felt herself relax a little at his well-chosen words, but it still bothered her to think he would try to control her. *I'm getting stronger. That time didn't tire me.*

"I noticed that. And, I'm not trying to control you, Ingrid. It's called concern; that's all."

Ingrid huffed and shook her head. "My parents used that same logic when they kept everything from me and tried to keep me in the dark about who I am. 'For my own good,' they said. I've had enough of people showing that kind of concern for me."

Jorg scrubbed a hand over his face. "Then at least let me come with you if anyone else needs your help. I won't do anything except what I did this time—watch and wait to see if you need me."

"I can live with that." She looked sideways at him and let a little curve tweak her lips.

A rustle in the bushes made them both turn toward the sound. Jorg pushed himself in front of Ingrid, earning him an annoyed growl as she elbowed her way back to his side. Before they could debate with each other further, Plintze and Lazuli stepped from the shadows.

"Where have you two been?" Jorg asked, a hint of levity in his voice.

"Playing," Lazuli stated matter-of-factly.

"I thought we were leaving? Are we or not?" Plintze asked, leaving no more room to question his whereabouts or doings.

"We are, right now, so I'm glad you're back." Ingrid said with a smile and tugged on Jorg's arm to hurry them all along.

After two long days and a quick night, they arrived at the monastery-turned-castle. Early in the afternoon, while still higher on the hillside, they could see down to what was essentially a small city. A large stone building with several smaller wooden ones to the side of it sat enclosed by a tall palisade and a deep ditch, creating an expanse of high ground.

A road led up to the trench on one side with a gate lowered as a bridge to allow entrance into the courtyard beyond the fence. There was an open area in the center of the buildings that appeared to have greenery. Selby, Ingrid, and Jorg stopped to take in the sight, with Bremen waiting with them as they looked.

"What is in the middle? It looks like grass, but why is it in the center of a structure?" Ingrid asked.

"That is the cloister, a place for monks to reflect on God. This used to be a monastery. Much of it was in need of repair from raiders but should be nearly complete by now."

Jorg flicked his eyebrows up with a little smirk, unapologetic for his countrymen. "Seems like a large place for you to acquire just to stay for a short time."

"We may need to return again, so it seemed a reasonable expense."

"Humph. Seems like a waste of land," Plintze said, surprising everyone that he'd returned after another time away with Lazuli.

"You are welcome to stay outside of its walls if it doesn't meet your satisfaction." Bremen smiled, but his tone left no doubt at his irritation.

Plintze snorted and sauntered down the road as the others followed. Selby and Ingrid continued to take in the sight of such large buildings and stonework.

A chill engulfed Ingrid, and she curled her arms around

her middle. The mental tar slammed against her mind at her temples, forcing her to squeeze her eyes shut tight.

When she opened them, she wasn't on the hillside any longer. She was in the center of the courtyard, surrounded by battle. This place, this instance—she'd experienced before.

Once again, she was in the center of the vision she'd had earlier. The first time she'd seen Jarrick. Ingrid turned slowly, unconcerned with the swords, axes, and clubs that swung around her because she knew she wasn't physically there.

Then she saw him.

Once again, Jarrick stood in the center of the fray, battling against the human foes. Her breath hitched as she saw Jorg fighting as well, near Jarrick. More and more men flooded into the courtyard through the open gate. There was no way to win against such numbers, even with Jarrick, Jorg, and their faster reflexes.

While Ingrid watched, helpless, a shadow covered the sun. Shielding her eyes, she peered toward the sky to see glass-like scales so black they shimmered with greens and blues like the oily sheen of tar.

No! This can't happen!

It was the same dragon that had attacked her months before. Her arm blazed with pain as if the injury was fresh. The beast swung its head from side to side, surveying the crowded courtyard before screeching as a stream of fire spewed into the fleeing warriors.

With a jolt that made Ingrid reach out to steady herself, she was flung from her vision back to the present. Tears streamed down her cheeks, and she had to brace against her knees to catch her breath.

Selby's wide-eyed stare flashed in front of her as she leaned over, keeping a steadying hand on Ingrid's back.

"What was that?" Shock and a touch of panic bled through Selby's voice. "Are you in pain?"

Slowly, Ingrid calmed, and she stretched to her full height. The others had come back and were standing behind Selby.

"I'm sorry to have worried everyone. I . . . I'm better now."

There was no way she was going to explain what she saw to the whole group. How could she tell them that they would be attacked—destroyed—by a dragon no less, because of her?

Betrayed by her stomach, Ingrid turned and wretched onto the ground. Selby's hand rubbed her back until the heaves subsided and she could stand again. Only Jorg and Plintze remained nearby when she looked up. Bremen had taken his men further up the road and Lazuli was nowhere in sight.

"Were you with Jarrick again?" Jorg's words were as sharp as a dagger, but his eyes held nothing but concern.

"No." Ingrid glanced over her shoulder to the view of the courtyard below. It's peaceful appearance ignorant of what was to come. "I'm bringing danger to everyone. Jarrick will never let me survive to bind that spell."

"What did you see?" Selby's hand rested on Ingrid's upper arm as if ready to offer support again.

"Something I've seen before—a battle that ends in dragon fire." Ingrid tipped her head toward the courtyard, then met with Plintze's gaze. "It's the same one."

The dwarf emitted a low rumble. He knew exactly what she meant; he'd nursed Ingrid back to health when she'd been attacked before. "We can prepare. I'll be happy to knock that flying lizard out of the skies."

"Yes, the vision is a gift. Now we can be ready and change the outcome. We can explain about it to Bremen as we walk and start to make a plan." Jorg brushed a piece of Ingrid's hair behind her ear. "We'll keep everyone safe, Hjarta. You'll see."

People rushed about at a frantic pace when the group made its way over the bridge and into the courtyard beyond the palisade wall. Rather than finding a peaceful scene of inhabitants going about their daily lives, the atmosphere was tense. Bremen was quickly entangled in a discussion with several men.

Jorg, Selby, and Plintze stood off to the side, out of the way, ignoring the stares and startled noises from those who hustled around them.

It's a good thing Lazuli isn't with us yet. Won't all these poor folks be surprised?

"I'm looking forward to that." Jorg chuckled.

"What is that?" Selby pointed from Ingrid to Jorg. "There is something going on between you two, and it's been like that since we left the village. Jorg says things that sound like he's answering you, except you said nothing."

"It's hard to explain. On our journey through the moors —" Ingrid stared at Jorg with a soft look on her face "—he heard my thoughts in his head. He tried to keep it from me for a while, but I caught on."

"So, you talk to each other in your heads?"

"It only goes one way. He can hear me, but I can't hear

him." Ingrid glanced at Jorg, expecting to see his typical grin about the subject, but he was staring at Bremen with a concerned expression.

What's happening?

"It's an elf skill," Plintze said. "Usually it can only happen between two elves, from what I've heard of it."

Selby started to ask another question, but Bremen strode up to them in a rush.

"My mother has sailed from Ireland and arrived on the coast this morning. There was no reason given in the message received, but I can think of nothing to make her take such a risk unless there has been terrible trouble back home. She should be here by tomorrow morning."

A sick feeling twisted in Ingrid's stomach. The darkness oozed lazily forward when she thought about the vision she'd had earlier. Now the queen was in jeopardy, too.

18

Selby pulled Ingrid aside the next day while they waited for the queen's arrival. "I'm such a fool." She charged right into the conversation. "When we were on the road and everyone was on the same level, it was easy to forget that Bremen is different from the rest of us. But this place, it's impossible to forget anymore. Now the queen—this is all too much."

She'd paced as she spoke, and Ingrid watched without interruption. Suddenly, Selby rushed to stand in front of her, grabbing her hand with wide eyes and causing Ingrid to lean against a stone column inside the nave of the former monastery. "Let's hurry and go. We'll say that you've learned where Eir is, and we have to meet with her. That way, we'll leave before the queen arrives."

Ingrid took Selby's hands between her own. "You don't need to run away from any queen. How Bremen thinks about you is all that matters. We've spent time with Queen Greta in Jorvik, and she was kind. This one will be, too."

"Greta is Norse. Bremen's mother, Galwain, is Saxon from

Wessex, by birth. Bremen talks about his mother and his little sister with such devotion. If she doesn't like me, what will that mean?"

"She will love you. Now relax and go stand by Bremen's side. Let his mother see you as the strong woman you are who belongs at the side of a prince." Ingrid spun Selby toward the front of the narthex where everyone was waiting and looped their arms together as they walked.

Selby groaned, but then took a deep breath and squared her shoulders. Every bit the shieldmaiden ready for battle as they headed nearer to Jorg.

The bustling bodies who'd prepared the church-turned-castle had disappeared. A few people stood around waiting for the queen, but most of the servants were out of sight. Jorg stood at the back of the room, and Ingrid stopped next to him.

"Where are Plintze and Lazuli? I haven't seen either of them this morning," Ingrid asked.

"Lazuli pressured Plintze to take her out for some fun. I think he agreed so they wouldn't be here when the queen arrived. That being said, whatever Plintze does for fun is something I really need to witness soon," Selby answered.

With a chuckle, Ingrid gently pushed her hand against Selby's back. "You know where you need to be."

Pale faced and holding her thumbs inside her fists, no doubt to keep from picking at them, Selby made her way to the front. Bremen instantly reached out for her hand, and Ingrid smiled.

A few of those standing around spoke in hushed tones and kept glancing over to Jorg as he stood near Ingrid. *Ignore them. They are jealous of me for standing near someone so handsome.*

Jorg snorted and kissed her temple before shaking his head. He smiled at a woman who stared, and she turned her face away as soon as their eyes met. "Yes, I'm sure that's what they're thinking."

Hoofbeats and commotion in the courtyard sounded just before the doors pushed open and boots clattered against the stone floors.

"Mother!" Bremen exclaimed.

Jorg and Ingrid faced the new arrivals, and Ingrid's chest suddenly became tight. A beautiful woman strode through the doors. She had a golden circlet entwined in her rich brown hair, and she wore a form-fitting gown of shimmering purple with sleeves tight to the elbow before flaring out and flowing down to the wrist.

Bremen embraced his mother and introduced Selby, who gave a hesitant smile and nodded. Galwain pulled Selby's hands between her own, and though Ingrid couldn't hear the words from where she stood, the warm acceptance radiated across the room.

I knew there'd be nothing to worry about.

Others greeted the queen as she made her way across the room. She smiled and spoke a few words to everyone, but when she turned toward Ingrid and Jorg, she halted ten steps away and gasped, her hand rising to her slender throat as she stared at them.

"What's wrong? Are you not well?" Bremen asked, taking hold of her free hand.

Ingrid felt an eerie stillness. All her muscles tensed, and a buzz of unease skittered through her middle. Perhaps they should have waited to meet the queen. Giving her time to greet her son alone might have been a better decision, but then she realized Galwain was staring at Jorg.

Ingrid snapped her attention to Jorg and watched as his face went from neutral to questioning. It looked like an answer to a question he hadn't asked was filtering into his brain and he was trying to process the information.

Ingrid reached out and touched his arm. "Maybe we should go." Jorg didn't move or respond to her. "Jorg?"

"Mother, what is it?" Bremen asked again, this time a hint of frustration lacing his words. "Perhaps you should go straight to your rooms. The journey has tired you."

"Alberich." One word was all she said, but it held enough emotion to fill the room—love, sadness, pain, and shock wrapped in a tone as beautiful as the woman herself. It floated through the air straight to Jorg, whose eyes popped open, and his chest hitched. For a moment, Ingrid thought he might fall to his knees, and she clutched the fabric of his shirt between the fingers she still held against his arm.

Bremen twisted toward them and saw Jorg's reaction. "What is this? Who is Alberich? Come Mother, sit and relax. You look pale." Bremen pulled his mother forward, sliding to her side and tucking her hand into the crook of his arm. She walked with him mindlessly while staring at Jorg with silver-rimmed eyes.

A torrent of emotions swirled over Jorg's face. As the duo neared, Ingrid could see his chest rise and fall faster, but still, he said nothing. When the queen stopped in front of them, a sad smile graced her lips but not her eyes.

"I never expected I would see you again. How did you know to meet me here?" the queen asked Jorg.

Bremen, Selby, and Ingrid looked back and forth between the two and amongst themselves. "Mother, what are you talking about?" Bremen shifted so his mother was behind his shoulder, then faced Jorg.

"I do *not* know you," Jorg finally spoke, directing his words to the queen before turning his attention to Bremen. "We need to be going," Jorg said, leaving no room for argument. He grabbed Ingrid's wrist and strode forward, bumping Bremen's shoulder as he dragged her along behind him. "Selby, you need to come as well," he said twisting to look at her.

"No." Selby's voice was strong and decisive.

Ingrid grabbed hold of the hand digging into her wrist and tried to pry his fingers off her arm. "Let me go. What is going on?"

When they got to the closed doors, four guards stepped in front to block their exit. Taking a deep breath and letting it out slowly, Jorg released Ingrid and turned around.

She rubbed at the red marks on her wrist and glared at him. "Jorg, what's wrong?"

"Stop! This is unnecessary. Guards, please step outside," the queen said, then looked to all of those standing silent around the edge of the room. "Everyone, please excuse us. I must speak to my son and his guests alone. I will be happy to meet with all of you later, after I've rested from my journey."

The guards stepped outside and closed the door after the last person had followed them. Jorg and Ingrid stayed to hear what the queen needed to say. With the doors shut, the room became uncomfortably silent.

Laying a hand on Bremen's arm, the queen smiled at her

son then faced Ingrid and Jorg. "Jorg is your name then?" she asked in a voice that floated across the room.

Jorg nodded but didn't move, every muscle in his jaw twitched as he stood still.

"I'm afraid I have misunderstood the nature of your visit. Let's find a place where we can sit and please allow me to explain myself."

Ingrid looked at Jorg, and even though she was angry at him for trying to drag her off, she worried more for why he felt it necessary. *Whatever this is about we'll face it—together.* The words were enough to soften his stance a small amount, and he cast a glance at her.

Jorg closed his eyes for a second and entwined his fingers gently with hers before he gave her a stiff nod. Together, they walked forward to stand in front of Bremen and his mother.

"The chapter house is now my meeting room. It's private," Bremen said and gestured for everyone to follow him as he took his mother's arm.

They found the room off the cloister where they'd talked with Bremen earlier. A large oval table took up the center of the room and several chairs sat around it. Cut stone walls with no decoration gave the room a cold, stark appearance. There were no sconces, so the only light came from a small, high window. Bremen quickly lit several candles and helped his mother to a chair.

All three of the others moved to sit across from the woman, and Bremen took a seat next to her.

"Bremen, please introduce me properly. Perhaps that would be the place to start."

"You've met Selby. This is Jorg and Ingrid. We met them along our travels a few days back as we headed home from our meetings. There are two others that travel with them as well—someplace, though I'm not sure where."

Bremen hesitated. Ingrid thought he seemed to be trying to decide if he should explain more. But he must have thought it best to leave it alone because he exhaled and said nothing further about them. "This is Galwain, Queen of Leinster, in Ireland."

Galwain smiled at Ingrid. "Are you from the same village Selby mentioned to me earlier?"

"Yes, we've been friends since we were small. She is more like my sister." The urge to help endear the queen to her friend filled her words.

Galwain's smile wavered, but she kept herself composed and focused on Ingrid. "What brings you so far from home?"

Ingrid gazed down into her lap and then at her hand entwined with Jorg's before she stared back at the queen. "I am searching for a woman whose help I need."

"Ingrid is a healer, Mother. She has special gifts, and she needs to learn how to use her abilities to save her village," Bremen interjected. "There are forces, both human and other, that are trying to stop her. We have run into some of them already on our travels and learned that a dark elf may be nearby now as well."

Galwain paled as she sat taller, and her expression grew very serious. Ingrid knit her brows together and worried that Bremen had said too much. She suspected Selby had told him even more.

The queen focused on Ingrid. "Dark elves are dangerous. Their magic does not adhere to the normal rules of nature. Whatever your gifts are, I urge you to find another way to help your village than facing one like that for any reason."

Ingrid stared at her. The woman spoke from experience, but she could not figure out how a woman—a queen—would have firsthand knowledge of someone like Jarrick. "If I could avoid him, I gladly would, but that's why I need to train. There's more at stake than just our village."

"Then that is why you are here as well? To help Ingrid with this situation?" Galwain looked at Jorg, and her expression was more pleading than questioning.

"Ingrid is special to me, and I will do whatever is necessary to keep her safe while she follows the destiny the Norns have woven for her."

It didn't escape Ingrid's notice that he sat rigid, not speaking of his own connection to the elven race. His hair was back and allowed his ears to be visible as evidence enough.

"I see. Perhaps I should explain why I have come. We may find that our goals are in line with each other's."

Bremen nodded. "Yes, please. I am anxious to find out what caused you to cross the sea. You hate sailing. Has there been news of father?"

"Your father's forces are faring well in Dublin; you can rest easy on that. He hopes to report an end to the war soon. I have come because of another matter." Galwain brushed at her skirt and arranged her sleeves. "When I first arrived in Ireland many years ago, I said it was because I had fled from Wessex, as I've told you before."

Bremen leaned his forearms on the table. "You said it was

because of your family. I didn't think it right to ask more of it."

"I have always appreciated that. Please understand that what I'm going to say has no bearing on my love for you. But my flight to Ireland was not the first time I'd run from my troubles."

Creases formed on Bremen's brow. Ingrid fidgeted in her seat. *Maybe we should go?* Jorg gave an almost imperceptible shake of his head.

"My father, Wilbert, was an ambitious man and spent years building relationships that would increase his social standing. He'd married my sister off to a man in Wales, and I found myself enjoying the simplicity and solitude of the forest. Not to mention it fed into my rebelliousness to protest the finery expected of me and ruin my dresses rummaging for mushrooms or climbing trees."

Ingrid and Selby exchanged an amused look. There were far too many memories in Ingrid's mind of similar experiences.

"After a time, the magical beings that lived among the trees began to show themselves to me, and I made wonderful friendships with sprites, pixies, shape-shifters that could take on the form of a variety of animals . . . and elves. It was great fun for me as a young girl to have an entire world of secret friends."

Galwain paused as she adjusted her sleeves. She then brushed at her skirts again before fiddling with a thin gold ring adorning her right index finger. She had met elves and sprites, had befriended them. She'd thought Jorg was someone else. Ingrid's breath hitched, and she glanced at Jorg. He was sitting so still it didn't look like he was breathing.

"The reason that I fled was because I fell in love with an elf. We spent every day for months walking through the trees, discovering more about each other, and discussing grand plans to make the future better. Then my father found out. He insisted that we give each other up, that it was not natural for a human and an elf to be together.

"Not only did he believe our union unholy, but he'd secured a marriage for me, and my relationship in the woods would ruin that agreement . . . as well as his reputation. It would destroy all his hard work and political scheming over the years. But I couldn't give up the love that I'd found. Father believed that elves could bend a human's will without their knowledge, and I was not of sound mind."

Bremen huffed. "Many of my men feared the same, and it caused some unfortunate consequences on our journey," he added, his voice low and thick.

While Jorg didn't notice the quick, apologetic glance in his direction, Ingrid did. She wasn't the only one, Galwain turned her focus to Jorg and held his stare. The silence in the room itched against Ingrid's skin as everyone sat rigid.

"I'm sorry." A shimmer lined Galwain's eyes. She sucked in a deep breath and continued. "When I left, my father developed a sense of hatred to all magical beings. So strong that I found out later he'd had the forest I'd frequented burned. His social status fell, and he was forced back into the life of a low ranking noble without influence. Recently, I received word that he was amassing an army to seek out and destroy all those from the otherworld that he still blames. It was the fact that he was searching for one individual in particular that brought me here."

This time when Galwain stopped speaking, she squared her shoulders and met Jorg's stare with strength.

"I was worried he had found out about my child. The son I'd given up to protect him when his father's ideas of a better future turned dark. I made the decision to run again, as I had from my father before. If I was found, I would face the consequences, but I couldn't let him turn my happy little boy into the monster he was becoming. There was a sprite that helped me find a family without children, and we hid him among the human world. Then I fled on my own to Ireland. I've come back to stop my father before he finds my son."

No one moved for seconds, though it felt like hours. Finally, Jorg blinked, once and then again before he spoke in a cold, but controlled tone. "And you believe that I am your son?"

Without hesitation, she nodded. "Yes."

"Because I happen to be here when you arrived? You know nothing about me to think that I might be that child."

Ingrid tried to reach over to Jorg, but he stood before she touched him. He walked to the side of the room with his back to everyone before he turned to Galwain once more.

"It's a shock, and you must have many questions, both of you." She faced Bremen and rested her hand on his arm before she returned her gaze to Jorg. "But I assure you that I recognize who you are. A mother knows her child. You've been as rigid as stone from the moment we saw each other because you feel it, too."

Ingrid was stunned and couldn't figure out what to do. Should she stand with Jorg or give him some space? She glanced to Selby for help, but her focus was on Bremen.

Finally, she turned to Galwain to ask the questions bothering her. "Did you look for him? Did you know the pain he had for being different and having to hide who he was?"

The silver lining Galwain's eyes slipped when she faced Ingrid. "I never knew where he'd gone. While elves don't have the ability to control someone's actions, they do have an ability to hear the thoughts of one they love. Jarrick would have been able to get the information from me if he'd found me, so I insisted that the sprite keep it a secret."

"Jarrick?" Ingrid spoke the name in a whisper that had the darkness in her head swell instantly.

Jorg made a shocked sound as he narrowed his eyes. "My father is *Jarrick*? The dark elf?"

The queen swallowed. "Yes."

"I need some air." With that, Jorg flung the door open and strode out of the room.

Ingrid sat stupefied for several seconds before rushing out to follow him. The darkness swirled in her head, and she couldn't think straight. It was too much to process and they needed to figure it out together.

When she ran into the courtyard, she didn't find Jorg, but she skidded to a stop as a woman walked toward her.

Eir had arrived.

19

———

Of all the times for the woman to show up. Ingrid stood staring at Eir, her chest heaving from running and the anxiety of Galwain's information.

"I've been searching for you." Ingrid's voice was barely above a whisper and tinged with relief.

"I told you I would find you when you were ready, and now you are. Come, there is much to do." Eir turned and walked away.

Ingrid hesitated and peered over her shoulder in the direction Jorg had gone. The ache in her head became worse when the sticky essence jerked like a fish pulling a line. She pressed her fingers against her forehead.

Everything that had happened—the entire reason they'd traveled so far—was to find Eir. With her free hand, she clutched the bead of her necklace. It hummed, and the energy in her middle sparked to life. The pressure behind her eyes eased, and she followed the goddess over the bridge toward the woods beyond.

When Ingrid reached the tree line, she hesitated once again before plunging forward into the darkness. After fighting through underbrush and tree limbs that snatched at her like claws, she came upon an open field. There, standing in the center was Eir, facing Ingrid and waiting.

I can do this. It's who I am. Act strong, be strong.

Ingrid straightened her shoulders, lifted her chin, and walked directly up to the goddess who radiated with an ethereal glow even in the daylight. She wore an indigo blue gown with embellishments of gold. Intricate embroidery crisscrossed between her breasts and around her abdomen, accentuating her shapely figure. A circlet of beading wrapped around her forehead and came to a point in the center above her eyebrows. Regal and steadfast, she held her hands clasped in front of her.

Ingrid couldn't pretend to understand what had made Eir decide the time was right, but she knew she was ready.

"My powers have grown stronger, and I've learned to use them as we've traveled," Ingrid said.

Eir smiled, more cunning than comforting. "Is that so? Perhaps you have no need of my help at all then?"

"That's not what I meant. I'm just more capable than I was before."

"You have much to learn, and healing a few injuries does not require the level of powers you possess. If you want to be a traveling völva and earn coin for work as a simple healer, then you are right."

Ingrid shifted on her feet and blinked several times. Eir's voice was soft and kind, but there was a sharpness to it that proved Ingrid had missed something. "I've never seen or heard of anyone who could do what I can."

"As long as you continue to pretend you command your abilities, you will not learn. Who are you, Ingrid? Why are you here?"

Ingrid stared and opened her mouth to speak more than once, but each time, no words would form. Her mind was blank. "I don't know who I am. That's why I need you," she finally said.

"There is the truth. Bravado and arrogance only fool others. Sight has many forms. It's not just about the ability to determine a person's fate or have visions. It is also the ability to follow the ebb and flow of life and death in all things. To connect with the power of the Yggdrasil tree and all creation on every realm."

The air warmed, and a small breeze rose up to rustle the grasses. Eir's long chestnut-colored hair floated around her shoulders as she stood tall and commanding.

"Many have magic, but they are pretenders compared to what is inside of you. The power to See from the source of unlimited strength is only experienced by those the Norns of fate have selected. Your power is less of a gift than a responsibility and obligation. One you must wield carefully if you accept it."

Ingrid didn't notice Eir move, but she suddenly stood inches away, her alabaster skin glowing with a brightness that made Ingrid want to shield her eyes. But she stood steady and did not flinch, even as the goddess placed her fingers against Ingrid's forehead and everything went black.

Her insides rolled, and the earth beneath her feet threatened to swallow her. The essence in her mind thrashed. The roar between the two unseen forces vibrated through Ingrid's mind.

Choose, Ingrid.

A voice in the distance, nearly drowned in the din, called out to her. Choose? *Choose.* Another surge of pressure made her entire body clench. Sweat rolled down her back.

I want to free you. Another voice, different from the first, called out.

Like a fog of shadows and mist, tendrils dark and light swirled around her. A battle waged unseen but tore at every fiber of who she was. Both held pain. Both offered power. The suffocating vortex ripped at her. A demand and an offer.

When there didn't seem to be a way to end the torment, she thought of home. Those she needed to fight for. Those she loved. She cupped the runes in her pouch, and they warmed against her palm. Home and protection—everything that truly mattered.

In the recesses of the darkness was a glimmer of light. The end of the cord that spread through her when she healed. Choose. She understood then. She controlled her own fate. The Norns chose a destiny for her, but she had to accept it for herself.

The pain flared, and she felt her knees buckle. She grabbed hold of the cord and pulled. Light burst from behind her eyes, and when she thought she couldn't hold on any longer, her mind went quiet and peace flooded through her.

"Open and See, Ingrid."

The golden glow that surrounded her vision when she healed was back, only this time it was as if she had been cocooned inside it. It seemed as if the amber bead that hung from her necklace had engulfed her.

Not trapped—there was no pressure or confinement. The golden light made everything clearer. Colors were deeper, edges sharper, and the patterns of every leaf, flower, and blade of grass distinguishable. Her body was light and airy; the darkness plaguing her mind no longer existed.

Unlike before, her senses picked up the smallest nuances. At the far-off tree line, a squirrel hopped into its den in the side of a large pine to feed her hungry kits. An owl adjusted its feet on a high branch of a different tree, sleeping the daylight away.

Her skin tingled with warmth all the way to her fingertips. It felt as if the sun itself wrapped her in its sweet embrace. Bees flitted from lavender to chamomile, sprinkling the air with their calming lullaby. Ingrid reached out and moved her hand through the air in a lazy ribbon-like motion, moving the particles around like dust motes.

The glove on her arm drew Ingrid's attention. With a slow, deliberate slide, she slipped it off and then the other. They fluttered like feathers, twisting over and landing with a whisper at her feet.

Ingrid allowed the peaceful tranquility to fill her soul. With each breath, each beat of her heart, it absorbed into her blood, her thoughts, and her emotions—like going home after a long absence. She felt whole.

Nothing escaped her senses, yet she was not overwhelmed. Flowers gave off their sweet scent, and she could somehow see the droplets of their essence flow out in all directions. A butterfly fluttered close, powerless to do anything other than kiss the gentle petals.

No single being acted alone. Every living creature, plant, and element breathed and connected to each other. Woven together in a pattern so intricate it was nearly impossible to separate.

But, at the fringe of her consciousness was the awareness of another pattern—another thread of the fabric as necessary as all the rest. Like a phantom, it seeped into the beauty as it wound its way among the brightness. The shadow gave depth to the light, working together in balanced harmony.

In the midst of the euphoria, a twinge of pain gripped her as a sparrow swooped down in perfect precision to pluck from the air the small butterfly she'd watched earlier. A mist of dust scattered in the breeze as the bird flew away, and every particle that landed on the grasses sparked with life as the two forces blended into one another. So quick, yet so necessary for balance.

"Your power draws from the forces of the realms and brings them into focus. Good and evil, life and death, side by side. One without the other cannot exist." Eir's voice sang into her ears as if she was standing right next to Ingrid, but as she looked around, the goddess was nowhere in sight.

Ingrid walked through the meadow, listening and touching the life all around her. "What now? How do I use this? When I heal, I follow the pathway to mend the injury I find. Is this the same?" she asked, believing the goddess could hear her from wherever she watched.

"This is the first step. The spell that was cast is layered. There will be choices you have to make where you need to understand the balance which must be maintained. The man Finian, who you healed on the road. Which choice did you make for him?"

"I stopped the poison." *How did she know about that?*

"How?"

Ingrid cringed. There wasn't any use lying to the woman, she obviously already knew what had happened. "I stopped the organ that was leaking. I couldn't figure out what else to do."

"Exactly, which is why you are lucky that he survived because it was a non-essential part of his body. The same decision could bring death. You will have to learn when that might be the appropriate response, and not by guessing."

"How would it be right to use my gift to take someone's life? I would never do that!" Ingrid was shocked Eir would suggest such a thing.

"And that is why you are not ready." Eir's voice was soft, kind, but also curt.

No. This couldn't be right. It wasn't what she should be learning. Her job—her destiny—was to ensure that all life had a chance. To make sure they would *all* live. How could Eir be telling her there might be a time that her gift would be used for destruction? That's what Jarrick had wanted.

"Show me. Show me what I need to understand to bring safety to my family. Show me so everyone will be safe."

Ingrid stumbled over the bridge, her mind a jumble of thoughts. She didn't know how long she'd been in the meadow. Hours? Days perhaps? Numbness coated her limbs, and she could only think about a warm bed and enough rest so everything she'd learned would make more sense.

"Ingrid!" Jorg's voice rang out from across the courtyard. "Where have you been?" He reached her before she had time to answer. Standing there in front of her, his grassy scent filled with the freshness of spring lightened the air. She sighed.

"I was with Eir, in the meadow."

"She's here?" He touched her fingers. "You were right then, this was the place you needed to be."

All around them, people milled about, doing their evening chores and eyeing the two strangers. They quickened their pace when they'd have to move near Ingrid and Jorg.

"You just returned, and you look exhausted, but will you go for a walk with me? Not far, just so we can have a moment alone." Jorg's voice was soft, and when Ingrid met his eyes, they were full of questions. They were so open and honest that her heart skipped, and she couldn't say no.

She smiled and nodded. *I always have time for you.*

Jorg closed his eyes and wrapped his hand around hers. He stepped to her side, and they walked back over the bridge.

In the cool darkness of the trees, they found a fallen log. Soft moss made a comfortable chair as they sat side by side. Damp soil gave an earthy smell to the air, and tiny tan mushrooms grew in a small ring on the ground near their feet. Ingrid dangled her hand over the edge and used one finger to trace the top of the mushroom closest to her that was illuminated by a ray of light filtering through the treetops.

"I found a ring like this once. Mama called them an elf circle. She said if you stepped inside, it would trap you in the realm of elves forever. It doesn't seem like a very fun story anymore."

"Unless we go there together. Then it wouldn't be so bad. Trapped forever without any worries. I might be convinced to give that a try." A wry grin tugged at one corner of Jorg's mouth.

"Where did you go? I followed you, but then I ran into Eir. I had to go . . . it's why we're here."

"I would have been upset with you if you hadn't gone." Jorg paused and rubbed his thumb over her fingers. "I thought you might be angry at me for trying to drag you off and then storming out alone. I'm sorry for all of that."

"Although, I could've done without the dragging part, I wasn't angry with you. Not after what Galwain said." Ingrid played with the end of her braid. On the inside, her stomach churned with the curiosity of how their lives were changing and what it could mean. "Where did you go?"

"I found men training and joined them. It took a little convincing, but when I offered to stay weaponless, they obliged."

Ingrid pushed away to look at his face, searching for marks or bruises. "Are you hurt?"

He scoffed. "I'm a good fighter."

She rolled her eyes and settled back next to him. "You still get injuries." They sat in silence, enjoying being alone together for a couple of minutes.

"Did Eir take you far? To Asgard?"

"We only walked out to a meadow, not far from here. I'm not sure I can describe what happened. It was as if she opened my Sight in a new way." Ingrid grew quiet as she recalled the new sense of power, both light and dark, and shuddered.

"Are you getting cold? We should go back.'

"I'm okay." So much was changing for her, and it was only the beginning. With Galwain and her news, it was changing for both of them. "I've spent my whole life fighting to do something grand, something larger than myself, without understanding that there was a bigger reason for my dreams than I could imagine.

"If I'd been given the chance to prepare and know who I am, what I'm expected to do . . . Maybe our families wouldn't be in danger now." She paused, then decided to push forward with what pressured her thoughts. "For so many years, you've had to hide who you are and wonder why." Jorg huffed but didn't interrupt. "Galwain has answers. You can finally understand and feel settled within yourself."

"Every time we had to move because people would find out about me, I'd get angry that I was different. That anger is still there, and I battle it constantly. When I met Hagen, his confidence amazed me . . . how secure he was with his place in the world. It was the first true friendship I'd ever made, but I'd still get angry at him sometimes."

Jorg shook his head and looked out into the space beyond Ingrid. "I'd wonder why I couldn't be accepted for who I am, like he was, or why I didn't get the chance to have his confidence. It would eat me up inside until I'd go out to the woods by myself and hit a tree, or run, or hunt, or something that would allow me to lose some control. I would embrace my anger. I'm not as good as you think I am."

Ingrid's heart ached. A sting threatened to spill tears at his childhood pain, but she forced herself to take even, steady breaths and keep calm. He was good and kind, and she would do whatever she could to help him see that.

"I love my mother, the one who raised me, but when *she* walked in yesterday, I couldn't breathe. In my heart, I sensed an instant connection. Yes, I would like to know her, but how can I accept . . . the other?" He stared at the elf ring at their feet, then continued in a low voice. "Why would you want to stay with me since I am part of *him*?"

Ingrid twisted on the log to face him. "I have watched you

for years. You are a *great* friend, a strong warrior, a sensitive son, and the most handsome man I have ever seen. Nothing Galwain has to say, or who your father is, will change how much I love you."

Then Jorg stiffened and sat straighter as he listened. Ingrid didn't move. She'd seen him act that way too many times not to recognize the danger he sensed interrupting their moment.

It wasn't just quiet in the shade of the trees—it was as if all life held its breath, waiting for whatever hid among its branches and leaves to show itself. When Ingrid faced forward again, he nudged her with a glance that said not to reveal her awareness. 'Let it come to us,' he seemed to say.

"We should get back. It's getting late," Jorg said calmly.

Ingrid rose to her feet and nodded. She didn't trust herself to speak, knowing the wobble in her voice would betray her nerves. It didn't matter, though. Before they could take three steps, a half-dozen or so men armed with weapons stepped out from behind the trees and rushed forward.

Jorg instantly drew his axe and charged. Ingrid pulled her daggers into each hand but hesitated as her powers flared to life.

I don't need these.

Once again, the world took on the glow that allowed her to see every detail as if time itself had slowed. Ingrid let the daggers slip to the ground as she held up her hands and concentrated.

Two men closest to her fell backward as if knocked into a wall. More came, and she faltered for a valuable few pulses as a trickle of fear rolled down her spine. A deep breath and another push, and three more men fell to the ground.

Ingrid heaved for air, her arms and legs trembling. Nausea rolled in her stomach. Her knees hit the ground with a thud. After all the training earlier in the day as well as her current efforts, she was drained. Jorg wasn't far away, fighting against the last two men.

Get up. Help him!

The clash of wood and metal pervaded the air. Shouts rang out. The metallic tang of blood and magic burned Ingrid's nose and coated her tongue.

A roar of pain caught her attention. Jorg struggled against the last man, a tall brute who held the advantage. Even with a gash along his side and a blood-soaked tunic, Jorg fought on. When he slipped to his knees, Ingrid screamed.

Angry and determined, she urged herself forward. She crawled through the leaves and twigs like an animal, her muscles too weak to stand. Mud squished between her fingers. Thistles caught in her hair and slashed her face. With a surge of strength, she lunged forward to trip the larger opponent.

An instant later, a crushing blow to the ribs knocked Ingrid to her back. A heavy boot smashed her chest and pinned her to the ground.

"I'll get to you next," a rough voice mocked.

Ingrid closed her eyes and seized the man's leg. As it had before, her breathing slowed and a pathway inside his body opened to her view. There were injuries, cuts and bruises. But she ignored those, a different destination in mind.

The muscles under her hand relaxed. The blood rushing through the veins slowed and thickened. She saw the rapid heartbeat turn sluggish, then stop. When the man fell with a thump near her, she held on. She didn't let go until his heart shriveled to nothing. She laid there, blinking into the bright sky.

A figure blocked the sunlight as it hovered over her with a halo of nut brown hair. "Ingrid! Say something." Jorg's voice was raspy as he slid a trembling hand along her shoulder, his touch light and seemingly afraid.

With a sigh of relief, she realized his wound was superficial as the rush of energy cooled inside her core, totally spent.

20

"We need to get to the bridge. Can you stand?" Jorg held his hands on either side of her face as he spoke.

The warmth of his palms seeped into her rapidly cooling skin. Her tongue stuck to the roof of her mouth as she croaked out a hoarse affirmation and made to sit up. Bodies lay scattered around them, and one man moaned. The initial blast of her power must have only knocked them out.

Was it wise to leave them alive to fight again?

"What should we do with those who live? Should we question them?" she asked.

"We know who they are and why they're here. Let's hurry to the shelter of the palisade." Jorg quickly tucked her to his side and hurried away as quickly as they could move. The wound on his side was warm and sticky on her fingers where she gripped his waist.

I'm sorry I can't help with this right now.

"It's only a scratch. Don't even try, or you'll take longer to recover yourself."

The tree line was ahead, and they could see the regular movement of people. Ingrid sagged in relief. There hadn't been an attack on the others. The motion caused Jorg to shift her tight against his side, so her feet barely skimmed the ground.

"You can let go. If I'd not spent so much energy with Eir, I could have lasted longer. I'm nearly better already, though." She didn't make any motions to pull away.

As soon as they entered the courtyard, two guards hurried over to them. One of them was Gavin. Jorg leaned close to him and spoke in a low voice that Ingrid couldn't hear.

Gavin called out to two other guards, and the four hurried out the gate toward the forest. The hiss of metal rang out as they drew their weapons while they jogged away. Ingrid stood rooted to the ground when Jorg started to move them forward again.

"Where are they going?"

Jorg scrubbed his hand over his face. The blood and dirt blending together as a reminder of what they'd just experienced. "Do you think we should have to face them again? What if next time they kill someone?" He nodded to the few people finishing up their chores before they went inside for the evening meal. "We've brought a lot of danger into their home. These people have helped us, and they deserve to stay safe."

It was true. If anyone was hurt or worse because of those men, she'd never forgive herself. Just then, two young boys ran from the stables, jostling each other and laughing as they headed toward a door leading directly into the dining hall. She tamped down her rising guilt and nodded.

"We should speak to Bremen and let him know what happened," she said. They moved forward again, away from the events taking place behind her among the trees. She'd exclaimed to Eir that she'd never use her powers to take another's life. Mere hours later, she'd done just that.

What am I becoming?

Rather than walking through the main doors, Ingrid and Jorg followed where the two boys had slipped through a side door. They were able to sneak unnoticed into the dining hall and stood along the back wall, searching a less direct path to the front table where Bremen dined with Galwain at his side. Selby should have been there, too, but before Ingrid could question her whereabouts, her best friend's voice rang out as she hurried toward Ingrid.

"There you are!" Selby's boisterous vocals took years to get used to. Ingrid hunched her shoulders and gave an apologetic smile to the men sitting near where they stood. "Where were you? I looked all over after you left—you worried me. And what happened?" Blood splattered over both she and Jorg, obvious that there had been trouble.

"I'm sorry," Ingrid said, ignoring an explanation for the moment. There wouldn't be any point to trying to stay on the fringes of the room anymore. They needed to warn the others and might as well let Selby lead the way.

Selby looped her arm through Ingrid's and dragged her toward the front as Jorg followed.

On their way to the front, the cook interrupted them as she called out to Selby. The woman hurried over with a scowl on her face. She appeared as though she'd wrestled a dozen errant boys. The bun atop her head fell limply to the side, and chunks of loose pieces of graying hair strayed down her neck.

"I do not want that flying beast in me kitchen again, do you hear? If she wants a pie, you make it for yerself and don't let me see one speck of a mess after you do."

Selby's eyes went wide, and she only nodded in response to the angry woman.

"She will be most careful, I assure you," Ingrid said and pulled Selby away. "What did you do?" she whispered after they were far enough away.

"Lazuli was pestering me to play with her earlier. I saw one of the serving girls and told Lazuli I had to help in the kitchens, thinking she'd go off to find Plintze or something. The next thing I knew, I was offering to make her a pie. I guess she didn't forget about that."

"She'll never forget. Don't make a promise to a sprite that you can't fulfill. Trust me, you don't want to be on the wrong side of her temper," Plintze said as he joined the others ambling to the front tables.

"I wish someone would have told me that," Selby moaned and plopped into a chair.

Under normal circumstances, Ingrid, and especially Jorg, would have enjoyed Selby's self-inflicted struggles, but neither could muster more than a hint of amusement.

Bremen's attention was drawn to Jorg as he glanced toward Selby, and his expression turned sour. Their disheveled appearance took immediate priority.

"I'm sorry to interrupt your meal, but we need to speak with you Bremen," Jorg said.

It took all of Ingrid's composure to keep the cringe off her face at Jorg's authoritative tone. Bremen's stone-faced expression said he shared her sentiment. The information Galwain had shared that morning—only just that morning—would be a hard adjustment for both of them. Instead of rising to go somewhere quieter, he leaned back in his chair and met Jorg's stare. Neither of them backed down from the challenge to avert their eyes.

Only the scratch of nervous feet or a muffled cough remained in the once bustling dining hall. The confrontation drew unnecessary attention, and several men stood with their hands rested on the hilts of their swords. With silent grace, the queen stood. "Perhaps we should all head back to the council room?"

A hint of competition sparkled in Jorg's eyes, waiting for Bremen to accept the invitation first.

"Now!" The queen's tone, though quietly spoken, made both men snap their gaze to her. The raised brow she directed to each of them had them giving her a nod as they turned to leave.

Gavin and those who'd gone into the woods with him strode toward the group as they left the dining hall.

"What is it?" Bremen asked, stepping forward. A nod toward Jorg had the prince looking between the two men with a mixture of suspicion and irritation.

"We are headed to the council chambers. You should join us," Jorg said.

A flush spread across Bremen's face, and Ingrid wondered how they were going to keep the two in the same confined space once they made it to the meeting.

Galwain strode past the simmering tempers and led the way down the hall, giving Ingrid the impression that the queen was of the same mindset.

The guards stayed outside the door while Gavin joined the rest of the party, and they settled into chairs around the large table. Without waiting to be asked, Jorg gave the details of the attack.

The images replayed in Ingrid's mind, and her chest tightened so much it was hard to breathe. When Gavin confirmed that all the men were indeed dead, she bit down on the inside of her lip in order to keep her expression strong.

"Do you think it was an isolated group?" Bremen asked. The anger aimed at Jorg earlier was now replaced with the calm demeanor of a leader.

"I doubt it. More likely a scouting party," Jorg said. "Greer led those men against us on the road, and he'd want to find out if we accompanied you here. I'd say we can look forward to more of them in the next day or two when those men don't check in."

"Unfortunately, that's true. I recognized two of them," Gavin added.

Plintze hopped off his chair and strode for the door. "I'm going to go find Lazuli and make sure she stays away from all of this," he said as he hurried out.

Bremen scrubbed his hand over his face. The simple gesture done in contemplation was familiar to Ingrid, and she glanced sidelong to Jorg. He sat relaxed and didn't seem to notice.

"Bremen told me of the trouble you had on the road, and I am so sorry for it." Galwain let her gaze drift to her lap when Jorg didn't respond, then turned her focus to Bremen. "So far, you have met with smaller groups, but now that word has had time to spread of Ingrid's identity and where she is, I have no doubt my father will be moving all of his forces this way.”

“Will he attack if he learns you’re here?” Selby asked.

It was a good question and worthy of considering. From what it sounded like, Wilbert’s focus was on finding Ingrid and didn’t know Galwain had ever given birth to a son. Two of them, though that might not be useful information to share under the circumstances.

Would it make a difference to a man so set on hate?

Galwain gave a brief pause before speaking again. “I couldn’t say if I would have any influence on him after all these years, but I’m certainly willing to try and speak with him.”

“He may be my grandfather, but he does not seem to be a man in his right mind. I’ll not take a chance with your safety,” Bremen said. “We can offer him a parlay, but he must come here where we can protect you.”

Galwain narrowed her eyes but smiled at her son. “The safety of everyone is of the utmost concern. I’ll not sit in safety if I can stop bloodshed. If I’d wanted to do that, I would not have boarded that awful boat again.”

“The men we’ve come across have no interest in parlays.” Disdain oozed from Jorg’s words. “That effort would only grant time for their men to breech the palisade while we are focused elsewhere. We need to be prepared to fight.”

“My father is a cunning man and may not march straight to the gate like regular Saxons. He has already proven his stubbornness by hiring such a ruthless army. He will be determined to breech the walls,” Galwain said.

“If we keep the archers spread out along the wall, we’ll control the high ground and can concentrate the rest of the men by the gate. Even if we have lower numbers of men compared to what they are sure to have, if they breech there it will be a bottleneck. We will have the advantage." Bremen spoke as a commander, no longer seeking peace but a plan of action.

"Yes, but how will we keep them from climbing the walls? If they have more numbers than we do, eventually, they will get their ladders on the sides and come over the top," Gavin said.

"How outnumbered will we be, do you think?" Ingrid asked.

"It's hard to say. We won't know until they arrive, but they'll be scattered about in the woods." Bremen stood and paced slowly. "The wagons will be here in two days, three at the most. Then we'll be up to our full compliment. We came for meetings with Mercia, not to fight. It is safe, and better planning, to assume they will have a larger force."

"Smaller numbers have won large battles. We'll need to keep them off the walls," Jorg said. Some of the antagonizing tone toward Bremen had dissipated. It seemed as though concentrating on the upcoming fight helped transfer his anger.

"It will be too hard for the archers to keep up. Perhaps we should think of an escape plan," Gavin said.

"No, we can't run. Besides, where would we go? We have too many to sneak past them through the woods. I won't leave anyone behind, and too many wouldn't be able to keep up." Bremen stretched his back and shook his head. There had to be a solution.

"What if we set fires all along the outside of the wall? It

would make it more difficult to reach us, and we could see them approach if they attack in the dark." Ingrid suggested.

"They would send a small force ahead to put those out before the rest of them rushed," Gavin said. Both Bremen and Jorg nodded in agreement.

The room was silent for a few minutes, the sputtering of a few lit candles the only sound as everyone sat in deep thought. Ingrid stared blankly at the flames while she tried to come up with a better plan until she considered one of the candles sitting inside a shallow metal cup.

"What about a kettle? Large ones filled with tar. If they were lit, it would be too difficult to put out the light. Even if they tried to knock them over, it would make it too hard for them to cross, even if the fires went out—"

"We could wrap a chain around them and pull them over. As the men rushed forward the hot tar would coat and burn them. That would give the archers more time and create a barrier that could keep them from getting their ladders across to the wall at all. Yes, that might work," Bremen said, his eyes bright as he spoke, not looking at any one person in particular.

Ingrid swallowed and glanced at Selby, who watched Bremen with a smile and a look of utter pride. *That wasn't exactly what I thought—it's even better.*

Jorg sucked in a deep breath and rolled his eyes at her, but she could see the recognition in his eyes that he agreed with the plan as well.

"The fire would set the grasses ablaze, and it would work its way through the ditch to the palisade. We would trap ourselves and do their job for them." Gavin looked as though it pained him to stomp out their hope.

"Every year back at home, there are fields left to sallow," Selby said. "Depending on the need, some of them are fired to better prepare the soil for the next year's crops. If we hurry, couldn't we do that to the ditch? That way, when the fires reach it, there will be nothing left to burn."

Bremen stared at her. His eyes glittered with a hardened satisfaction, a warrior ready and eager for action.

21

Preparations for the upcoming battle were in full swing the next day. Forges blazed as smiths pounded more chains into shape. Every kettle that could be found was heated over small flames, wafting the pungent aroma of tar through the air.

Every man met in the courtyard to sharpen steel or fashion arrows between exercise sessions and drills. Selby trained alongside Bremen and the other men, while Ingrid sparred with Jorg so he could teach her how to use different weapons.

After the meeting in Bremen's council room, Gavin had given Ingrid back her daggers which he'd found in the woods. She'd thanked him, especially relieved to have the bone-handled blade Jorg had given her returned.

"I still don't understand why this is necessary? I can use a hammer and my daggers. Besides, I proved I can fight without weapons in the forest," Ingrid said. She gave a quick shudder as she recalled the hammer made especially for her in Jorvik, and the shipwreck that caused her to lose it.

"A hammer is a strength weapon. The one you had was lighter, unique. You used it well, but it is not the right choice for you," Jorg said as he held out an axe. "And using your abilities in the forest left you drained. A smart warrior will give themselves options."

Ingrid rolled her eyes and bit her cheek as she stared at him, finally taking the axe. "I'm not that weak, you know."

Jorg gave her a challenging, blazing stare that made her heart leap and distracted her focus on fight training. Too fast for her to react, Jorg was behind her with an arm around her throat and her wrists trapped by his other hand.

"So, use your strength against me then." His voice held the timber of a man ready for battle, and while it was a bit exciting, especially said into her ear, it was also frightening. Ingrid swallowed hard and tried to wrench herself free, without a sliver of progress.

"Have you tried yet?" Jorg taunted.

Ingrid flattened her lips, no longer warmed by his touch but annoyed at her helplessness. Frustrated with another failed attempt to wiggle free, she closed her eyes and reached for the energy coiled inside herself. It responded in a flash, and she pushed it into her hands before letting it loose. She stumbled forward once she was free from Jorg's grip and standing alone.

"Ha! See, I can . . ." she teased but froze when she turned around. Over her shoulder she heard Selby gasp. The entire yard, full of training soldiers, halted and stared between Ingrid and Jorg. She held her breath, and her pulse beat like a drum in her ears.

Across the yard, Jorg picked himself up from the ground

amid a pile of broken crates, but before he could get to his feet, he fell backward again. Ingrid screamed and ran toward him as did several others.

"Get back, let her have room," Selby yelled.

Ingrid ignored everyone else as she bent over Jorg, his muscles rigid and his face contorted into a grimace. "Where does it hurt most?" she asked. Jorg let out a groan and grabbed his side with a hiss.

Gently, Ingrid placed her hand just below his ribs and felt the warm, stickiness of blood as the coppery odor filtered into the air. Because of the angle of his body and the other pieces of wood all around him, she couldn't get a good enough grip to pull out the broken shard sticking into his side. She pulled her hand away from his body and heard mutterings from the onlookers.

"Help me! I need to get him out of this pile and onto his side."

Bremen and another man pushed forward and shifted Jorg to the smooth dirt of the courtyard. Ingrid wanted to break apart inside, but instead, she closed her eyes and brought forward her energy once more. Shaky and irregular, she fought for control of her emotions. Bremen held Jorg's shoulders to keep him positioned on his side, and Ingrid kneeled next to his back.

With a hard swallow, she closed her eyes and took a firm hold of the protruding stake before she pulled with all her strength. It took two tries and Jorg grunted, his knuckles white as he clenched through the pain.

As soon as the wood was removed, Ingrid immediately placed both hands over the wound while blood spilled between her fingers. Sounds around her slipped away as her energy washed through her and out her hands, like it always did.

The blood slowed under her palm, and the tissue of his skin knitted back together. Then flashes of light hindered her vision along the pathway she tried to follow. Something fought against her, and she pushed harder. Locked in a battle of wills, exhaustion crept through her. As she rallied to force another attempt, hands ripped her away from Jorg, so she landed hard on her backside.

"No! I'm not finished," she screamed, and scrambled back toward Jorg. She was again pulled away and held tight, so she couldn't move. Drained, her powers faded back into her middle and sounds returned to her.

"You need to stop, something isn't right."

Ingrid shook her head. It was Selby's voice she thought she heard and turned toward the sound to see her friend's wide eyes staring back at her. Selby placed her hands on both sides of Ingrid's face.

"Look at me. Blink when you can focus again," Selby said.

Ingrid let out a whoosh of air and blinked several times. "I can hear you," she whispered. "What happened? Why did you stop me? He isn't healed yet."

"You were hurting him. I don't understand how any of this works, but he was screaming."

The blood left Ingrid's face, and everything inside grew cold. "Let me see him."

Selby released her, so she could turn toward Jorg. He lay on his back, unmoving with his eyes closed and a pained expression on his face. She stared at his chest, watching for it to rise and fall, nearly collapsing in on herself when it did.

How could she have done such a thing? She'd learned so much about bringing her powers forward, but she had no control of them. He had to be okay. *Please don't leave me.*

Deep creases furrowed his brows, and his skin looked clammy. Unable to stop a tear from falling, it landed on his cheek. "Jorg?" *Please open your eyes. Tell me that you're okay.*

A whimpering sound escaped as she tried to contain her worry, but when his fingers slid over and touched her hand, her tears flowed unrestrained. Without thought to anything except relief, she laid her head against his chest and mumbled "Thank the gods." Over and over.

"Let's get him inside," Bremen said softly over Ingrid's head, but she didn't want to move.

"Ingrid, let us move him so he can get somewhere more comfortable. Come with me." Selby gently pulled Ingrid away. They stood off to the side as Bremen and another man lifted Jorg and carried him, while Gavin cleared the way ahead, so they could walk faster.

Selby and Ingrid followed closely behind. Ingrid wasn't sure how she was able to walk because her knees felt so weak, so she was thankful for Selby's arm around her waist. Her mind was a jumble of thoughts trying to figure out what had happened.

The men carried Jorg up the stairs and into his room. He moaned when laid onto the mattress, and it pierced Ingrid's heart like a spear. With heavy legs, she approached his side letting the others fall back to give her space.

Jorg's face was pale as she scooted onto the side of the bed next to him, watching his shallow breaths and pain-lined face. Tears stained her cheeks, and her hand shook as she touched two fingers to his lips.

I'm so sorry. Please forgive me for what I've done. I never meant to cause pain, especially never to you.

Jorg rolled his head toward her, opening his eyes to little more than slits. He brushed her thigh with his fingers. Ingrid startled at his touch and picked up his hand, holding it between both of hers.

"I made things worse, not better. You have to be all right," she said.

Jorg whispered something she couldn't hear so she brought her ear close to his mouth. "I will recover. Don't worry."

"I almost killed you," her breath hitched, and she stuttered. "Something went wrong. I . . . I didn't know what to do."

A slight pressure on her hand made her look down. Jorg was so weak, his touch barely registered as he tried to squeeze. She laid her head on his chest, letting tears soak into his tunic.

Ingrid shifted herself onto the bed and curled herself against Jorg as he lost consciousness, refusing to leave him. The others in the room slipped quietly away and shut the door, leaving them to themselves.

Ingrid stirred later in the night, her body stiff from lack of movement, and stared at a part of the moon that showed through the narrow window of Jorg's room. Not until she'd let her head rise and fall with Jorg's breathing—his heartbeat faint, but steady, under her ear—did she allow herself to believe he would be safe.

Slowly, she sat up and stared at his handsome face. He seemed more peaceful in sleep than he had been earlier. A hint of a smile crept across her face, and she brushed a lock of his hair away.

She'd grown too dangerous. Without more control over her abilities, she couldn't be trusted. Gavin had fallen with a burn from her touch, and she'd been dizzy then. This time, she didn't even have to touch Jorg for him to fly backward, and she had remained strong and steady.

There was more she needed to learn before the next person she injured didn't survive.

"I will come back. Grow strong while I make sure nothing like this ever happens again. I love you," Ingrid whispered before she kissed his cheek and then another quick one to his still lips.

Sliding off the bed, she looked over him one more time before crossing the room and heading out into the hall. Leaning against the closed door, she steadied herself.

"I'll never make a difference . . . not until I can figure out how to heal without hurting. Please understand why I had to go," she whispered into the darkness.

She made her way outside and kept to the shadows across the courtyard to avoid confrontation or the need to explain herself. When the guard turned his back at the gatehouse, Ingrid left through a door next to the closed bridge, then scrambled through the ditch and into the trees unseen.

Alone in the center of the meadow, Ingrid closed her eyes and felt for her power. Coiled deep, it held a faint hum that stayed where it was no matter how she tried to pull it forward. Tears rolled freely down her cheeks as she stood there.

How can I ever expect to fulfill my destiny? The Norns have made a mistake charging me with such a task. Even my powers recognize that I am not worthy to command them.

Anger welled up in her chest as she cried. Lifting her chin to the skies, she yelled to the stars. "No, I will not believe that! Glory and honor are still ahead of me if I will only work harder. I am stronger, but I don't have control. I can learn, and I will."

With her eyes closed once again, she renewed her attempt to call upon the powers hiding within her and felt them spark to life. She sighed in relief and pulled them up through her chest and down to her fingertips, ready and available.

When she opened her eyes once more, the meadow was bright as midday through her golden-hued vision, and she ambled forward, aware of every living plant, animal, and insect that surrounded her.

Drawn to the base of a tree, she found an owlet on the ground suffering from a fall out of its nest. She kneeled and scooped the young bird into her hand and gently massaged its small chest with two fingers, until the tingle of life flowed into its body.

When the owlet squeaked and tried to rise, she stopped her fingers and smiled at its fuzzy awkwardness. Looking up into the tree she saw two glowing eyes peering down upon her and nodded, placing the tiny bird onto the ground before she stepped away.

A brush of wind ruffled Ingrid's hair as silent wings swooped past her, picked up the owlet with gentle talons and disappeared into the treetops.

While resuming her walk, she touched trees, brush, and

flowers, causing them to flare with new growth. The shimmer of a web caught her attention, and she watched a spider almost half the size of her fist spinning and weaving an intricate pattern through the leaves of a gorse bush. The plant's vanilla fragrance blushed the night air as she stood watching. Ingrid tore her eyes away from the industrious web-maker and stared at the ground.

A curiosity provoked her. *I need to know . . .*

As close to the web as she could stand without disturbing it, she reached out with one finger and touched the spider. Within seconds its legs curled and shriveled in on itself as life left its body.

A hiccupped sigh escaped Ingrid as she looked at the carcass of the once-living being she had destroyed. But a spark of fascination simmered in her brain, bringing forth an idea. She reached out to touch the spider once more.

Her mind filled with thoughts of life and vitality. The flow of energy pulsed through her fingers, and her eyes snapped wide as the spider unfolded its legs. Once again it hurried on its way to weave its web as if it hadn't been interrupted by death.

Ingrid pulled away and gasped. Though she'd induced the scenario, it still startled her. *How is that possible?*

A sense of life behind her pricked at her nerves, and Ingrid twisted to see Eir standing a few feet away from her, watching.

"Did you see what I did?" Ingrid asked, a slight shake to her voice.

"Of course," Eir answered.

"How? I don't understand."

"If you didn't think it was possible, you wouldn't have tried it. Look inside of yourself and you will find the answer you are not allowing yourself to believe. You have far more abilities than you will accept, but it is within your grasp."

"I almost killed Jorg earlier." The words burst out of her, gaining a small sense of relief at the admission.

"Yes."

Ingrid swallowed. "Would I have been able to bring him back like the spider if no one had stopped me?"

"Would you have believed you could?"

"No."

"Then you have your answer. Come, Ingrid, it's time to devote yourself to your abilities." Eir reached out her hand as Ingrid shuffled closer, placed hers into the goddess's palm and held her breath.

A gentle breeze brushed against her cheek, her eyes fluttered, and she was no longer in the meadow. All around her was a forest, thick with trees whose branches flowed in all directions as if floating in water.

Lichen and hanging moss draped them in colors from light yellow to deep emerald. Mushrooms in every hue of pink, purple, and orange sprouted from everywhere. Cool but not uncomfortable in the shade, Ingrid turned a slow circle and let the sweet aroma of flowers, honey, and ginger fill her senses.

Life and energy pulsed into the air. It flowed through her, mingling with her own forces as if she wasn't bound by the limitations of her body. It was no ordinary forest. Soul-deep nourishment revitalized her senses and awakened pathways of awareness she'd never known before.

"Where is this?" she asked in a voice filled with reverence.

"This is, Lyfjaberg, the Healing Mountain of Asgard, my home. We will stay here in a small cottage that I use for myself when I need to study. It's located away from the Castle of Menglod, at the top of the mountain, so you won't be distracted. The Healing Mountain is the lifeblood of Asgard. The branches of the Yggdrasil tree make up this forest, and there is no other force of nature more powerful or pure."

The base of an ancient looking tree next to Ingrid was so large, she knew that if she held hands with Selby and Jorg and they all stretched their arms wide, they'd still only make it half-way round. Ingrid was so awed by the gnarled trunk and bark that looked rough but felt soft like velvet, she almost missed Eir as she sauntered around the bend.

Ingrid hurried after her. The air in front of the goddess shimmered as a arched door appeared in the center of the massive trunk. She gasped, remembering how the völva's cabin had appeared the same way.

"How do you do that?" Ingrid asked as she crossed through the secret entrance.

"It's a simple glamour to keep out prying eyes. I prefer my privacy."

The inside opened to a cozy room. One large cushioned chair with a padded footstool sat in the corner facing a fireplace on the opposite wall. The mantle looked carved from branches, but on closer inspection, it was the actual roots of the tree wrapped and woven into a pattern and shaped around the opening.

Ingrid turned a slow circle and realized that everything in the room gushed strength and vitality. Life flowed around her in a tangible way, tingling on her face like a soothing mist, absorbing into her skin, just as it had done outside. She closed her eyes and inhaled deeply, the coil of power in her middle seemed to sigh as if it, too, felt refreshed.

Eir stood behind her under an arched doorway leading to another room. Ingrid twisted and smiled over her shoulder. "When can we train?"

"Follow me," Eir said and stepped into the adjoining room.

Upon entering, Ingrid stopped and stared. It was a large room with shelves and workbenches lining all the walls and several oversized wooden work tables arranged in the middle. Every shelf or surface was full of glass jars, wooden boxes, books—some on shelves and some laying open and piled on top of others.

Dried herbs hung upside down from the ceiling, giving off an intoxicating array of scents that made it impossible to differentiate individual smells. No sconces hung from the walls. There were no windows and not a single candle flickered anywhere, yet the room was as bright as midday.

The hairs on Ingrid's arms lifted, and a swirl of unrest twisted her gut. She'd been in a room like this before, and it had assaulted her senses in the same way. *How can this be?*

Eir chuckled under her breath, and Ingrid whirled around to face her.

"What is this place?" Ingrid clamped her mouth tight, and her nostrils flared as she tried to control her breathing. The cloying smells choked her throat and spots danced in her vision.

"This is my workroom."

"I've been here before. How is that possible? Should I have waited for you there?" Ingrid leaned forward and put her hands on her knees. Everything that had happened after they buried the woman—meeting Bremen, Lazuli, the battle, Jorg—rushed back to her, and it was too much.

"Ingrid, slow down and calm yourself. I will explain." Eir's voice washed over her, and Ingrid stood. Her chest still heaved, and her fists stayed clenched. A three-legged stool rested under the bench, and Eir pulled it over for her to sit. "The room you were in before was not this one. It tested the level of your abilities. Minimal exposure left you overwhelmed and told me that you were not ready to handle the experience of coming here."

"It was a test?" Ingrid said the words more to herself. She huffed a wry laugh. "Who was that woman? Did she die just so you could test me?"

"No, that situation was unexpected. But you will need to put that experience behind you. The others you've had since helped you to develop the awareness of your abilities, to know what is inside of you is powerful. Now it is time to move forward. What you need to learn is beyond the capabilities of a mortal. The Norns have granted you strengths that defy the order of the realms, and we haven't much time for you to waste."

"Waste? You think that's what I've done? I've been searching for you, trying to train to save everyone. You let me wander and put Jorg at risk because I didn't know what I was doing." Ingrid stood and paced further into the room. When she turned to march back, Eir stood in front of her blocking the way. Ingrid's breathing rasped as she fought her emotions.

"I did not say that your experiences were for nothing. It was vital for you to prove yourself capable, to continue forward despite obstacles and not give in to the temptation to follow the easy path."

The memory of Jarrick's outstretched hand, beckoning Ingrid to his side through the shadows gave her chills. How close she'd come to giving in sapped all the frustration and fight out of her. There was no more time to debate the past, it was time to become who she was meant to be.

22

"Everything is so cluttered and jumbled together. It's not what I expected." Ingrid rubbed her nose and tried to take in all the sights as she scrunched her face. Eir had strolled to the other side of the room and asked Ingrid to assess the room.

"This is your first lesson. How do you think the room should look?"

"Clean and orderly, with space to work. This is like trying to weave cloth from tangled yarn."

"Then close your eyes and picture how it should look. Instruct yourself to see the room as it should be, believe it will be so, and then open your eyes again."

Ingrid did as she was told. She pictured the books put away on the shelves, jars and boxes lined up and stored properly, the tables dusted and free of clutter. Once she had in her mind's eye how everything should look, she opened her eyes.

As expected, everything still looked the same as before, only this time she was even more bothered by it since she'd been able to picture it cleaned.

"What do you see now?" Eir asked.

"What do you mean? It's still the same as before." Ingrid reached up to fiddle with her bead and realized she'd taken it off sometime in the night as she lay next to Jorg. She rolled her lip between her teeth, afraid to say anything and afraid to not to. What if she couldn't clear the room because she didn't have her necklace?

"Well, when you can open your Sight to the room as it should be, come and fetch me. I will be in the other room reading."

Eir walked past her and left the room. Ingrid could hear her humming to herself as she hung a kettle over the fire and rustled around.

What am I supposed to do?

Eir poked her head back into the workroom. "Also, you must not pick up anything in this room without my permission or help—is that clear?"

"How am I supposed to put things away, so I can *see* it clean?"

"That is what you need to find out." And with that, she left again.

Ingrid let a small sigh escape under her breath and closed her eyes again. *This is madness.* Once again, she pictured the room in her mind, seeing all the clutter and trying to visualize where it would all go if it were put away. *There's not even enough space for everything.*

Blowing a wayward strand of hair away from her face, she slumped down onto a stool and let her arms hang between her knees as she looked around. She fingered a couple of jars that were close to her, not breaking the rule by picking them up. Eir hadn't said not to touch anything, after all.

With a careless wave of her hands, as if she were shooing away an animal, she giggled and commanded. "Be gone. Put yourself away." To her amazement, however, the jars she had touched rattled on the table then settled back the way they were.

Ingrid jumped to her feet and stared at the wooden surface and its contents, her stomach a flurry of knots and butterflies. With her pulse pounding through her ears, she closed her eyes and took several breaths to steady herself and then raised her arms. She was immediately aware of the pull of her coiled energy.

Starting at the back of the room, farthest from where she stood, she pictured the various items lifting and floating to their spots. Excitement puffed inside of her chest, and she continued to watch as more jars, boxes, books, pots, and bowls found their way to niches on the shelves and in cabinets.

This is so much fun!

When the last book slid into its place, and nothing except broken petals, leaves, and dust remained, Ingrid dropped her aching arms and opened her eyes.

"What?"

Her mouth dropped open as she gasped and nearly came to tears. Everything she'd seen in her mind was for naught. The room looked exactly as it did before when it lay in chaos. In reality, nothing had changed. She crumpled onto the stool again and buried her face into her hands.

"I knew it couldn't be true. I don't have power to do that kind of thing. My power heals living beings, and it doesn't even do that right."

Exhaustion settled onto her shoulders like a scratchy

wool blanket. She could fall asleep right where she was and not wake up for days. *How am I going to learn in time to stop Jarrick?*

"You don't seem as happy as you were a while ago. Why not?" Eir asked from the doorway behind her.

"See for yourself, I thought I was getting it done and nothing happened for real," Ingrid said, without looking up.

"It's late, you must be exhausted. Come get something to eat, and you can try again later."

"What good will that do? Do you want me to clean it by hand?"

"Self-pity is pointless and unseemly. Come eat and then rest. We'll work together tomorrow, and maybe you'll figure out what you overlooked today."

Ingrid slid off the stool and moped out to the other room, following Eir. "There's not much time left. How will I make it back to save my family?" She accepted an offered bowl of soup and bread, then sat on a chair that wasn't in the room the last time she'd been there.

Her tired limbs were like fallen logs and her feet felt rooted to the floor. A quick peek at them reassured her that they had not, in fact, become part of the room. She could have sworn the mantle quivered as if laughing at her.

Eir bent over a flat pan which sat on a rack over the fire and turned slabs of ham. Another lidded pot nestled into a pile of coals.

"I'll explain a few things while you eat." Eir launched right into a story, and Ingrid perked up, listening with eagerness. It had been too long since she'd been home to hear her father tell sagas around the fire after meals.

"Freya married a god named Odr, and they bore two children together. You've met the younger daughter, Hnossa, and your mother met Gersemi when she was about your age."

Ingrid smiled and nodded, her mouth too full of bread filled with a berry she'd never seen nor tasted before. It was so light and fluffy it practically melted in her mouth.

"At some point, Odr left. No one knows why—" Eir, rolled her eyes and lowered her voice "—they *do*, but no one dares to cross that woman." She shrugged. "He didn't say why or if he'd be back. He was just gone. Freya didn't believe he would leave her and suspected foul play. Because *no one* would leave Freya."

Again, Eir flicked her eyebrows up and shook her head. Ingrid tried to muffle a laugh that came out like a little snort and listened with a grin while she ate.

"To this day, Freya leaves Asgard for long stretches of time and searches the realms for Odr. The entire time she's gone, she cries and cries as she calls for him. I've lost track of when she was on Midgard last, but when she's there, if her tears fall in water, they become amber."

"That's so sad. She really cries the whole time? And she has never gotten over his loss?" Ingrid stared at Eir with heavy lines furrowed on her brow. A pain squeezed her heart as an image of Jorg flashed in her mind. The bread she enjoyed dangled precariously between her fingers, forgotten.

"I'm glad you like that bread. It is made in Valaskialf only for Odin, but I convinced the cook that he only feeds it to those two wolves of his anyway, so she gave the recipe to me as long as I only make it here and not in Fensalir where Frigg would find out."

Setting the sweet bread onto her plate, Ingrid gave a sheepish grin, afraid to waste even a crumb. Eir spoke of

Odin and Asgard as if they were as familiar as the sky or the grass, and Ingrid shook her head at the thought of such a thing.

"My bead started as one of Freya's tears?" She brought the conversation back to her amber necklace, and heat flushed up her neck from the thought of having left it behind.

"Yes. Since the amber holds Freya's essence, I chose it as a talisman for the healer. You do not gain your powers from the bead—it answers to the power already within you."

"Because . . . I'm . . . from . . . Freya." Ingrid sat stunned, staring into the air. It's what the völva meant by her message. It made sense, and she'd have known it all along if she'd let herself think it through. "That must be why my eyes get brighter as well."

"Yes, dear. What you have experienced is the power of Freya that flows within your veins, and the amber has reacted to it. You are the source, and now that you are here, you need to learn to harness it completely. The bead is not necessary for you to train. It was only a guide. Later, it will have more importance, but for now, it is not essential."

As expected, the workroom looked exactly the same when they returned the next morning. Ingrid shuffled her feet as she entered. Even learning the amber bead was not the source of her powers, thus not the reason for her failure, didn't help her confidence.

"I don't understand how you want me to put everything away without my hands. I thought I had done it yesterday only to open my eyes and see it like this again," Ingrid said, trying unsuccessfully to cover the whine in her voice.

"When you were putting things away, were you focused on each item and the importance that it holds, or were you so enticed by the concept of moving objects that you only enjoyed the sensation?"

Ingrid shifted her weight and rubbed the top of one foot with the other while she rolled her bottom lip between her teeth. "It felt like a game," she said in a small voice.

"Every item in this room holds significance to the healing arts. Are you familiar with the word alchemy?"

Narrowing her eyes, Ingrid gave it some thought and finally shook her head in denial.

"It is how all the ingredients come together in perfect harmony to heal the body and soul. Within that is the belief that all living things are connected, and when one part is damaged, all parts suffer. It is perhaps the most serious of all concepts on any realm. I suggest that you try again today. Let the importance of every individual item flow through you as you touch it and see if that does not make a difference in your efforts."

After Eir left her alone, Ingrid once again took her seat on the stool nearest the door, letting her eyes roam over the myriad of objects scattered about.

I don't know how I'm supposed to feel everything in here. Nothing is alive.

Once again, she calmed her breathing before she focused on the first object. It was a jar that held a lotion, sitting on the edge of the farthest table. At first, she only stared at it, noting its ale-colored glass, the bright blue ribbon tied around the neck, and the light brown stopper stuffed into the top.

The slightest hint of a smell blew across a nonexistent breeze and burned her nose with the powerful odor of mint. Ingrid pictured the bottle moving to a spot on a shelf where it would be far from the edge. The jar slid into position in the exact spot she chose.

A breath of relief left her lungs, and she focused on the next item, an open book laying precariously on a box. Again, she noted the yellowed pages of vellum, the worn edges, the leather binding, and loose stitching.

Then once more, like a tendril reaching out to her, a wave of musty air, acids, and a hint of vanilla tickled her senses. With as much care as she could, she thought of the book closing and then sliding into place next to others on a high shelf.

One by one, item after item, she took notice of small details and found a spot where the piece in question would be placed in safety. Without concern for time or thoughts of anything else, Ingrid continued until a soft voice entered her mind and begged her to listen.

"It is time to stop now. Everything will wait for you to have something to eat."

Ingrid's breath suddenly felt labored and her body weak as she lost her concentration. If not for a pair of hands that caught her, she would have fallen to the floor. A face came into focus, and she looked up at Eir in a state of confusion. "What happened?"

"You have done well. Now you must nourish your body and take a rest."

After some soup and a foggy memory of crawling into bed, Ingrid awoke the next morning refreshed and invigorated. She bounced into the main room to find Eir again making breakfast.

"Did anything that I put away yesterday stay? I don't remember."

"Eat first. After that, you can go back and check your progress," Eir said.

Ingrid moaned and rolled her eyes but took the offered trencher of roasted meat and bread. "This is delicious, thank you so much. Is all of this food from Asgard?"

"Of course. That's where we are."

Who knew I could miss Selby's continuous chatter so much?

"Many who reflect and pay attention to the details of the world around them need not fill the air with careless words. It is not a flaw, but a gift of observance that few understand," Eir said.

Ingrid stopped chewing and stared. "Did you hear me?"

"Your thoughts are open and easily heard by those with the skills to hear."

"Jorg does that, but he explained it was because he is half-elf. Can anyone of another realm hear like that?"

"Not everyone. Most, regardless of what realm they are from, concern themselves more with their own thoughts, and they don't take time to listen to others, whether they are speaking internally or out loud. Listening with intention can be illuminating."

"I'll remember that. Is there a way I can block my thoughts from others? What if Jarrick can hear me?"

"We will work on that before you leave."

Ingrid then tried to keep her mind from anything but the buttery bread and meat that tasted of exotic spices.

As they made their way to the workroom, Ingrid rubbed her moist palms on the sides of her thighs and took hesitant steps. She realized how much it meant to her that the things she'd put away still sat where she'd placed them. It squeezed her heart to think that they would be treated so carelessly again.

She stopped within two steps of the door and braced herself for disappointment. With a deep breath, she hurried through the threshold to stand in awe. The room wasn't perfect yet, but she'd made significant progress the day before, and it had lasted.

"I did it," she whispered and sighed a satisfied breath.

"You paid attention and learned what each jar, bottle, or box contained, what each book teaches, and placed them in spots that made sense. Belief in one's abilities doesn't come from raw power, it comes from how to think of what's best for others and to do that, regardless of self-interest. It's the most powerful lesson you can learn."

"Can I finish?" Ingrid's voice felt raw, and her heart pounded in anticipation.

"Yes. It shouldn't take you as long today now that you can identify what's important."

Ingrid looked around at the remaining items strewn about. It was still a good number of books, boxes, and glassware, but she understood it now. She knew the best places to store everything. She was eager to begin and sure she could finish faster.

"When can . . ." She looked to where Eir had been standing and found she was alone in the room. "I can start now, I guess." She shook her head and set her sights on a wooden box.

Eir returned when Ingrid had finished. "Well done. We can move on to more difficult tasks now."

"How much longer will this take? I need to return in time to make Jarrick's deadline, or he'll destroy my village," Ingrid said.

"Have no fear. I will return you in plenty of time."

Ingrid swallowed the rest of her complaints. There was no hope of changing the goddess's mind, and she would worry regardless of Eir's assurances until the spell was bound. The best option was to hurry and train as she needed.

"Midgard is limited, and it is why you have so much to learn. That's also why you could not heal Jorg—his elven blood was fighting against you, and you didn't recognize it."

"What? Could I have helped him? I knew I should have tried again."

Eir sighed and stared at Ingrid. "It wasn't a matter of just doing more of the same. You needed to See. Which is why you have to concentrate on your studies." With that Eir turned from Ingrid and pulled several large books from the newly organized shelves. "These will get you started on the basic healing runes and herbs. You can practice what you learn tomorrow."

"Could you have helped him if he needed it?"

Eir pointed at the books. "He didn't need my help. Now read."

Ingrid looked a bit lost. The task seemed even more impossible than moving objects around a room. It was a lot of reading in such a short time. "I have to read these tonight? And know how to use them by tomorrow?"

"Believe you can, and you will. No one outside of Asgard has ever had the ability to read the language of the gods.

You've shown that you have that skill. Trust in it and the knowledge will come to you."

Ingrid stared at the large tomes stacked in front of her and swallowed. "Which one should I—oh," Ingrid tipped her head toward the ceiling and groaned. *I wish she'd say something when she leaves.*

With careful fingers, Ingrid pulled the top book closer and opened the cover, if this helped her to bind the spell and get home quicker, she'd do her best. As it was in the workroom of the völva's home, the language made sense to her, opening her mind to wisdom she'd never learned but somehow knew.

23

R estless that she'd wasted too much time learning about plants and runes, Ingrid itched to be back with her friends. She wanted to help stop the druht and save her village.

She reached her hand into her waist pouch and removed the rune stones. The weight against her palm gave her some peace, yet it also made her long to protect her home as the message on them told her.

All this reading and training and I've learned nothing I can use right now. How much longer will I be here? I need to know that Jorg has healed from his injuries. What if he needs me?

"He is recovering well, if that will help you concentrate."

Eir's calm voice from behind made Ingrid's shoulders scrunch. The information she acquired was valuable—she understood that. It was just taking too long.

"It's been days and while I sit here, my friends and family are in more danger. I need to be there. I feel so helpless . . . and selfish. I should be with them."

"The skills to control the powers inside of you is not

complete. As you have seen twice now, you need to understand the will of the Norns and the destinies they have woven for each person. When you heal in battle, you do so because that person is not marked for Valhalla. If you refuse to understand that, you will not find the path to follow and could sway against your true purpose."

Ingrid tried to stay calm, and respectful, like she knew she should, but the thought of home and family was weighing heavy on her heart. "I appreciate all that, but isn't there a way for me to learn faster? Or maybe to train on Midgard instead of here, away from everyone and everything I love."

"You have a great responsibility in front of you." Eir smiled, and her face softened. "Have patience and you will be ready to face everything before you. Now, show me how to protect one's mind from an unwanted essence."

Hours later, as Ingrid tried to put a book away on the shelf while holding an armload of various jars and containers, she knocked a neighboring book from its place. It fell to the counter below.

Frustrated, she lowered the breakables from her arms so that one accident didn't turn into several. A sketch caught her attention as she started to close the fallen tome. It was the drawing of a portal like Hnossa had created to bring her to Asgard all those months ago.

With a quick glance over her shoulder to make sure Eir hadn't walked in unannounced like she was apt to do, Ingrid let her hand roam over the page. Several methods were possible to create such a travel device, depending on the need for it. Immediately discounting the ones that were too complicated and beyond the simple seiðr magic she'd already practiced, Ingrid committed to memory one process to travel short distances.

Finally, something useful. If I can figure this out, then I can learn one that opens travel between realms. Even if I have to go with Jarrick, I'll be able to leave on my own. This should be what I'm learning!

She closed the book and slid it onto the shelf a little farther back to remember which one it was for later. As Ingrid hurried to finish her cleaning, she picked up one jar she'd set aside earlier. Eir's voice from the doorway startled Ingrid, and she dropped the jar, breaking it into countless pieces all over the floor.

"That's exactly what I hoped to avoid," Ingrid mumbled with a moan.

"I was about to say you've done well for today and see if you wanted to join me on a walk. I'll wait in the other room until that's cleaned. Then we can go."

The walk turned out to be a test over the use of many plants Ingrid had to identify. It frustrated her because she wasn't sure that any of the lichens, ferns, or mushrooms she'd seen were available on Midgard. Still, she had to admit it was a welcomed change from inside the workroom.

"I think I'm extra tired this evening and will go to sleep early, if you don't mind," Ingrid said.

"Not at all. Sleep well." There was a smirk on Eir's face that made Ingrid's stomach flop. There was no way she could have learned of Ingrid's plan. *Was there?*

Inside her room, Ingrid leaned against the closed door. She would wait until later to be sure that the other room was quiet before trying to open a travel window.

"Why isn't this working?" Ingrid created a thread in her mind that she knew was the key to opening the window, but she couldn't get the portal to form. She'd been at it for hours and knew she needed sleep but couldn't help trying once more.

Recalling the words and drawing the runic symbols into the air with her fingers, a string once again formed in her mind, hovering as if waiting for her to tell it what to do.

Ingrid scrunched her nose and concentrated on her memory from the book to see if she'd missed anything. Everything was correct. As she watched the thread, it seemed to push toward her and then retreat again to wait.

Realization struck her to reach out and take hold of the thread in her mind. When she did, it felt as though her entire body lurched forward, and she had to lean backward to keep from falling. The far end of the string bunched up on itself, and a pinpoint of light appeared. Ingrid gasped and stared in amazement.

"It's like gathering fabric—slide it on a loose thread until the ends meet," she whispered into the air.

Then with a gentle, steady pull, she watched as the far end of the string bunched and moved closer, while the point of light grew larger. When the oval-shaped light was about the size of a platter, Ingrid could make out shapes on the other side. As it grew to the size of a shield, she could see the tables of the workroom.

Tingles bubbled through her veins, and her hands grew slick with moisture though she held the thread with her mind. She continued her slow, deliberate draw until the end of the string brushed against the open pathway.

The large oval, less than a foot away from her, illuminated the darkened workroom in the other part of the cottage. Ingrid sucked in a deep breath. Unsure if she should mentally let go of the string, she took a hesitant step forward.

After her second foot touched the workroom floor, the string pulled against Ingrid's mind, twisting her around to watch as the window, now showing her own bedroom, closed in on itself, leaving her standing in the dark room.

Should I have let go?

Conducting the symbols and words again, she stared at the thread. This time, she grabbed it with more confidence and pulled faster, yet still steady. The bedroom appeared in front of her once again. She bit back a squeal of joy. But this time she dropped the string to see what would happen.

The portal stayed open, shimmering in the dark. Dry-mouthed and breathless, she stepped through to her room and spun around to check the gateway. The window stayed open. The string was there, dangling off to the side, waiting for her to pull it when she was ready.

She stepped back through and gave the string a tug; the portal shimmered and winked closed in the blink of an eye. Excitement bubbled inside of her, and with her hands over her mouth, she danced around the workroom in silence.

Several more times she opened and closed the travel window, until she could draw the string, step through, and close it in one fluid motion. Exhausted, yet relieved, she flopped onto her bed and fell asleep in her clothes.

"Which books will I be studying today?" Ingrid asked with a yawn the next morning.

"None," Eir said. When they were standing near the center of the room, the goddess turned and stood before Ingrid with a crooked grin on her face. "Try opening a doorway to outside the house this time."

"What?" Ingrid swallowed hard and shivered, suddenly cold.

"Did you really think you could open a portal inside of my home without my notice? Show me what you learned."

The morning meal rolled over in Ingrid's stomach, and she regretted eating the extra helping of Odin's bread. Is this a test? *Should I really open it?*

"Yes, you should, and I'd rather not wait all day."

Ingrid glanced up at Eir before dropping her gaze back to the ground. Several deep breaths later, she made the rune motions and pulled at the string when it appeared. When she peeked at the oval, however, it wasn't the forest that she saw, it was her bedroom again.

"I did say outside, did I not?" Eir asked.

Heat flushed Ingrid's face, but when she glanced at Eir, the goddess held a smirk on her lips and a glint in her eye. "I only practiced going to the bedroom."

"Well, then, let's work on that."

For the rest of the day, they opened and closed portals all around the mountain, going farther away with each one. Exhausted from the effort, but excited with the possibilities of her new skills. Ingrid was eager to find out how far she could go, but it would have to wait. Eir said she had a different kind of training to start.

"Every type of being that you encounter from each realm has a different spirit that must be ministered to in its own distinct way. That is the reason your beloved didn't heal as you expected, but I will help you learn those differences, so you can be ready next time."

Eir closed the gap between them with slow steps. "First, you also need to recognize how to determine between light and dark energies as they form so you can control them instead of the other way around. Jarrick was right about that."

Ingrid nodded, unable to speak and surprised by how Eir towered over her.

"As you learned when you fought in the forest, the dark energy can be useful in battle and to protect yourself. But when you are healing, you must not allow that energy to surface. Control is the highest priority."

Eir narrowed her eyes at Ingrid. "You also need discernment to detect the difference between an ally and an enemy." Ingrid stared and dared not move as the goddess leaned forward, inches from her face. "Which am I?"

Frozen in place, Ingrid stared as the hair on the back of her neck tingled. Seconds ago, she'd have bet her life the goddess was an ally, but at that moment, waves of heat radiated off the beautiful woman and made Ingrid want to turn and run.

"Whatever you do, do *not* run. Do you understand?"

Ingrid nodded, but her chest tightened and a bead of sweat trickled down her spine. *No, I don't understand. Everything has gone from peaceful to terrifying in the space of a heartbeat.* "Why is the air pressing against my skin as if I'm in danger?" Ingrid asked.

"Because you are a smart girl and part of your powers of Sight are to recognize the signatures of good and evil in every being. Right now, your senses are aware of danger, but you are blocking yourself from seeing why. Glamours can hide a variety of things, including a dangerous beast capable of devouring you. What have you learned to counter or dispel a glamour?"

"To trace the runes of knowledge and discovery into the air in the direction that seems different from what it appears."

"Do you sense an area in this room where something may be delusory?"

Ingrid stared at Eir, weighing whether she should be honest and possibly offend a goddess of Asgard or point somewhere else.

"Honesty will keep you alive."

Ingrid released a heavy breath, then raised her hand in the air and shaped the rune marks in front of Eir.

A radiant smile flashed before the goddess disappeared and standing in her place was a gigantic wolf with glowing eyes, licking its lips with a low rumble coming from its chest.

A whimper escaped from Ingrid, and she summoned every bit of effort to keep her feet planted to the floor. Her eyes roamed over the thick gray coat tinged black on the tips, the yellowed teeth, and the challenging gleam in its copper eyes that were level with her own.

Though something wasn't right, there was a hint of anticipation as well that made Ingrid pause. Honesty, that's what Eir had said. While keeping her hands near her sides, she traced the runes again slowly. The air rippled, and the wolf shifted back to Eir.

"Fantastic. That wasn't so difficult, was it?"

Weak in the knees, Ingrid sagged. "I'm not sure what to think at the moment. I need a chance to calm my heart."

Eir laughed, full and joyful. "Don't worry. You'll come to

find this part fun—I promise. Now, shall we try something challenging?"

Later, peace settled over Ingrid as she was granted a small rest. A camaraderie had grown between the goddess and herself. In some small way, she was no longer separate from Eir's world.

Tall, slender, and dressed in a blue gown the color of a summer sky, Eir's beauty seemed to glow brighter than ever. Dark blue eyes rimmed with long, curling lashes sparkled as she smiled at Ingrid.

Without realizing she was doing it, Ingrid reached up to smooth down her hair, then snapped her hand down behind her back and tried to sit a little taller.

"You learned more today than I would have expected from months of study," Eir said, disrupting the quiet. "It does not surprise me, though, since you have inherited some of Freya's seiðr magic."

"That is not possible is it?" Ingrid held her hands over her middle. "Won't Freya be angry and think I've taken something from her?"

"Ingrid, calm yourself. Freya knew what she was doing when she bound her own blood to the spell. For you to have some of her magic is unexpected, but not surprising."

"Not surprising? It is to me. What does it mean?" Skeptical that the goddess of fertility, love, and death would accept such a thing easily. Years of offerings to placate the temperamental ruler told Ingrid that she wouldn't, despite Eir's casual attitude.

"We will have to see how it develops. One thing is for sure, Jarrick must not find out about this. He only knows of your involvement in keeping Midgard protected. If he believes he can access even a small portion of Freya's magic, you will be in greater danger."

Ingrid tried to squelch the memory of dark shadowy tendrils caressing her skin as Jarrick's voice promised her freedom and power.

"What if he already suspects? He came to me in a vision before you arrived and wanted me to go to him. He said something about being more powerful than Freya and making me a queen."

"I'm sure he doesn't suspect Freya's abilities run through you, or he would not have cared about the agreement his underling made with you. You would be in Alfheim already." Eir spoke almost as if to herself and then formed a mischievous curl on her lips. "That's the reason I let you travel to find the völva—to see what would happen and how much power you might already have."

"I wondered why you didn't just come like you did in Jorvik."

"I needed to gauge how much you'd grown on your own and who else might have been aware of who you were."

"Who was the woman we met with the glamoured cottage? Was she an ordinary völva? Those men tortured her, and I never found out who she was, but her workroom held such power. And it was as messy as yours when I first arrived." Ingrid snorted, conscious she did not sound at all as ladylike as her mentor.

"Ordinary? That's a little offensive." Eir looked insulted and tried to hide a grin. "I must say though, all of you treated her with the utmost respect. Especially Jorg as he tossed her about over his shoulder. He is fit, isn't he? I can see why he holds such attraction for you." The goddess waggled her eyebrows, shocking Ingrid and making her face warm.

"How do you always know about everything that has happened?"

"I am connected to all living beings, Ingrid. Also, I could follow you through your bead," Eir said.

Ingrid huffed and shook her head. "Like Jarrick and his sticky tar in my brain."

"It is a testament to your strength you managed so well and didn't give in to his pressure. I gave the bead to you as a child because I needed to keep track of when you were ready to study with me. It was a way to check in on you from time to time as you grew, nothing more. That's why I had to go to you in person twice more," Eir added with a smirk.

"Twice? I had only met you the one time in Jorvik before. Hadn't I?"

As she'd witnessed many times throughout the day, Ingrid watched as Eir's features transformed. Taking her place in the chair was a woman with long dark hair in a burgundy gown with smudges of dirt all over it. Ingrid gasped, wide-eyed and slack jawed, unable to get a full breath. "You! But we buried you," she said when she could finally process the sight.

"Yes, that was unpleasant, but touching," Eir cooed.

Ingrid put her head in her hands and folded herself onto her lap. "I'm too tired to deal with any more of this right now. I'm afraid I'll learn I can sprout wings or something. It was cruel to make me think a poor woman had died because of me."

"I didn't realize how sensitive you'd be about that, and I felt bad. But now there is no need for any guilt."

Ingrid groaned and stared at Eir, who gave her an ingenuous smile, looking like herself again. "What more do I need to learn to bind the spell? How will you determine when I'm ready?"

"There will be a need for you to release all your current human desires and attachments in order to do what must be done for all the realms. You will then meet with the Norn, Skuld, at the Well of Urd, and she will show you the final step needed in order to connect with the life-force in the water."

"We should go there now. Let me finish this so everyone will be safe."

"Right now, you are still unable to detach yourself for the good of all, and that makes you vulnerable. It's why you are susceptible to Jarrick's influence and need to stay here until you can overcome these sentiments."

"How do I do that? I don't think I can let go of my worries for those I care for most."

"That's when you will be truly ready, not before."

Ingrid stared into space. How could she set aside her feelings for everyone she loved? The only reason she accepted her fate was because she worried for the safety of her family and friends. Nothing was more important than those she cared about. That was too great a sacrifice, and she'd have to find a way to compromise.

"Maybe if I can go back and see that everyone is safe, then I will be able to move forward," Ingrid said.

"It's best that you continue to strengthen your skills here, away from where Jarrick can reach you. It's the optimal place to clear your mind of your concerns."

"Skills like the ability to make portals? Will I be able to travel between realms on my own soon?"

Eir gave a huff that somehow still sounded ladylike and graceful. "That skill differs greatly from just moving short distances within the same realm, and it is dangerous. One small misstep, and you slip between the worlds, where it is impossible to return." She narrowed her eyes as she spoke and made Ingrid swallow hard and want to shrink into the nearest wall.

"I understand." *No, I don't, but that's okay.*

"We need to work on your ability to block your thoughts better. Come." Eir held out her hand to Ingrid.

Seconds later, Ingrid stood alone inside the doorway of Bremen's council room.

24

Jorg and Bremen were bent over some papers on the large table, arguing with each other. Several other men were in the room also talking with agitated voices while apparently making battle plans. Gavin noticed Ingrid first, tipping his chin to her.

A wave of nausea rolled through Ingrid at the abrupt change of location. *I guess I won't be learning how to move between realms myself then.*

Jorg snapped his attention to the door and stood tall, staring at Ingrid. His chest heaved in and out, but he said nothing.

"It's nice to see you're well," Ingrid said, suddenly concerned. She worried her arrival was not welcome, considering the last time he saw her she'd almost killed him. It was made worse by the silence that descended.

"Ingrid! Thank God you're back," Bremen said, relieved.

Jorg moved around Gavin and walked with slow steps, his stare locked on her as if she might not be real. When he stood in front of her, blocking the rest of the room from her view, she saw the silver lining his eyes and flung herself against his chest.

I'm so sorry I left, but I almost killed you, and I needed to train so it would never happen again.

Strong arms held her like iron even as Jorg's body trembled. Voices filled the room again, and Ingrid tried to pull away but couldn't budge herself free.

"Not yet." His voice was ragged as he whispered.

Relief washed over her, and she relaxed inside the protective hold. Jorg's muscles tensed more than before so that Ingrid could barely breathe.

"I need to finish here, but do not think you are leaving this room without me." Jorg leaned his face back, relaxing his hold the smallest bit. "I might have been . . . forceful, in some of my plans to find you." He cocked a brow at her and tipped his head at the front of the room.

Ingrid grinned and soaked in his presence. He was healthy and making plans to find her. The wound in her heart created the moment she'd hurt him knitted together and sealed closed. "I'm not going anywhere."

Jorg huffed but released his hold on her long enough to slip her hand inside his and take her with him to the front. Bremen stood with Gavin and several of his other top men.

"Mother will not stand for being locked in this room with posted guards, no matter how safe it makes you feel. We can make sure she stays away from the walls, but other than that, she won't listen. Besides, we need every man outside, not babysitting a door," Bremen said.

"I don't care if she likes it or not. She's the queen and needs to keep away from the battle at all costs. If we can't make her stay in here, we need to find another location to move her—completely away and out of danger," Jorg said.

"The queen is *my* top priority," Bremen said between his teeth, "not yours. My decision is final, and I will not discuss it further. Gavin, divide the archers into groups to fortify the wall in every direction. Martin, make sure the extra arrows, spears, and axes are on schedule from the smithy, then have them distributed properly to all the men." Both men nodded and hurried from the room. "The rest of you, make sure everyone is gathered in the courtyard in an hour."

Ingrid stood close to Jorg as all the other men left the room. After they'd gone, Bremen turned to face Jorg. "These are my men, and you will not challenge me in front of them again. If you have something to discuss, do it privately or not at all."

"Galwain is the queen of your people and your mother, I understand that. But, she is my mother also, whether or not you like it, and I will do what I need to do to keep her safe."

Ingrid looked between the two men, both with tense shoulders and tight jaws. The idea of being brothers would take time for them to work through.

"It's good you've returned and look well, Ingrid," Bremen said with a genuine, yet forced curve to his lips. "I sincerely hope it helps ease some tension." After a swift glance at Jorg, Bremen strode away from the table. Stopping at the doorway, he turned back to Ingrid. "Also, please don't wait too long to find Selby. She has worried over your disappearance as well. I believe you will find her in the kitchen." The corner of his mouth twitched into a grin before he left the room.

"What was that about?" she asked.

"I don't care." Jorg rubbed his hand over his face. "Ingrid, stop doing this to me. When I woke the morning after the accident and you weren't there . . . I couldn't look for you. It took two more days before I was strong enough to comb the woods. The druht has gathered throughout the forest preparing for an attack, and I thought they had you."

He sat down in the nearest chair with a sigh, resting his forearms on his knees. "I came back only yesterday to check if you'd returned here. Then I found out Galwain has been training with Selby to join the fighting. Why do women have to be so stubborn?"

"I'm guessing that's not a real question," Ingrid said as she moved herself between his knees. Jorg smirked at her and wrapped one hand around her waist to steady her as she perched on his leg. "I am very sorry. I stayed with you through most of the night, but I was restless to learn how to control my powers, so I didn't hurt you again. I wandered to the meadow, then Eir showed up and took me with her to Asgard."

She felt his body tremble. "I couldn't hear you anymore, and it was like a void inside my mind."

Confusion muddled her thoughts as she tried to figure the time left until the deadline. The days with Eir blurred together with those since they'd left the village.

"It makes sense that we couldn't communicate across realms. Does it cause you pain?" she asked.

"It did this time. It was like a head ache that doesn't go away, ebbing and flowing constantly. Living that way, if some-thing happened to you . . . I couldn't bear it."

Ingrid sank her fingers into his hair and tucked it behind his ear. "I'm sorry," she whispered. She wanted to tell him he'd never have to live like that. She hated to think that when she left to bind the spell, he would be in pain yet again.

No, she could not make any promises for the future.

Now that she knew Jorg was better, if she could be sure that the village was safe, too, it would free her mind to go back to Asgard and bind the spell. It must be the reason Eir sent her back. She'd have to hope that Jorg would accept her absence and that would help ease the pain in his mind. Before she could explain her thoughts to him, a harried-looking Gavin swept into the room. Jorg stood and held Ingrid against his back.

Really? Ingrid clamped down on her frustration, giving him some leeway because of his heightened state of emotions. Instead, she just listened to Gavin from her hidden position.

"Bremen would appreciate it if Ingrid could come to the kitchen. He believes that since she's back, her presence will help to calm the situation in there."

Jorg let his arm drop from where he braced Ingrid, and she slid to his side with only one quick glare at him. "Yes, we will come at once." She turned to Jorg. "Won't we?" He rolled his eyes and gestured for her to follow Gavin out of the room.

When they arrived in the kitchen, it was in chaos. A dusting of flour coated everything. Pots and pans littered the worktable and floor, something slick and shiny was splattered in patches. Apples, carrots, and other vegetables lay scattered around, and in the middle of the fray sat Lazuli on the table. Her arms were crossed over her chest and a huge pout weighed down her face.

Selby was in a heated debate with the cook, both of them covered in flour and other remnants, including a few broken eggs. Bremen was between the women and looked to have taken a couple of hits from flying debris as well. Taking ginger steps on the slippery floor, Ingrid made her way across the room.

"Can I help with anything?" Ingrid asked.

Selby whirled around at the sound of her voice and rushed over to embrace her in a crushing hug. "It's about time you made it back here." She pulled away and looked into Ingrid's face, now smeared with egg from Selby's hair. "You went to Asgard, didn't you?"

Ingrid nodded while wiping her face with the edge of her sleeve. "Is this part of a welcome home celebration for me?"

The cook turned with an incredulous expression aimed at Ingrid. "Celebration? You think I'd ever in my right mind let a wee devil like that into me kitchen for any reason? No, that's the answer. I'm glad you're back, Miss, but I want that beastie out of me space." The cook spoke with animated gestures and a red face as she pointed to an angry Lazuli sitting on top of the center worktable. The poor woman looked ready to collapse.

"I remember how you kept such a tidy kitchen and I understand this is—" Ingrid looked around at the messy room "—*unsettling*. Where is Plintze?" she asked Selby.

"Right here."

Ingrid peeked around Bremen and saw Plintze sitting on an upturned crate resting his head in his hands as they leaned on his knees. Ingrid had to bite her lip to keep from laughing in pity at his dejected countenance.

"Glad you're back safe," he said.

Taking hold of the flustered woman's trembling hands, Ingrid squeezed them and let a bit of calming energy seep through her fingers. "I give you my word that I will personally make sure that this kitchen is back to your standards before the day is through. Will you allow someone to escort you to your room, so you can rest?"

"Rest? In the middle of the day like I'm some fine lady? There's too much work to be done and none but me to do it, especially now."

Ingrid thought for a second and used a different persuasion, squeezing the hands she still held. The cook swayed on her feet a little and Bremen threw his arms around her before she fell.

"Ach, I don't know what come over me," the lively woman said as she fought to keep her focus.

"I think you have overworked yourself, Vevina, and with good reason. Please allow one of the others to help you to your rooms as Ingrid suggested," Bremen said. Another woman who assisted in the kitchens stepped closer to the pair.

"Aye, all right. But I'll not leave before that winged devil does."

Ingrid released the cook and turned to face the sprite. "Lazuli, is this about a certain pie that Selby promised to make you?"

"Yes. I was trying to make it myself since the friend—who is no longer my friend—never made me one like she said she would. And no one understands that!" She yelled straight up to the ceiling as she continued to sit on the table with her back to Ingrid.

"If you will go outside with Plintze and find something fun to do for a while, I will make sure that Selby cleans up this mess *after* she makes you a pie. When she's all finished, she can deliver it to you in the courtyard. Will that be acceptable?" Selby snorted behind Ingrid, who swatted at her without taking her eyes off Lazuli.

"Thank you! I knew you were the nicer one. Come on, Plintze, let's go chase those snooty butterflies," she said as she fluttered her wings in the air and headed for the door. She blew a raspberry with her tongue at Selby before disappearing outside.

"Plintze, please try to keep her outside," Ingrid begged.

"Humph. As if I could keep her from doing anything." Shaking his head, he hobbled off through the door to follow his troublemaking friend.

"Thank you, miss." A heavy sigh escaped from the cook, and she sagged against Bremen.

"If you will lead the way—" Bremen nodded to the woman standing by "—I'd like to accompany you both to Vevina's room to ensure her safety," Bremen said.

"Oh no, I'll not have ye waiting on me like that. I can make it on me own." As she stood tall and tried to brush down her apron, she faltered again, needing Bremen to help her.

"I won't hear of it. You can let me walk next to you, or I must carry you. Which shall it be?" Bremen asked with a mischievous tug to the corner of his mouth.

Vevina stared at him with wide eyes as one hand fluttered to her throat. "We'll walk then."

Bremen nodded and looked at the woman. "Lead the way, please."

After they left, Ingrid scanned the kitchen and spoke to the rest of the servants pressed around the room. "This has been a trying situation for all of you. Will you please do me the favor of taking the rest of the day to relax as well, while I help Selby with this mess?"

They looked around at each other, unsure if it was acceptable to listen to her. "I don't think we should, Miss. Vevina would want us to stay and help," one older woman said while the others nodded in agreement.

"A time of rest after all of this is a fine idea,' Bremen said as he returned to the room. Every one of the staff immediately lowered their faces and mumbled quick words of thanks before hurrying away. "This is impressive," Bremen said with a chuckle as he walked up to Selby and pulled a lettuce leaf from her hair, which made her groan and cover her face with her hands. "You made a big promise to clean this up and make a pie by the end of the day. Can I assume that you have dismissed the staff for a reason?" he asked Ingrid.

Jorg crossed the room to stand at Ingrid's side and surveyed the damage. "I'm guessing you have a new skill to show off to us?"

"Oh, I hope she does. I'd love to find out what all that time in Asgard accomplished," Jarrick said as he sauntered into the room.

25

Jorg spun around, and Bremen stepped next to him, placing themselves between Jarrick and the girls. "You are not welcome here," Jorg said. There was no mistaking the tall elf sauntering into the room as Jarrick.

"Such chivalry you young men have. Does it really impress the girls? Ingrid can take care of herself, and the other one looks capable, too." Jarrick angled himself to make eye contact with Selby. "Yes, quite capable," he said with a leer.

Bremen lunged, but Jorg caught him by the arm and wrestled with him to stay put. "That's what he wants. He's baiting you to get you out of the way," Jorg hissed between his teeth as he held Bremen's arms behind his back.

"All right! Let me go," Bremen yelled and straightened out his tunic when Jorg released him. "Leave now or be removed," he snarled to Jarrick.

"Not yet, little boy," Jarrick flicked his fingers and Bremen flew across the room, slamming into the wall.

Selby screamed and hurried over to him. Bremen slipped in the lard still spilled across the floor as she helped him to right himself, but he was unharmed.

"Ingrid, I simply want to see what that crone taught you while you were in her care. And why, for that matter, is it acceptable for you to go with her and not me?" Jarrick said. His voice dripped with sarcasm, and anger rolled off him from across the room.

"Is that what bothers you most? That I accept her help but not yours?" Ingrid asked.

"You have more power than you think, and she will stifle you . . . hold you back from your true potential. She is trying to keep you from seeing the truth for her own selfish reasons."

"And you aren't? You want her with you in Alfheim for the benefit of others?" Jorg stood next Ingrid, and the tremors in his arms belied his calm exterior as he held himself in place. Whatever he may have wanted to do, he stayed at her side instead of pushing his way in front of her.

Bolstered by her training and Jorg's belief in her, Ingrid raised her chin and stared Jarrick in the eye. No one would treat her as helpless any longer; she'd make sure of it.

"Yes. There is far more at stake here than that valkyrie will ever tell her. I doubt she even understands all of it as Frigg's little puppet." Jarrick sauntered nearer to Ingrid and Jorg stepped up to block his path. "You don't want to make me hurt you—now move out of my way."

"Funny, I was thinking the same thing," Jorg said as they stood eye to eye.

Bremen and Selby had moved up to stand behind Ingrid as Galwain walked into the room. "Mother, get out! Run and call the men!" Bremen shouted and startled Ingrid, breaking her concentration from the standoff.

Galwain gasped, her face going pale when her gaze locked with Jarrick's. A sound that could have been a whimper emanated from her as she took a step backward. Jarrick spun away from Jorg and stared at her. Bremen used the distraction to charge but, Jarrick flicked his hand at him again. Instead of tossing him across the room, he bound him in place.

"That one is your son?" Jarrick asked, taking a step closer to Galwain.

"Yes." Her usual graceful voice, squeaked.

"Your *only* son?" he asked, his eyes narrowed.

Galwain clasped her hands together to keep them from shaking, but before she could answer Jorg did.

"No, he's not."

A smile spread across Jarrick's face as he glanced over his shoulder.

"Jarrick, please let me explain." Galwain rushed to take hold of his sleeve.

"Mother, stay back!" Bremen called out and then growled against the force restraining him.

Ingrid stepped closer to Jorg and slipped his hand into hers. Though his focus remained on Jarrick, his grip was gentle.

"What is there to explain, Galwain? How my wife, the love of my life, stole my son and disappeared? Why would I want to hear that old story again? What's important is that you've brought him back and at the most opportune time. In fact, I'm feeling so generous I might even forgive you."

"Jarrick, you scared me. I loved how passionate you were

to rebuild Vanaheim, and I supported you in that, but then you began to study the dark arts with Urkon and believed that Asgard had to fall. You weren't the man I fell in love with anymore. When you talked about the plans you had for our son," Galwain hesitated.

Tears streamed down her face, and her voice faltered as she continued. "I was too afraid of what you would turn him into, so I asked Thelonius to help me, and he sent me back to Midgard. He was as concerned about our son as I was. I hid with a friend for several months, but eventually that brought harm to him as well—"

"*Him*? You ran away from me, straight into the arms of another man? With the help of my brother no less! Is that where the other one comes from?" Jarrick's voice boomed into the room, making the walls shake.

"No! It wasn't like that. I met Cerball later. The friend was not from Midgard, and he paid severely for helping me. When I had to uproot again, I convinced myself that it would be better to hide Alberich. If I sent him to live with another family, where he wouldn't know who he was—away from both of us—he would have a good life. If you found me, it wouldn't risk his safety. So, I gave him to someone who took him away to a village. The only information given to me was he would go to a woman who wanted a child but couldn't have one of her own. I thought she would love him and give him a better life than I could."

"Not a better life than *we* could have given him together," Jarrick said through his teeth. "He would have wanted for nothing, raised with his own people."

Ingrid felt Jorg flinch and looked as though he was going to say something, but then clamped his mouth tight.

Jarrick tipped his chin to the ceiling before he stared at Galwain again. "I loved you more than I ever thought possible." He reached up and brushed his fingers along the side of her face. "I don't know who kept you from me, but I will destroy them when I find out," his voice calm, cold, and deadly.

"They've suffered much already. Can't we try to move on from here?" Galwain spoke softly and put her hand over his. The gold of the band on her index finger glinting in the light.

Jorg stiffened as he watched, clutching Ingrid's hand tight enough to break bones if she wasn't protecting herself. Bremen struggled in vain to free himself, while Selby tried to calm him and explain that it was useless. She had been bound in the same manner before.

Faster than anyone could blink, Jarrick stood behind Galwain and stared at Jorg. Leaning down, he spoke next to her ear while he wrapped one arm around her waist to pull her tight against his chest. "Let's listen to our son's story about this woman he calls mother instead of you, and then we can decide if you did the right thing." Standing to his full height, he tipped his head to Jorg. "Your turn, *son*. Explain how your life was so much better without your true parents."

Jorg smirked and shook his head. "I have nothing to say to you."

"That's a shame. From how close you are to Ingrid, I would guess you grew up near her, possibly in the same village—the village that I will destroy if she doesn't come with me, and yet you take that chance. You must not have that much love for the imposters who kept you from me."

"He has people there who he loves and love him. My

family does, almost as much as I do," Ingrid smiled at Jorg. "If you kill them, it will hurt Jorg, too."

"Then you're aware what needs to happen, Ingrid. Are you ready? Eir was smarter than I gave her credit for, taking you to Asgard, but if you want to protect all those people you both claim to love so much, come with me."

"Why do you want her? What's your goal in this?" Jorg asked.

Ingrid had tried to explain it before, but she didn't understand enough herself. She was as eager as Jorg to hear Jarrick's reasons.

"It is a long story of an idealistic boy who thought he could rebuild a broken realm to its former glory, bringing honor back to his family in a way they deserved." Jarrick wove his finger through a curl of Galwain's hair, a dreamy look on his face as she shuddered. "The more I learned about how it all came to be, the more I was determined to make things right.

"Odin cheated the Vanir, persuaded them to accept a deal that only benefitted himself, and because of it, Vanaheim lays in ruins. A once vibrant and rich culture of artists, poets, and philosophers stamped out by the greed of those who care only for themselves. It is a society and realm that deserves—" he jerked Galwain hard against his chest as he tightened his grip, making her gasp "—to thrive as the true leaders of the realms.

"The Vanir could have won the war of the gods, especially if the elves had joined them like they should have. This time, they will. They will rise and restore Vanaheim to glory, and Asgard will receive its justice."

His voice was full of passion and grew stronger and

angrier as he spoke. Tears streamed down Galwain's cheeks as she listened.

"You don't need Ingrid. She can't help you with any of that," Jorg said.

"Yes, she can, and she will. There was a reason that Odin and Freya cast their net around Midgard. Odin represents Asgard, and Freya is still Vanir. I believe it as strongly as I live; she has been waiting for someone to break her out of that prison. Midgard is in the center of all the realms. The gods who control it, control all the others. Freya used Odin's arrogance against him and set up a way to defeat Asgard. Ingrid holds inside of herself the blood of Midgard and Vanaheim."

A cold fear slithered down Ingrid's spine. Jarrick *did* know that Freya's blood flowed through her veins. So why hadn't he forced her to go with him to Alfheim? Was that why he'd come now?

"Even if she adds her powers to the spell without me," Jarrick continued, "the balance will be in the Vanir's favor, leaving an opening to break Asgard's rule once and for all. It's why Eir is trying so hard to keep Ingrid from learning exactly how powerful she can be and what she truly means to all the realms. Odin wants to control her, and he is doing it through his wife's handmaiden. I don't want to control you, Ingrid—I want to join you."

"Join me? My destiny is to keep Midgard safe and protected from the evil of the dark realms, from creatures like dragons that you let into our world and used for your purposes."

"I controlled that dragon. It did not hurt you."

"Really?" Ingrid pulled up her sleeve to show the jagged claw mark that disfigured her forearm. "I almost died."

Jarrick rolled his eyes and let out a long breath. "*Almost* is the key. You were being obstinate. But I've realized now that we should work together instead. In fact, the more I have studied the spell, I believe that Freya's intentions were to make sure that her descendant didn't just restore Vanaheim as a realm but rule it as well. I am convinced that you, Ingrid, are to be the new Vanir Queen."

"Ha! That is the craziest thing you have said so far," Ingrid said. "And who is to be the king? You?"

Jarrick laughed. "I'll admit, the thought crossed my mind, many years ago." He tightened his grip around Galwain and used his right hand to let his fingers roam up and down her arm. When he reached her hand, he pulled it to his lips and kissed the ring on her finger. A flicker of light bounced off the matching one he wore.

Galwain closed her eyes and let her shoulders sag in defeat.

"But look at you, standing next to my son. It's more than I hoped for. When I dreamed of building this legacy, I couldn't see past the restoration. Who would lead and where they would come from wasn't clear to me. Not like it is now. Alberich, royal elven and Vanir blood flows in your veins. Together with Ingrid, you are *both* the rightful heirs to Vanaheim."

Ingrid shivered, her energy coiled so tight and deep down it left her feeling vulnerable. Part of her struggled to ignore what he was saying as lies. There was an odd truth to it, but in her heart, she knew it was a twisted version of Jarrick's form of truth. It had to be.

We need to get away from him. He is confusing me.

"Why is it then, that you only want Ingrid to go with you

to Alfheim? If I'm to be a part of your plans, shouldn't I go as well?" Jorg asked. "In fact, you should take me instead. I have much to learn about the homeland I was denied."

Jarrick let a slow grin split across his face. "Now that is not an offer I thought I'd ever hear. My son willing to join me despite the years he was kept from me—"

"Jorg, please don't." The urgent panic in Galwain's voice billowed into the room. "You don't understand what is at stake. Let me explain why I did what I did, and you'll see it was the only way. Even your uncle, the king, felt the same. It's why he sent us back here to our own lands."

A low rumble echoed against the stone walls. At first, Ingrid thought it might be a storm brewing on the horizon, but it was much nearer. The sound emanated from Jarrick as he clamped his mouth together so tightly that his lips were translucent.

"Apparently, your mother thinks so little of your heritage she can't even use your proper name. I am not of the same mind, Alberich. However, while I appreciate your offer, I must decline. There is a reason Ingrid is essential, and until she does her part, nothing else can proceed," Jarrick said.

Once again, the dark elf turned his focus to Galwain. "Marriage on Alfheim is eternally binding. You know that or you would have removed your wedding band." Jarrick touched Galwain's golden ring.

"I expected that Ingrid would choose to join with me when I arrived, but another day won't hinder my plans. Now that you and I have so many things to discuss, my love."

"Mother!" Bremen yelled out as Galwain's eyes grew wide and then she disappeared in a flash with Jarrick.

Released from his constraints, Bremen scrambled and

grabbed hold of Ingrid, spinning her to face him. "Where did they go? Can you take us there?"

"Let. Her. Go." Jorg kept his voice low but spoke through his teeth. Ingrid had no doubt he would lose every bit of his anger on Bremen if he didn't release her arm immediately.

Moving slowly, she laid her free hand over Bremen's and eased his pulse to a steady rhythm. He relaxed and let go of her, but the expression of loss on his face ripped a hole in Ingrid's heart. A desire to climb into her own mother's arms and forget about her destiny squeezed her like a vice.

"Most likely, he took her to Alfheim. And I'm sorry, but I can't make portals between the realms."

Bremen raked his hands through his hair and spun around, striding several paces away before the upheaval of Lazuli's tantrum stopped him. Selby stared at Ingrid, speechless as the loss for Galwain covered her face.

"Go to him," Ingrid whispered to her friend. She saw the shine of tears pooling in Selby's eyes before she gave a weak smile and made her way to Bremen. When Ingrid faced Jorg, his features were hard as he stared in the direction Jarrick and Galwain had stood only moments before. "He'll bring her back," she said, though not with much conviction.

"Why? What would make him bring her back? He believes she's still his wife." Jorg made a sound that crossed between disgust and a dangerous predator. "You said you can't make portals *between* realms, but you can make them within one?"

"Yes, but—"

"Do you need to practice? Will Eir help you with that?"

"Jorg, please try to stay calm and let me explain." Ingrid reached out for him, but he stepped out of her reach.

The growing heat of his temper rolled off his shoulders and constricted the air in Ingrid's lungs. She stood staring at his back. Did he blame her? After all, Galwain would still be there if Jarrick hadn't come for her. "He'll come back for me. We can make a trade."

"No! That's not what will happen." He spun and closed the gap between them. The emotions swirling among the green and gold in his eyes. Ingrid sank into his palm when he cupped her cheek in his hand. "If you could make a portal, I would go and get her, but I won't sacrifice you for anyone."

Ingrid sighed. "It may be the only way, and I'm prepared. I've trained, and I'm ready."

"The spell is complete?" Selby asked as she and Bremen moved closer.

All three sets of eyes bore down on Ingrid as she felt the weight of their hopes on her shoulders. Eir had said she needed to release her worries and cares for those she loved before she was fully prepared to bind the spell. How could she do that now when another person close to her was in danger?

"No, it's not complete yet. There's one more step I need to take."

"If you do that—bind the spell, whatever that means— will my mother be able to return?" Bremen asked. "If this realm is protected, will it trap her outside of it?"

Oh gods, could that be true? Ingrid clutched her stomach and opened her mouth to speak but had to close it again. She didn't know, but she'd have to find out. How many more days were left before Jarrick's deadline for the village? Eir said she'd return in time, but was it enough?

"There has to be a way to bring her back, even with the

protections in place." Jorg's face was pale, the reality of Bremen's questions soaking in.

"I will have to go. There isn't any other way. Either Galwain is trapped, or the village is destroyed . . . unless I convince Jarrick to make the trade." Ingrid straightened her shoulders. She'd do whatever she needed to make everything right.

26

L ater that afternoon, after helping to deliver a warm pie to Lazuli and ensuring the kitchen was back in working order for Vevina, Jorg and Ingrid sat in the chairs of her room staring into the quiet darkness. The weight of the next day wrapped around them.

Jorg rested his forearms against his thighs. The waning sunlight angled through the window to shine on his face. "If I can convince him that I believe in his cause, maybe he'll take me with him instead of you. Then I can keep him from hurting you while you do what you need to do for the spell. At the very least, maybe I can gather some information that will help stop him. Whatever it takes to keep you from going to Alfheim with him, I need to try."

It was what she expected him to say, and Ingrid didn't bother to wipe the tears away from her cheeks. She was unsure if they fell from pain or anger—both were viable reasons. "You asked me to trust you, but you won't trust me. I'm stronger now, and he won't hurt me. He thinks he's making me some kind of queen." She let loose an ironic chuckle at the absurdity of Jarrick's comments, even as part of the sentiment enticed her.

"That's the same reason he'll take me instead. He'll be eager to teach me everything he thinks I missed out on, and I will keep him preoccupied enough for him to stay away from you. There's so much about myself I don't know, and I hate it, but at least he can explain who I am."

"From *his* point of view. He uses dark magic, Jorg."

"I understand that." Jorg stood and paced behind the chairs. "But he wasn't always dark. He became that. I won't."

"And what if you do? How can you be sure you can avoid his manipulation? Jarrick is strong, and if I have to fight him with you by his side, I won't be able to. The protections will fall. If I have to choose between you and the rest of the realms, I'll choose you." Ingrid stood and faced him. "Please don't put me in that position."

"She's my mother." The words were soft, and Jorg hung his head, not looking at Ingrid. "I can't let him take both of you."

Ingrid slipped her arms around Jorg's waist and pulled herself close to him, breathing in his grassy scent. His body trembled, and his heart pounded through his tunic against her cheek. The thought crossed her mind to ease his pain, but it would be a violation. His grief was true, and it wouldn't be fair to take it from him.

"For a time, while we walked along with Bremen's men, I couldn't help but think it might have been best if we turned back. Persuade Bremen to use his forces to help the village and battle Jarrick that way instead of continuing to search for Eir."

Jorg sat down again, holding Ingrid tight against him and allowing them to speak face-to-face.

"I had a grand picture in my mind of how it would all work, and everyone would be safe and happy. But, that's not sensible . . . no more than you going to Alfheim alone."

"It's different." Jorg stared into the space above Ingrid's head when she glanced up at him. His hair had grown longer since they'd left the village, and it mingled with hers. Light and dark, just like they would be if Jarrick had a chance to teach Jorg his ways.

Before Ingrid could say anything more, a commotion rang through the halls from outside her door. They both sprang to their feet and rushed into the corridor.

Bodies scrambled everywhere grabbing weapons as shouts ordered men to their posts. The druht army had arrived. Ingrid and Jorg hurried down to the courtyard to find the others.

"Close the gate! Close the gate!" a caller from the watch tower yelled over the din of preparations as he waved a flag.

Chaos erupted at the sight of men sprinting across the bridge through the open gateway. They were out of time.

Bremen emerged from the building and yelled for the archers to fire at will, and men to gather at the front. Ingrid fell backward as a set of hands grabbed the side of her tunic and yanked her from behind. A jolt of pain shot up her spine from the hard landing but disappeared in a heartbeat. Plintze stood in front of her, sword drawn.

Not anymore!

Ingrid stood and moved herself next to the overprotective dwarf. The days of feeling helpless and hiding behind others were gone. Ingrid pulled her daggers and steadied her breath.

The vines and leaves on the carved bone dug into her palm as she tightened her grip.

This was not like the forest, where she had concentrated on only a handful of men. Now there were too many streaming into the courtyard and blending in with Bremen's men. She would have to fight like the others.

Men charged over the bridge and through the gate, despite the arrows flying at them from the archers above. There were so many of them. Ingrid gulped down a hard lump rising in her throat and wrapped her fingers tighter around the hilt of each dagger. The runes in her pouch seemed to vibrate as if reminding her of her destiny.

A wave of doubt flashed through her mind. Eir said she would be ready to bind the spell only when her desire to save and protect all the realms transcended her loved ones. How could she do that knowing they faced such a danger as the angry warriors flooding the courtyard? The army was there because of her.

She had to fight—to keep everyone safe.

From the corner of her eye, she saw Selby. Each of them gave the other a nod. There was a slight grin on Selby's face and a confident set to her shoulders.

For a quick second, Ingrid closed her eyes and relaxed into the same confident pose. When she opened them, heat crept up from her middle as Jorg brushed the back of his hand against her arm and gave her a wink.

Ingrid charged, a battle shriek ripping from her lips, and Plintze and Jorg moved on either side of her. Seconds later, the grunts of bodies slamming into each other surrounded them. Swords clanged, and wood splintered as axes smashed into shields. Ingrid let her body take over and ducked under the swing of a sword and swiped the leg of an oncoming fighter as she spun low.

Before she could stand, a foot landed in her middle and she flew backward onto the hard, dry earth. Shaken, she quickly righted herself and ducked away from a shield, spinning as she did and sinking her dagger into the back of her attacker.

Sweat and blood stuck to her face, the metallic taste on her lips. She charged again, not caring if it was hers or someone else's.

Her arms grew as heavy as iron, and her chest heaved with the effort. Someone yanked her hair, and she stumbled to her side, landing on her knees. The stench of a filthy hand covered her mouth and nose as it exposed her neck.

She'd lost one dagger, but the other found purchase in the leg of her captor. His grip loosened enough to pull away, but only for a second as a hand grabbed her again. Facing the angry man, she brought her knee hard into his groin. He fell face-first, and she slammed her bone-handled dagger into the side of his neck with both hands.

Ingrid nearly fell on top of the crumpled body as her knees wobbled. The world slowed as she watched the chaos through the dimming skies of twilight. Bodies filled the courtyard.

Jorg fought men from all sides with his double-sided axe. Plintze surprised men with his strength and speed. Lazuli had arrived and zipped among the throng, leaving a colorful trail and bloodied bodies.

There were so many. More of the druht still streamed through the gates. Somewhere among them was their leader, Wilbert. Bremen's—and Jorg's—grandfather. Would he call off the attack if he knew it was his family that he battled?

Through the dusty haze churned up by so many feet, Ingrid caught sight of Bremen and Selby heading for the gate.

We need to help get the gate closed.

"This way!" Jorg grabbed Ingrid's wrist until she saw where he was going, and Plintze followed.

They raced their way to the edge of the combat, fighting until they reached where Bremen and several men were shoving a wagon. The three of them fought off attackers while the others tipped the wagon to block the gate. Another group did the same from the other side. It wasn't enough to stop every druht warrior from entering the courtyard, but it created a bottleneck and slowed their progress.

Breaking away from the steady onslaught, Bremen sent four men to climb ladders and shoot flaming arrows to the burning kettles outside the palisade walls. Black smoke billowed into the sky as they hit their targets.

Still locked in the battle, Ingrid found a small, round shield and used it along with her dagger to continue to fight. A flash of light drew her attention to a spot twenty paces from her as Jarrick arrived in the courtyard.

A tug pulled at her senses, and Ingrid's eyes met Jarrick's. The mayhem fell away from her ears as her eyesight tunneled. Everything was as she'd witnessed in her vision.

I knew it was only a matter of time until things got worse. Much worse.

27

Jarrick pulled a sword from his hip and began to battle against the druht around him. Ingrid watched, in stunned silence. Wondering why he would fight hand-to-hand, or help confront the druht when he could overpower everyone with little effort.

Then she noticed the curve of his lip. He wasn't fighting—he was toying with them, like a cat in the center of a colony of mice. At that moment, she knew she had one option left.

If she was going to save the realms, she had to get back to the Yggdrasil tree and secure the veil of protection. Jarrick could destroy the entire courtyard easily if he wanted. There was no way she could stop him from taking her to Alfheim with him unless she removed herself.

I have to go. There's no other way for this to end unless I bind the spell. I need to draw him away before things become worse. She remembered her vision and the thunderous crack of dragon wings she'd heard within it.

Ingrid saw Jorg's face snap toward her before she slashed out with her dagger at another attacker. The fighting had separated them so much that Jarrick was now closer to Ingrid than Jorg.

He swung his arms and spun in almost a dance as men fell all around him. Jarrick's eyes glittered when they met Ingrid's. His eyes widened for a moment as someone landed a crushing blow to his back while he was distracted. Stumbling down to his knees, a broad-shouldered man stood over him.

Ingrid gasped as Bremen rushed in and blocked the man's sword from coming down onto Jarrick. *Why would he do that?* She didn't understand why Bremen would protect Jarrick, but then she noticed Bremen leaning into the man and speaking to him. As the two pushed apart she noticed the resemblance.

It had to be Wilbert. He would have recognized Jarrick, and Bremen had made the connection also. It still didn't excuse the reason he didn't let his grandfather kill the dark elf. Ingrid gritted her teeth as she lunged away from an axe that was aimed at her head. Rolling to the ground, she swiped at the man's legs and crushed his throat with her shield.

When she stood, she ran for Bremen, watching as Selby rushed in from the other side. Wilbert raised his sword to strike Bremen, and before the latter could defend himself, Selby sliced her short sword through the older man's arm.

At the same time, Jorg reached Ingrid and pulled her to him in a suffocating embrace. "You need to go." Silver lined his eyes, but his jaw was tight.

Ingrid shook her head. The weight of leaving them to their fate slammed against her, and she faltered. "I can't. I can't leave all of you. Not now."

"You have to. No one will *ever* be safe if you don't." His mouth covered hers for a brief moment in a crushing kiss before he thrust her away from the battle toward a tall stack of crates near the palisade wall. "I love you. Now, go!"

As she hesitated, her gaze found Jarrick once again staring back at her. A curl tilted his mouth with an evil satisfaction. Ingrid's heart raced. Blood pounded in her ears. What was he doing?

Then she heard it.

A crack of thunder—except it wasn't. She'd heard that sound before. The scar on her arm pulsed.

"*Run!*" she screamed. It was the final piece of the vision she'd seen coming to fruition.

No one could hear her over the din of fighting bodies. The clang of metal and thud of wood drowned her voice.

Jorg, run. Dragon!

Selby was closest, and Ingrid bolted for her, screaming as she went. "Dragon—run!"

The screech filled the air as she reached her friend. All around her, the fighting slowed as faces turned to the skies.

Grabbing Selby's sleeve, Ingrid spun her away from the fighting and together, they darted for the front doors. Selby yanked her arm back midway there and halted, nearly making Ingrid topple trying to avoid her.

"Where's Bremen?" Selby asked.

The crack of wings in the air thundered again as a second silhouette darkened the courtyard. The sight of two dragons tilted the battle into a frenzied chaos. Men screamed and clambered over each other to get away. The druht nearest the gate turned and raced back for the forest. Those inside tried to follow or spring for the narthex, friend or enemy no longer a concern.

"You have to get inside!" Ingrid had to scream even though they stood face to face. "I have to go."

Tears immediately sprung from Selby's eyes as Ingrid backed away. The dragons circled over head, getting closer to the ground with each pass. "Go, please!"

Selby shook her head, wetness creating streaks through the dirt and blood splattered on her cheeks. Ingrid knew neither of them had time to wait, and if she could create a portal, Selby might hurry to safety after she was gone.

I love you. She sent her message to Jorg as she made the rune symbols. A portal opened, but Eir's words of warning that she could be trapped between the realms if she'd not done it right, rang in her mind.

As she hesitated, she heard Selby scream a warning and then the weight of a large body slammed into her side, knocking her to the ground. Large arms encircled her, getting caught on the string of her necklace. Her beads scattered across the wartorn ground. The amber bead landed in the dirt several feet away. The portal winked closed. Hot, acrid breath washed over her face as a voice spoke in her ear.

"You aren't going anywhere." Greer twisted her arm behind her back and yanked her to her feet.

The entire courtyard fell into blackness as one of the dragons sailed by with another screech. It was close enough that Ingrid could see each scale on the beast's underbelly shimmer like glass with iridescent blues and greens. The rising moon illuminated through its outstretched wings as if they were made of delicate indigo silk and twinkled off the razor-sharp claws.

"Let me go! You are condemning everyone to die if you

don't!" Ingrid screamed and kicked out at Greer as he held her from behind.

Before he could let go, the dragon curled in on itself in a serpentine twist and headed directly for them. Panic seized Ingrid, and she threw her hands up as high as she could with Greer's heavy arm around her shoulders.

Power surged from her, much like it had done in the forest, but this time her back arched and pain ripped through her from the inside out. Greer flew backward, and Ingrid fell face first into the dirt.

A horrendous, bellowing gurgle came from the dragon as it careened to the ground outside the palisade. The earth shook when the giant body crashed and then silenced.

For a few seconds that seemed like days, the entire court-yard came to a halt. Then with a startled urgency, everyone rushed back into a panic. The second, larger dragon let out a screech so fearsome that Ingrid's blood drained from her face. Her legs were too shaken to stand, but strong hands pulled her to her feet.

Selby didn't wait to find out if she could move. She just snatched Ingrid's hand and took off. Stumbling along behind as they hurried their way toward a wagon, Ingrid saw Bremen thrust his sword through Greer before he sprinted in their direction.

A wooden wagon wasn't going to provide any real cover from the dragon, but as they huddled under the darkness it provided, she wanted to believe it could. Bremen made it just as the dragon opened its mouth to spew fire, the heat already blazing through the air.

Directly in the line of fire stood Plintze, waving his arms wildly to get the beast's attention. He appeared to be drawing it away as he shuffled sideways. Realization cut through Ingrid like a dagger—he was moving away from the narthex. Away from the stream of warriors taking shelter within its walls.

No! The scream caught in Ingrid's throat, and she could only gape at her friend. Her pulse pounded against her temples, and the edges of her vision tunneled around the flapping dwarf.

Out of nowhere, Lazuli flew directly at the monster. She pestered the beast around its eyes. Her badgering made the creature halt its flame. As she tried to dart away, she almost made it, but the beast managed to snag her between teeth that were larger than the sprite's little body.

It threw her into the air, and she tumbled lifelessly end over end out into the forest. Her glittering trail of light dissipated into the air as her detached wings fluttered to the ground.

Sobs seeped into Ingrid's consciousness next to her, but she was numb. Lazuli was gone. A chasm cracked wide in her chest as she thought of Plintze.

Before she could process her grief, she screamed and covered her ears as a voice burst through her mind. Unlike the pressure of Jarrick's essence she'd known before, this was a sharp, stabbing agony—unrelenting as she tried to make out the words. She hoped that if she could understand it would make it stop.

"Come out of there, Ingrid, before I let my second pet torch this place to dust."

Bremen and Selby both pleaded with her to stay, but she twisted away from them. On hands and knees, she crawled from cover, unable to open her eyes from the pain.

28

Ingrid pushed herself to her feet, the headache fading as she stood before Jarrick. The courtyard was mostly empty, those still outside were hiding behind crates, barrels, and wagons. The second dragon undulated through the moonlit skies. Every few minutes it would let out a mournful howl and hiss a stream of fire. The acrid stench of sulfur choked the air.

The memory of crystalline lilac-colored eyes, purple hair, and a spunky rebellious personality made Ingrid hope that the gigantic lizard burned with pain more than she did. But she knew that wasn't possible as her chest squeezed in on itself.

"Your powers have grown stronger since we spoke last," Jarrick said. His frosty tone pierced through Ingrid. "It's time you learned better ways to use your skills."

"I learned what I needed, and there's nothing that you can teach me." She glared at him with the desire to test her skills. She'd sent men flying before. Over Jarrick's shoulder, she could see Plintze and Jorg moving closer. Bodies lay strewn at odd angles, and the ground darkened where dirt mixed with blood. "Where is Galwain?"

"My wife is not your concern—"

"She *is* mine," Jorg called out. Jarrick didn't so much as glance back as his son strode closer.

"Your mother is safe and happy to be in her rightful home. At some point, you will join us as well, but that will have to wait until Ingrid has finalized her part in the process."

There was a shuffle of bodies behind her as Bremen and Selby crawled out from the wagon. "Tell me where you've taken her," Bremen shouted.

Ingrid cringed on the inside from the hard stare Jarrick continued to level at her. That look darkened even more at the sound of Galwain's second son. It took much of her concentration to stand tall and act as though she was confident.

Without taking his eyes away, Jarrick spoke directly to Ingrid. "You and I are alike, Ingrid. We each have a gift that makes us stronger than those around us."

"Ha!" Ingrid curled her lip and fought back rising bile, the sting of it aching in her jaw. "I am *nothing* like you. You want to destroy and call it salvation. All the realms will suffer if you have your wish."

He shook his head. "Now, you know that isn't true. That's the sentiment of that old crone who filled your head with nonsense and left out all the best parts."

"You know nothing of what she taught me. I will not go with you. I will bind the spell."

Jorg circled around to stand by Ingrid's side, while Plintze stayed at Jarrick's back.

"It will be wonderful to show you Alfheim, my son, so you

can understand exactly what you've missed out on." With an exasperated shake of his head, Jarrick flourished his hand, sending Bremen, Selby, and Plintze backward in different directions as they tried to advance.

Muffled sounds of swords and shouting could be heard from the narthex where those who'd taken refuge from the dragon must have begun to fight again. Those who hid in the courtyard, however, remained silent.

"This is madness, Jarrick. You can't force me to follow you. The Norns granted me this destiny, and I will complete it."

With a tilt of his chin, Jarrick gave a wry grin. "Why should you care anymore? You haven't asked about those precious family members in that hovel of a village you have worried yourself sick over."

Ingrid let her nostrils flare as she tried to keep her expression calm, her breathing steady. Everyone would be safe if she was successful, including those in the village. Wouldn't they?

"Have you considered the cost of your allegiance with Eir? I allowed you two moons to come to your senses, and instead of choosing the wiser path, you chose to squander the opportunity I offered. I came to retrieve you yesterday." Jarrick angled his brow at Ingrid when he finished and let silence creep between them.

Ingrid's mind faltered to understand the implication of his words. Her nerves were too rattled to pick up on the subtlety of what he clearly wanted her to realize. Jorg shifted closer to her. She heard his breath hitch, and the muscles of his arm tensed where it brushed against hers.

What was she missing? What was she ignoring?

Then it hit her. Her eyes traveled to the sky where a

bright, round full moon shone low on the horizon. Two moons, that's the timeframe she'd been given, and she'd counted out the weeks, but she'd lost track. Starting like a small crack that quickly splintered into a cavern so deep it threatened to cleave her in two.

Yesterday. Jarrick had come for her yesterday.

No. No! He can't mean it.

Tremors erupted through her body as she shook her head. The air left her lungs and wouldn't return. She clutched her middle and fell to her knees. The village was destroyed—everyone dead. She'd failed.

Sound failed her even though she opened her mouth to scream. The world shifted out from under her. Nothing would ever be the same. Her home, her family—there was nothing to go back to. She fell to the ground, her fingers clawing at the cold, damp earth.

Finally, a scream—louder in her ears than even the dragon's had been—erupted from her core. The world went dark, and her powers turned to ice. Nothing had prepared her for the emptiness of such a devastating, crushing loss. How could it?

Someone touched her, and she lashed out, screaming and swinging her fists. Rising to her feet, ready to strike again, she found Jorg standing in front of her. His hands were at his side, his shoulders slumped, but what held Ingrid like a vice were the glistening streaks that slid down his cheeks.

Her family was gone, and they had been his family, too. Hagen, Jorg had told her, had been his first true friend, and now he was gone. Did he get to fight? Would they meet him in Valhalla one day?

Never again would she work side-by-side with her mother

at the loom or nestle against her father. Tattooed runes of Odin's bravery were etched on his neck—had they helped?

Ingrid's chin quivered as she stared, but she did not break down. The runes in the pouch at her waist felt as heavy as boulders. Home and Protection; no longer her destiny but her agony. Crumpling into Jorg, she curled her arms around his waist and let his crushing embrace remove the world around her.

As the heat from Jorg's body melted into her own, a new sensation pricked at her middle. The gentle warmth of her powers grew red hot. She pushed herself away from him and ignored Selby's muffled sobs from somewhere behind her as she faced Jarrick.

Every fear she'd held, every concern about being strong enough when the time came, dissolved. She'd never known hate before—until that moment.

The strength she'd developed in Asgard was but a drop of what she summoned within herself. It rumbled through her body and into her limbs, but she did not waver. Steady, with a hardened resolve, she stepped toward the dark elf, ripping her arm away as Jorg tried to stop her.

A glint in Jarrick's eye seemed to welcome, even enjoy, the challenge as she moved closer. When she raised her hands and gathered the energy into her palms, invisible and ready, he grinned.

With determined force, she thrust her arms upwards. The release of her power purred under her skin as it slammed into Jarrick. Shock flickered in his eyes as he registered the violence of it and stumbled backward several steps. He caught himself, closing his eyes and smiling as if drinking in the experience.

Ingrid let another wave fly, this time sustaining it so that it kept pushing against him. Sweat beaded on her brow, but nothing except anger filtered into her consciousness.

This time, his legs buckled and he went down on one knee. From somewhere off to the side, a roar caught Ingrid's attention a split second before Plintze rammed into Jarrick.

With a shriek, Ingrid closed her fists and raced to where the duo had tumbled. Neither was moving, and her rage turned into utter panic for Plintze. Before she could reach the crumpled dwarf, a cold hand wrapped around her wrist.

Jarrick was on his feet and yanked her to his side in the blink of an eye. Shouts and one desperate scream—Selby's—rang through her ears. But as the flash of a portal opened around her, the last noise she heard was the screech of a dragon as the heat of blistering flames warmed her skin.

Heaving for breath and muddled in confusion, she blinked against the bright light and sweet air that filled her lungs seconds later.

"Welcome to Alfheim, Ingrid," Jarrick cooed.

29

———————

JORG

The flash of the portal was so quick. Jorg stood motionless, the shock of what happened pushing in on him so that all else faded into the background. An earth rattling screech cleared his head instantly, and he raced toward Plintze. He managed to drag the dwarf's body behind some barrels as the dragon spewed it's fire.

We need to get out of here, further from the courtyard.

He checked Plintze for signs of life and let out a relieved sigh that his friend still lived. *Thank the gods.*

Whatever it was that Ingrid had done was powerful enough to knock Jarrick to his knees. But he'd have to think on that later, the first concern was to get away.

Hauling Plintze to his shoulders like a deer carcass, he bolted toward the nearest building. He leaned against the back wall of the smithy and waited for the beast to fly higher into the air as it circled for another pass.

With a hitch of his shoulders, he headed toward the kitchen garden. He thought if he could get to the northern most side of all the buildings, keeping to the farthest section of the palisade, he might escape.

Sorry for the rough carriage, but you are heavy my friend. A pulse of fear nagged at his thoughts for Selby . . . and Bremen, but he had to bury that deep to concentrate on his current effort. The dragon had to leave at some point, and he'd look for the others then.

Along the farthest section of the outer wall, beyond an odd arrangement of mounds, Jorg found a tall oak. Its branches spread out, creating shade, and also seemed to be out of the dragon's path. He set Plintze down in the tall grass at the base of the tree and crouched beside him. If he stayed still, perhaps the dragon wouldn't notice them.

The giant, slithering beast made two more passes over the courtyard. Billows of black smoke rose into the sky. Much of the building, where the bedrooms were, was reduced to rubble and char.

Jorg waited until he heard birds chirping in the tree over head to signal that the danger had subsided. He checked Plintze once more and decided to leave the unconscious dwarf where he lay, giving him a pat to the shoulder.

I'll come back for you. Sleep tight.

Stretching to his full height and scanning the area before he moved, it seemed eerily quiet. Sulfur, smoke, and burning flesh filled the air, but there weren't any human noises.

With heavy steps, he trudged toward the ruins. The cloister was exposed, and two walls of what had once been Bremen's council room remained. The room where he'd wanted Galwain to hide so she'd stay safe. He wanted to scream and punch something but instead picked his way over the timber and stone and made his way toward the nave.

Finally, he heard the rumblings of speech, and even though they might have been the surviving druht, it gave him hope that the others had made it inside as well. As he entered from the back, he startled several men clustered in small groups. He recognized a few of the faces but not many. No one stopped him as he continued toward the front. Most who glanced his way seemed too stunned to care.

Once in the narthex, however, there was a different scene. The two factions were separated and arguing forcefully, but no one was using weapons—yet. As Jorg stayed in the doorway assessing the room, he noticed that many of the men no longer had their weapons. Most likely they'd dropped them as they'd run for their lives.

Finally, near the main doors he spotted Selby. She stood near Bremen who was on one knee. He spoke to a man on the floor who leaned against the wall, pale-faced from the amount of blood on the bandage wrapped around what was left of his arm.

With a deep breath and a resolve to avoid a confrontation before he reached the two, if he could help it, he strode for the doors. He didn't concern himself with the makeshift battle lines and pushed through both groups until he'd drawn Selby's notice.

"Jorg!" Like an arrow, she hurtled herself toward him and slammed against his chest. Her arms squeezed around him, taking him by surprise. He wasn't sure how he stayed on his feet.

Relief flooded through him as he wrapped his arms around her, too. *I couldn't have dealt with having to tell Ingrid that Selby had been lost.* "Thank the gods you are all right." Jorg pulled back to see her face. "You're not hurt, are you?"

Selby said nothing but shook her head, even though tears streaked her cheeks. "Ingrid's gone."

His throat suddenly dry, and he waited to answer until his resolve was solid. "Yes. Jarrick pulled her through a portal. Who is Bremen speaking to?" A couple of the men near where they stood tried to taunt Jorg, but he ignored them as he kept hold of Selby. It comforted him in a way he didn't expect. But the tensions were too high, and fighting would break out any minute if he didn't help Bremen keep things under control.

"That's Wilbert. Galwain's father and his grandfather," Selby said, releasing her hold on Jorg and turning toward the two men. "Oh!" She stared into Jorg's face. "He's *your* grandfather, too."

The concept was difficult to fathom. He'd spent his entire life with so few family ties—until he'd met Ingrid's, of course. He shook his head as Selby led him closer to Bremen.

That man started all of this to rid the world of those like me. I doubt he's anxious to meet me.

Wilbert's eyes widened when Jorg came near, drawing Bremen's attention. It was worse than Jorg had already guessed from across the room. Wilbert was missing half his arm and was not long for this world.

"This is your other grandson, Jorg," Bremen offered.

"He's not my kin. No product of the monster who stole my daughter is related to me," Wilbert said. His voice was barely over a whisper, and the effort sent him into a coughing spasm.

Jorg scoffed and shook his head. "I'm not surprised to hear that. Look around at how hard you worked to spread your hate. You're no better than he is."

"Grandfather, whether you accept him or not, he *is* your relation, and so you know, the agreement you and I have made about your properties—I will share with my brother," Bremen said in a cool even tone.

Wilbert coughed again and leaned his head against the wall, his chest heaving as he tried to gather the energy to speak.

Brother. That's going to take some time to get used to.

Jorg crouched down so that he was eye to eye with Wilbert. "I don't care what deals you've made, but while I won't mourn you, I will remember you. For the rest of my days, I'll know what a sad and depraved man looks like. When I speak to my mother, I will help her understand that sorrow for your death is unwarranted as well."

"Leave me . . . to die in peace . . . I don't care . . . what your trollop mother . . . feels." He hesitated as he wheezed with the effort of speech. "Nor . . . you." He leveled his stare at Bremen until it became glassy and his chest no longer moved.

For a few minutes, the room sank into silence. The men had quieted when they realized the moment taking place between the two leaders. Bremen rose to his feet and slowly turned toward the men, though he said nothing. Jorg rose as well, and together with Selby, they stood on either side of the prince.

"Those of you who were hired to fight here today are released from your contract. Your leader is dead, and your cause is over." Bremen's voice rang strong and reverberated against the stone walls.

Unease filtered through the crowd once more. It was one thing to acknowledge that their campaign had ended, but Jorg suspected it was another to walk away. Many of them undoubtedly had expected to be paid. Some may even have learned to believe in the hatred Wilbert spewed. The realization hit Jorg that without Plintze, or Lazuli, he was the only nonhuman representative.

"What if we don't think it is?" a man near the middle of the room called out. "There's some sense to destroying those like that creature next to you, before they do the same to us. It was one like him that called the dragons."

Thankful that he'd slipped his axe into his belt before hefting Plintze, Jorg put his hand on it and let his eyes grow cold. He wouldn't say no to a fight right then. The weight of losing Ingrid was pressing in on him as he stood in silence. It would be a welcome relief.

"You'll drop your weapons and leave. If I'm not mistaken, there are more of my men in this room than yours. Your sacrifices will be in vain," Bremen said, as he moved his hand to the hilt of his sword.

Out of his side vision, Jorg saw Selby ready her short sword not attempting to be subtle. He'd never said as much, but he admired her warrior attitude.

Without another word, the remaining druht made their decision. Whether with weapons or fists, they charged forward. The clash of bodies, the clamor of shouts, the taste of vengeance flooded the space. Jorg let it absorb into him. Like a berserker on the battlefield, he only had eyes for the enemy and the single thought to destroy.

The vibration of his axe as it landed against bone or shield urged him forward. Every pain within begged to be released until there was nothing left—as if there could be an end. Sounds escaped and faces blurred as he let his rage unleash.

When the last man fell at his feet, he stared in silence. Chest heaving, he let his arms fall to his sides. As exhaustion swept through him and rational thought returned, he dropped his chin—defeated in victory. As much as he'd wanted to purge himself of his pain, it seeped back in, relentless and suffocating.

Jorg rubbed his hand over his face but snapped around when a light touch landed on his shoulder. Fire crackled in his veins, and it took every ounce of control not to strike out at the man, his brother, in front of him.

Bremen leaned in and spoke so only Jorg could hear. "It's done."

As they stood face-to-face, Jorg studied his eyes. They were strong, determined, and honest, but not challenging. There was a hidden plea in them that the broken pieces of his spirit responded to, and his anger leaked away. He gave a tight nod.

The courtyard was charred, and bits of it still smoked. When Jorg made his way outside with Bremen and Selby, sulfur and burning flesh stung his eyes and made his stomach roll.

Buildings, carts, and piles of crates still smoldered from the dragon attack. The palisade wall was broken in several areas, and one of the gate towers had fallen, destroying the gate and bridge in the process.

Jorg thought of Ingrid as the destruction around him billowed his resolve to find her and destroy the one who took her—the cause of all his pain.

It wasn't supposed to happen this way. I was supposed to save you, to prevent all of this. Ingrid, I will find a way into Alfheim. No matter what, I'll get you away and make Jarrick pay for what he's done.

"How do you plan to find her?" Selby asked, startling him as she walked up.

He knew she couldn't hear his thoughts, but she must have read the expression on his face. There was only one solution he'd been able to think of. "Since the spell was not bound, it means Midgard is still open to other realms. If there is a pathway to Alfheim, I intend to find it."

"Whatever you decide to do, I am coming." Selby clamped her lips in a set line. The stone-like glint of her stare challenged him to deny her.

Before Jorg or Bremen could answer her, the sound of a gravelly voice made them all spin around.

"I can help get us to Alfheim." Plintze stepped closer as he spoke. Covered in dirt, his coarse hair was matted in some places and singed in others. The sleeves of his shirt hung in tatters where the fabric remained at all, and he looked ready to collapse.

Both Bremen and Jorg rushed forward and held him from each side. They guided him to an overturned broken barrel with enough remaining support for him to rest against.

"Did he take her?" Plintze's shoulders slumped further when Jorg nodded.

Jorg let a few seconds of silence hang in the air before he spoke. "But I'm going after her."

"*We—we* are going after her." There would be no arguing with Selby on that point.

"I know a way, but it will not be an easy task," Plintze said. "It will require going through my home realm first."

Bremen placed his hand against Selby's face and rubbed her cheek with his thumb. "Jarrick also has my mother. Wherever we need to go to find them both and stop him, I'm coming, too."

Jorg's middle clenched at the loving gesture and shared moment between Bremen and Selby. It added tinder to the ember of anger smoldering within himself. He needed Ingrid. The silence where her voice should've been, clawed at his mind.

Old pains from his childhood, which were buried deep and thought forgotten, were surfacing unexpectedly. Jarrick had forced his mother to abandon him as a baby. Now he'd stolen his chance to get to know her. He needed to run, to fight, to scream—to hunt. He would make Jarrick pay for the pain he'd caused.

Stay strong, Hjarta. I am coming for you.

ACKNOWLEDGMENTS

There is an African proverb that says it takes a village to raise child. Proverbs 27:17 of the Bible reads, "As iron sharpens iron, so one person sharpens another." It also takes an army to publish a book!

At least it has for me—especially this one. I got lost in the weeds with this story for a while. Quite literally as those early beta readers can attest. But, with a few thousand tears and a lot of hand holding, I believe I've found the story it was meant to be. It took longer than I expected, but I will be forever grateful to everyone who helped make it the success it is.

To my husband, Craig, your patience to listen while I ramble on and on about plot holes and "stupid commas" is such a blessing to me. Thank you for bringing out your inner little boy to help me figure out fight scene actions with blanket cloaks and pencil swords. As well as spending time with me watching hours of research videos. You are my favorite warrior superhero!

I don't know what I did to be so lucky as to work with Ashley McLeo, my critique partner extraordinaire. Your work ethic, drive and skill encourage me to do my best everyday. Thank you for reading the really ugly pages and asking for more! I can't imagine life without our coffee shop meetings, or someone else who understands the sheer number of story ideas that can filter through one mind.

Without my Indie Author Marketing group, I don't know where I'd be. Every book needs the best promotion to succeed and every author needs a support system like all of you. There will always be more to learn and I love our meetings together.

Sometimes I need a good kick in the pants to do what I know I should anyway. For those who trudged through a beta read early on - bless you! You insisted that I do my best and you were exactly what I needed. Your artistic ability to speak kind words with a red pen will always be appreciated.

Jennifer Roop, thank you for giving me such a great start and being quick with a kind word. Jen McDonnell thank you for answering my questions, teaching me how to find all those fun symbols, and being an all-around great person. Also, for introducing me to Candy. Candy Crum – you are a treasure! You came along when I needed it most and lifted me up more than I can express. At some point we need to share a glass of wine, a big ol' hug, and a lot of laughs! Just like this story – you are full of magic. My heart is full of an absurdly abundant number of exclamation points when I think of you.

To all my family, friends, and readers who constantly shower me with encouragement and love – thank you so much. I will strive to make you proud because you fill me with joy always!

ALSO BY KELLY N JANE

ABOUT THE AUTHOR

Kelly is a USA Today bestselling author who writes heroic epic fantasy immersed in elaborate worlds rich with myth, magic, slow burn romance, and fast-paced action.

In her office, there's a chihuahua on her lap and a cat nearby. Coffee always flows and she believes that dessert goes with every meal. When she's not in front of her keyboard, she's probably reading, playing with yarn, or on a wild rabbit chase down an interesting research trail!

www.kellynjane.com

www.ingramcontent.com/pod-product-compliance
Lightning Source LLC
Chambersburg PA
CBHW050755190726
48285CB00005B/1678